Pra

# Sprinkle with Murder

"A tender cozy full of warm and likable characters and a refreshingly sympathetic murder victim. Readers will look forward to more of McKinlay's tasty concoctions."

—*Publishers Weekly* (starred review)

"McKinlay's debut mystery flows as smoothly as Melanie Cooper's buttercream frosting. Her characters are delicious, and the dash of romance is just the icing on the cake."　　　　—Sheila Connolly, author of *Bitter Harvest*

"Jenn McKinlay delivers all the ingredients for a winning read. Frost me another!"

—Cleo Coyle, national bestselling author of the Coffeehouse Mysteries

"A delicious new series featuring a spirited heroine, luscious cupcakes, and a clever murder. Jenn McKinlay has baked a sweet read."

—Krista Davis, author of the Domestic Diva Mysteries

*Berkley Prime Crime titles by Jenn McKinlay*

*Cupcake Bakery Mysteries*

SPRINKLE WITH MURDER
BUTTERCREAM BUMP OFF
DEATH BY THE DOZEN

*Library Lover's Mysteries*

BOOKS CAN BE DECEIVING

# Death
## by the
# Dozen

## Jenn McKinlay

**BERKLEY PRIME CRIME, NEW YORK**

**THE BERKLEY PUBLISHING GROUP**
**Published by the Penguin Group**
**Penguin Group (USA) Inc.**
**375 Hudson Street, New York, New York 10014, USA**

Penguin Group (Canada), 90 Eglinton Avenue East, Suite 700, Toronto, Ontario M4P 2Y3, Canada
(a division of Pearson Penguin Canada Inc.)
Penguin Books Ltd., 80 Strand, London WC2R 0RL, England
Penguin Group Ireland, 25 St. Stephen's Green, Dublin 2, Ireland (a division of Penguin Books Ltd.)
Penguin Group (Australia), 250 Camberwell Road, Camberwell, Victoria 3124, Australia
(a division of Pearson Australia Group Pty. Ltd.)
Penguin Books India Pvt. Ltd., 11 Community Centre, Panchsheel Park, New Delhi—110 017, India
Penguin Group (NZ), 67 Apollo Drive, Rosedale, Auckland 0632, New Zealand
(a division of Pearson New Zealand Ltd.)
Penguin Books (South Africa) (Pty.) Ltd., 24 Sturdee Avenue, Rosebank, Johannesburg 2196,
South Africa

Penguin Books Ltd., Registered Offices: 80 Strand, London WC2R 0RL, England

This is a work of fiction. Names, characters, places, and incidents either are the product of the author's imagination or are used fictitiously, and any resemblance to actual persons, living or dead, business establishments, events, or locales is entirely coincidental. The publisher does not have any control over and does not assume any responsibility for author or third-party websites or their content.

PUBLISHER'S NOTE: The recipes contained in this book are to be followed exactly as written. The publisher is not responsible for your specific health or allergy needs that may require medical supervision. The publisher is not responsible for any adverse reactions to the recipes contained in this book.

DEATH BY THE DOZEN

A Berkley Prime Crime Book / published by arrangement with the author

PRINTING HISTORY
Berkley Prime Crime mass-market edition / October 2011

Copyright © 2011 by Jennifer McKinlay Orf.
Excerpt from *Red Velvet Revenge* by Jenn McKinlay copyright © by Jennifer McKinlay Orf.
Cover illustration by Jeff Fitz-Maurice.
Cover design by Lesley Worrell.
Interior text design by Laura K. Corless.

ISBN: 978-0-425-24405-0

BERKLEY® PRIME CRIME
Berkley Prime Crime Books are published by The Berkley Publishing Group,
a division of Penguin Group (USA) Inc.,
375 Hudson Street, New York, New York 10014.
BERKLEY® PRIME CRIME and the PRIME CRIME logo are trademarks of Penguin Group
(USA) Inc.

PRINTED IN THE UNITED STATES OF AMERICA

10  9  8  7  6  5  4  3  2  1

For my brother Jon (Jed) McKinlay.
Thanks for never letting me quit.
I love you forever.

# Acknowledgments

Big, fluffy cupcakes to my agent, Jessica Faust; my editor, Kate Seaver; and her assistant editor, Katherine Pelz. I couldn't do this without all of you.

More cupcakes to Tori and Brad Niemiec for entering the contest at the annual Scottsdale Cupcake Love In to win a walk-on part in this book. Have fun finding yourself, Tori! Special thanks to Tree and Susie Matazzoni for hooking me up with the Love In and to Sheila Levine for going halfsies with me on all of those cupcakes! Next year we don't start with the mini Bundts!

A big thank-you to Kelly Garcia of Butter & Me (she doesn't need any cupcakes) for being so gracious in answering my cupcake questions and for baking some seriously spectacular cupcakes for my book signings!

And lastly, but with sprinkles on top, extra yummy cupcakes to all of the McKinlays and the Orfs, and especially to my dudes Chris, Beckett, and Wyatt, the best sous-chefs and hug givers a girl could ever have!

# One

"Fifteen minutes!" Angie DeLaura yelled. "We have to turn the registration form in by ten o'clock or we're locked out of the competition."

Melanie Cooper scrambled into her tiny office with Angie hot on her heels. Paperwork was scattered all over the top of her desk. There was a reason she was a cupcake baker and not a bookkeeper. She did much better with her pantry organization than her file cabinet.

She ran a hand through her short blonde hair in exasperation.

"I know I put it here," she said. "Why didn't I turn it in last week like I planned?"

"Because you had a hot date with my brother," Angie said. "And you forgot."

"Oh, yeah," Mel said. She couldn't stop the silly grin that spread across her face as she remembered her romantic evening with Joe DeLaura. A heavy sigh escaped her, and Angie snapped her fingers in front of Mel's face and said, "Snap out of it!"

Mel shook her head, trying to regain her focus.

"You start on that side of the desk, and I'll start on this side," Angie ordered as she dug into a stack of cookware catalogs.

Mel shuffled through a pile of flyers advertising Fairy Tale Cupcakes' unique flavors and special-occasion cupcake tiers. Sure enough, stuck by a smear of royal frosting to the back of the flyers was their registration form for the Scottsdale Food Festival. "I found it!"

Angie glanced at her watch. "We have twelve minutes."

"We'd better run," Mel said.

Together they bolted through the kitchen and the bakery. Mel turned and locked the front door behind them. Then they pounded down the sidewalk of Old Town Scottsdale, passed a Western-wear store, a Mexican import store, a jewelry store, and around the corner they passed a tattoo parlor and a hair salon.

Mick, the owner of the tattoo parlor, stepped outside as they whizzed by. At six foot four with a shaved head and covered in ink, he was fairly intimidating, but Mel and Angie knew he was a big old softie, who had a weakness for Mel's Moonlight Madness coconut cupcakes.

"Where's the fire?" he called after them.

Angie opened her mouth to retort, but Mel grabbed her arm and kept running. "No time! Chat later."

They hit the entrance to the Civic Center Mall and had to dodge an elderly couple, who stood admiring the bronze sculpture of three horses running entitled *The Yearlings*. Mel loved the sculpture, too, but this was not the time to stop to admire it.

They had to turn their registration form into the Scottsdale Art Association office, which was housed in one of the small buildings that encircled the many fountains and sculptures that made up the Civic Center Mall. The mall, a large twenty-one-acre park, was one of Mel's favorite spots in the city. She frequently walked to the library on the opposite side just to enjoy the lush flowers, trickling fountains, and beautiful public art that filled the meticulously tended area.

A small group of tourists blocked the path ahead as they admired a short fountain that formed a ball of water. Mel followed Angie as she cut around them and onto the grass. Like track stars, they jumped over the narrow stream that fed a larger fountain, and they raced down the slope farther into the park.

Mel could feel a stitch cramping her side, and she was wheezing just a bit as Angie skidded to a stop in front of the darkened glass doors of an office building.

"What office do we need?" Angie asked.

Mel glanced at the papers in her hand. "Twelve-B."

"Second floor," Angie said. She glanced at her watch. "Seven minutes."

Mel suppressed a groan as they pulled open the doors and hit the stairs on the right. They wound up in a tight turn. Mel jogged up the steps, breathing hard, when she slammed into Angie's back.

"Ow!" She grabbed the rail to keep from falling backwards and glanced up to see why Angie had stopped.

Blocking the way upstairs in a fair imitation of a brick wall was Olivia Puckett, owner of the rival bakery, Confections, and Mel's own personal pain in the patoot.

"Step aside," Angie growled.

Olivia spread her beefy arms wide. "Make me."

Angie took a step forward as if she would do just that,

but Mel grabbed her arm and held her back. Angie was known for being a bit of a firecracker, and Mel didn't want her sending off any sparks here.

Olivia obviously didn't know what kind of trouble she was inviting when she challenged Angie. Although it had been more than twenty years, Mel still hadn't fully recovered from the day Angie had bloodied the nose of their seventh grade class bully, Jeff Stanton, when he dumped chocolate milk over Mel's head at lunch one day and called her "Bessie, the chocolate cow."

Although that incident had only gotten Angie a week's detention, Mel was always afraid that one day Angie's temper was going to land her in a jam that Mel wouldn't be able to fix.

"Breathe, Angie," she said. "I'll take care of this."

Angie gave her a mutinous look, but she complied. Mel stepped around her and faced Olivia.

"You can't seriously think you're going to stop us from registering to compete in the challenge to the chefs," Mel said.

"Oh, yeah, I can and I will," Olivia said. "I called my contact in the Arts office last night, and she told me you hadn't registered yet. I knew your last chance was this morning. I've been waiting since eight. You are not going to get by me."

"You've been waiting here for two hours?" Angie asked. "You're mental. You know that?"

"No little snot-nosed Scottsdale princess is going to beat me out of my title," Olivia said. "I've won it five years in a row, and I'm not giving it up, not now, not ever."

"Who are you calling a Scottsdale princess?" Mel snapped, feeling her temper begin to heat. "I'm a Southie, born and raised off of Camelback Road. I am no princess."

"Look at you. You're tall, blonde, and thin," Olivia snorted. "For someone who says she isn't a princess, you sure look the part."

The irony was almost too much to take. When Mel was a chubby adolescent, she was derided and called "Bessie, the chocolate cow." She would have given anything to be considered a princess back then.

Now, after years of struggling with her weight, she had developed a healthy relationship with food and felt good about her body and herself. And she was being mocked for it. It was all so ridiculous.

"Olivia, you need to step aside," Mel said. "I have just as much right as anyone to enter."

"Maybe you didn't hear me," Olivia said. "You're not entering my contest."

She puffed out her chest, and Mel was sure she was going to expand to fill the entire landing. She was stocky with corkscrew gray hair that she wore in a stubby ponytail on top of her head. She also wore a blue chef's coat that Mel suspected she thought made her look like Cat Cora on the *Iron Chef* TV show. Mel wanted to tell her that it just made her look like Grumpy Smurf, but she didn't think that would get Olivia out of her way.

"Five minutes," Angie hissed from behind her.

Mel felt her panic swell. Olivia was not known for being reasonable, and the clock was ticking.

"'I don't scratch my head unless it itches, and I don't dance unless I hear some music. I will not be intimidated. That's just the way it is,'" Angie muttered.

"Coach Boone in *Remember the Titans*," Mel identified the movie quote. She and Angie and their other childhood friend, Tate Harper, were old movie aficionados and frequently quizzed one another with movie quotes. But why was Angie doing it now? Didn't she know they were in a crisis? But then, she'd chosen a football movie quote, and Mel realized that was no coincidence. She knew what Angie was thinking.

"No, we can't do that," she said over her shoulder.

Olivia was watching them through narrowed eyes.

"We have no choice," Angie said. "It's got to be the fall-over feint."

Mel groaned. Angie had seven older brothers, who loved to play touch football, and Mel had spent enough time at the DeLaura family gatherings to be drafted into play. When they were younger, she and Angie had never been able to get their hands on the ball, and the brothers only allowed them on the field to humor them and keep their mother from scolding them. So naturally, Mel and Angie had been forced to create a few plays of their own, one of which was the fall-over feint. It was guaranteed to get them where they wanted to go with the ball, but usually resulted in someone getting fairly banged up.

"Three minutes," Angie said through gritted teeth.

"All right, all right," Mel said. "On three."

Olivia was beginning to look concerned.

"One," Angie counted.

"Two," said Mel.

"Three!" they said together.

Mel fell over to the side, curling up into a tight ball as she went, as Angie sprung over her. Mel felt Angie's sneaker kick the side of her head, but she came out of her crouch and crawled past the collision of bodies, barely registering that Angie had Olivia pinned to the floor as Mel hurried up the stairs.

Olivia let out a furious bellow, and from her splayed position on the landing, she reached out an arm and tried to grab Mel's leg, but she was too late. Mel reached the top of the stairs and took off in a sprint.

The door to 12B was open, and Mel skidded into the room and glanced at the digital clock on the wall. It read 10:00. An elderly woman was working the counter, and she squinted at Mel through her reading glasses. She held out her hand, and Mel shoved the papers into it. As the woman hit it with a rubber stamp, the clock flipped to 10:01.

"You're cutting it pretty close, miss," the woman said. Her short hair was dyed a champagne color, and her purple lipstick matched the frames of her reading glasses.

Mel sagged against the counter and glanced at the woman's name tag. "You have no idea, Jane."

Angie came tearing into the office. Her T-shirt had a small rip, and her long brown hair was hanging haphazardly out of her hair band. "Did we make it?"

Too winded to speak, Mel held up her fist, and Angie banged knuckles with her.

"Excellent!" she said and then sagged against the counter beside Mel.

Jane, the clerk, looked at them in concern and then left the counter. She came back with two Dixie cups of water.

"Thanks," Mel said. She held hers up toward Angie, and they clinked paper.

"Let's take Olivia down for good," Angie said.

"I hear that," Mel agreed. They downed their water and crushed their cups. Tossing the cups into the wastepaper basket, they left the office calling a thank-you to Jane. There was no sign of Olivia on the stairs, just a smudge of flour on the floor where she'd been sprawled. Mel took it as a good sign.

# TWO

"How did it go?" Tate asked as he pushed open the front door of the bakery. "Are you registered? You didn't forget, did you?"

"Why would you think I'd forget?" Mel asked.

Tate was wearing his usual power suit. Today it was an Armani in navy with a crisp white shirt and jade green tie. His wavy brown hair was cropped in a conservative cut to suit the investment clients he dealt with each day, and he looked every inch the wealthy businessman that he was.

Having known him since he was riddled with acne and shooting rubber bands out of his braces, Mel often forgot that her childhood chum had grown into a man that most husband-hunting women would happily hold at gunpoint to force a proposal.

Tate stared at her. Then he looked at Angie, who was restocking the display case with Mel's latest creation, the Choco-Pom Cupcake, a chocolate and pomegranate concoction that was Mel's current favorite.

"How did she do?" he asked Angie.

"Made it with a nanosecond to spare," Angie said.

Tate shook his head. "Mel, you've got to get your game face on."

"It wasn't my fault," Mel protested. "We would have been there in plenty of time if not for Olivia."

"Olivia Puckett?" he asked.

"Yep." Angie said. "She tried to block us from turning in our paperwork."

"How did you get past her?"

Mel and Angie exchanged a look. Angie ducked back behind the display case and began rapidly unloading the Choco-Poms. Mel grabbed a rag and began wiping down the counter even though she had just finished doing so minutes before.

Tate lowered his head and pinched the bridge of his nose as if bracing himself for a migraine. "You might as well tell me. It can't be any worse than what I'm imagining."

"The fall-over feint," Mel mumbled.

"Sorry, I didn't quite catch that," Tate said. He cupped his ear and leaned close.

"The fall-over feint," Mel repeated with a grimace.

"You didn't," he said. He looked as if his knees might give out, and he lowered himself into a nearby chair.

"We did." Angie popped up from the display case with an empty tray. "And it worked, too."

"Of course it worked," Tate said. "It always works! Last time it worked so well, your brother Tony ended up in the hospital with a concussion. Please tell me Olivia is unconcussed."

"She got up on her own power," Angie said. "As soon as I got off of her."

"Does the word *lawsuit* mean anything to you two?" Tate asked. He looked as if he might have a seizure.

"She was blocking our way," Mel said. "We really had no choice."

"If Joe hears about this . . ." Tate's voice trailed off, and Mel blanched.

Her boyfriend, Joe DeLaura, one of Angie's older brothers, was an assistant district attorney. There was no question. He would be very unhappy to find out she and Angie had tackled someone, even someone as annoying as Olivia Puckett.

"Well, I don't see why he would unless someone shoots his mouth off," Angie said. She glowered at Tate, making it very clear who she thought the weak link might be.

He raised his hands in a gesture of innocence. Angie scowled, picked up her tray, and pushed her way through the swinging door back into the kitchen.

"What did I say?" he asked Mel.

"'It has been my experience that men are least attracted to women who treat them well,'" Mel said.

"Miss Bowers in *Death on the Nile*," Tate cited the quote without blinking. "Played by Maggie Smith, I believe."

"Correct and correct," Mel said.

"So, enlighten me," he said. He leaned forward, resting an elbow on the table, eagerness etched in every line of his body. "What's going on with Ange?"

"Don't get your hopes up," Mel warned him.

"Too late." He grinned. "Did she dump him? Is it over? Was he crushed?"

"No, no, and no," Mel said. "In fact, I'm worried about her. He hasn't called her in two days."

Tate let out a groan and leaned back. "That's it?"

"He's never missed a day," Mel said. She put away her cleaning rag and wiped her hands on her bright pink bib apron that had *Fairy Tale Cupcakes* scrawled in glittery script across the front.

Tate rolled his eyes. "Why is she still dating him? I mean, what can she possibly see in him?"

He was referring to Angie's boyfriend of three months. Brian Malloy, known to his fans as Roach, was the drummer in the popular rock band the Sewers. He and Angie had met when his father had been murdered on a date with Mel's mother. Roach had made the mistake of accusing Mel of harming his father, and Angie had gone nuclear on him. Mel suspected very few people got in the rock star's face, and he had been bowled over by Angie and asked her out immediately.

"Um, let's see, he's hot," Mel said. She came around the counter and sat across from Tate. "Oh, yeah, and he's hot."

"Only if you go for the 'skinny, tattooed, with stringy hair' type," Tate grumped.

Mel pressed her lips together. Over the past few months, she had become a master at knowing when to keep her mouth shut. Whatever happened between Angie and Tate, she fervently hoped they would all come out friends at the end of it.

It had been the three of them against the world for as long as she could remember. Then Tate had gotten engaged, and Angie had finally come clean to Mel about her feelings for him. She was in love with Tate and had been since they were kids. Oy.

But after his tragically ended engagement, Tate, being a typical male, had wallowed and whined and refused even to consider dating anyone ever again. Then Roach had come to town and swept Angie off her feet. Now Tate had come to realize that he was in love with her, too, but so far he had not declared himself but sat ever hopeful, waiting for Angie's relationship to implode.

It was only a matter of time before the situation was resolved. Roach had asked Angie to move back to Los Angeles with him, but she had told him she wanted to wait until he was done with his current tour. Mel knew that once Roach was back, decisions would have to be made.

Mel hated the idea of losing her best friend and partner, but Tate had it much worse. He stood to lose the love of his life without ever having told her how he felt.

"He'll call," he said sourly. "He'd be an idiot to let her go."

Mel reached over and patted his shoulder. "Hang in there, champ."

"I have a choice?"

"No."

"Okay, I've worked out a schedule," Angie said as she came bustling back through the kitchen door. She was carrying a clipboard and had a red pen in her hand. "We have three weeks, and we're going to need every second of them."

"Three weeks for what?" Mel asked.

"Until the competition," Angie said. "Now here's what I was thinking. We get up at four thirty every day and—"

"In the morning?" Mel asked in horror. The only part of running a bakery that didn't suit her was the early mornings.

"Yep," Angie said, plowing on and ignoring her. "Tate will drop off a bag of mystery ingredients, and we'll set the timer to give ourselves one hour to whip up a fabulous dessert."

"And we can't do this during regular operating hours because . . ."

"We need to have complete, uninterrupted focus," Angie said. "Tate, can we count on you?"

"Absolutely," he said. "Any idea what the mystery ingredients should be?"

"If I gave you a list, they wouldn't exactly be a mystery, now would they?" Angie asked. "However, I made a list of everything they've used over the past five years, so that should give you some ideas."

Tate took the list she handed him and scanned it. "Why are pickles on this list?"

Angie gave a long-suffering sigh. "Because that was one of the mystery ingredients one year."

"For the pastry competition, really?" Mel asked.

"They try to make it difficult," Angie said. "Have you even looked at any of the information I've given you?"

"Yeah . . . uh . . . no," she admitted.

"How do you expect to cream Olivia's tartar if you don't study up?" Angie asked. "You can't just waltz in there and expect to win, you know."

"I don't expect it to be easy. I've just had other—" Mel began, but Angie interrupted, "I know. Now that you and Joe are finally together, you are useless. You know, I have a good mind to ban you from seeing Joe until this competition is over."

Mel opened her mouth then shut it quickly before something better left unsaid flew out. She and Angie locked stares. They'd been doing this since grade school. Whoever blinked first lost, not only the staring contest, but also the argument.

"Would you look at the time?" Tate asked without consulting his watch or a clock. "I'd better get back to the office. So, I'll see you tomorrow morning at four thirty. Bye."

Mel felt her eyes begin to burn. It was agony.

"You blinked," Angie said. She spun on her heel and stomped back to the kitchen.

Mel turned and glared at Tate's retreating back. Big coward!

✦ ✦ ✦

"Hey, Cupcake, wake up," a voice whispered in Mel's ear.

She cracked an eyelid and then closed it. It was still dark. She must have been dreaming.

"It's four twenty-five," the voice said. "Angie is going to bang in here and drag you out by the hair."

"I don't care," Mel mumbled and burrowed deeper into her pillow.

"Yesterday she dumped ice water on you," the voice reminded her. "And the day before that she pressed the test button on your smoke detector to blast you awake."

Now Mel's eyes opened. She turned her head and saw Joe smiling at her from the neighboring pillow. As always when she found him watching her with his warm brown eyes, she was struck by how much he seemed to like her, and her breath caught in her chest.

She'd had a crush on Joe DeLaura from the first day she set eyes on him when she was a sturdy twelve-year-old and he was a gangly sixteen-year-old with a killer grin who looked out for his little sister, Angie, and by extension his little sister's best friend, which was Mel. They'd gone separate ways in their twenties, but then, six months ago, he'd walked into Fairy Tale Cupcakes and noticed that Mel was all grown up. They'd been dating ever since.

She felt too much when she looked at him, so she turned

her gaze to the ceiling and teased, "You just don't want to get caught in the back splash again."

"Well, it was kind of harsh," he said. "Even for Angie. No telling what she'll come up with today."

Mel groaned. "I'd better head her off."

"Call me later," Joe said.

"I will." Mel kissed him and rolled out of the bed. She ducked into the bathroom, threw on some clothes, and slipped on her sneakers. Joe was snoring softly as she locked the door behind her.

She turned to head down the stairs and found Angie halfway up, holding two pot lids, which she had obviously intended to use as cymbals.

"I'm going to take back the key to my apartment," Mel said. "You're abusing the privilege."

Angie shrugged. "You're up, aren't you?"

Mel followed her down the stairs and into the back door of the bakery, which led into the kitchen. The large steel worktable in the center held a brown paper bag, presumably full of mystery ingredients. Tate was hovering by the coffee machine in the corner as if willing it to brew faster.

"Morning," Mel mumbled.

"Hunh," he grunted. He handed her a mug before filling his own.

"So, what's the ingredient today?" Mel asked. She took a sip of the refreshingly strong brew and tried to defog her brain. They'd been at this competition prep for two weeks, and she wondered if Tate had run out of mystery ingredients yet.

"Good question." Angie fished in the bag with a frown. She pulled out a bunch of what looked like white carrots by their leafy green stems and frowned. "What are these?"

"Parsnips," Mel and Tate said together.

"Seriously?" Angie asked. "What are we supposed to do with these?"

"Sorry, I'm beginning to scrape the bottom of the barrel on unusual ingredients," Tate said. "I figured this would throw Mel a nice curve. Call me when you're ready for a taste test. You have one hour—starting now."

"Where are you going?" Angie asked.

Tate usually stayed to watch them work, but today he looked more exhausted than usual. Mel figured the early mornings must be catching up to him. He sipped his coffee and headed for the office. "I'm going to stay out of the way and read the paper."

He shut the office door behind him, and they heard Mel's desk chair creak as he tilted it backwards.

"Five bucks says we hear him snoring within ten minutes," Angie said.

"Sucker bet," Mel said with a shake of her head. "You're not earning a fiver off of me that easily."

"Fine. Clock's ticking," Angie said. She held out the parsnips to Mel. "What's your plan?"

Mel studied the parsnips. "Peel and shred these into three cups then steam them."

"Roger that," Angie said and set to work.

Mel walked over to her pantry and examined her stores. She knew the judges in the competition would be looking for originality in presentation as well as taste. She wasn't going to be able to present them with cupcakes every time—she had to show diversity—but if she made it to the finals, she wanted to win with a cupcake to give the bakery the most promotion possible.

Now parsnips were known to be a cross between a potato and a carrot or a mild turnip. Mel figured she had two ways she could go with this. It was either a parsnip spice cake or a carrot cake with parsnips in lieu of carrots. If she made the spice cake, she wanted a plain cream cheese frosting. If she went with the carrot-type cake, she could get funky with the frosting. That decided it. In competition, funky frosting would be much harder to ignore.

With that in mind, she started gathering ingredients. She raided the pantry and the walk-in cooler. Because they were only making a small batch, she used her pink KitchenAid mixer instead of her industrial Hobart. She fitted it with a paddle and let it go to work, creaming the butter, sugars, and oil.

She prepped the cupcake pan with foil liners, and in a separate bowl she sifted her dry ingredients. Angie handed her a bowl with the shredded and steamed parsnips.

"What next?" she asked.

Mel glanced at the clock. They were ten minutes in.

"I need you to toast some walnut halves in the small oven and then make a batch of cream cheese frosting," she said.

Mel slowly added the dry ingredients into the mixer then the parsnips. When the batter was done, she scraped the sides of the bowl and grabbed an ice cream scoop. She filled the cupcake pan and put it in the oven. She set the timer for 25 minutes.

Angie was toasting walnut halves in their smaller conventional oven and mixing the frosting at the same time. Mel dashed back to the pantry and found her container of crystallized ginger. Using her best chopping knife, she minced a quarter cup of the sugared ginger root.

She glanced at the clock. Fifteen minutes for the cupcakes to be done, and then they had to cool. It would take both her and Angie icing them at the same time in order to beat the clock.

Angie shut off the mixer and delivered the cream cheese frosting to Mel. She went back to the walnuts and pulled them out of the oven.

Angie poured the walnuts into a bowl, shaking it to help the walnuts cool. Mel added the crystallized ginger and a teaspoon of ground ginger into the cream cheese frosting. She stirred it in with a rubber spatula, scraping the bowl and making sure the ginger was well mixed.

The timer on the oven buzzed, and Angie grabbed two pot holders to retrieve the cupcakes. They were golden brown and sprang back to the touch. Perfect.

Angie glanced at the clock. "These are too hot. How can we frost them when we only have fifteen minutes left?"

"Let them sit in the pan for five minutes," Mel said. "Then we'll put them in the walk-in for another five minutes. They should be cool enough to frost by then."

Mel got a steel tray and laid out some circular paper doilies. This would be the base of their presentation. While they waited for the cupcakes to cool in the freezer, they each loaded a pastry bag with a large plain piping tip and filled the bags about two-thirds full of the ginger cream cheese frosting.

Five minutes to go. Mel could feel her heart pounding as adrenaline coursed through her. Was this what the real competition would be like?

Angie brought the rack of cupcakes out of the cooler and set it on their steel worktable.

They each took a cupcake, and starting at the outer edge, they piped a circle of icing toward the center. Mel stopped squeezing the bag and twisted her wrist to give the frosting a center swirl. Then she carefully perched one of the toasted walnuts on top. They managed to finish the cupcakes with seconds to spare.

Tate banged out of the office just as Joe came in the back door. The clock struck six o'clock, and Mel was ready to go back to bed.

"Wow, those look spectacular," Joe said. He meant it, which was just one of the many reasons that Mel adored him. "Do we get to taste-test now?"

He looked as eager as a kid, and Mel grinned. Joe suffered from an advanced sweet tooth disorder, and she was sure one of the many reasons he was so fond of her was her baking skills.

"First, we have to judge the presentation," Tate said.

"Looks awfully plain to me," a gravelly voice said from the back door. "What kind of lame teachers did you have at that culinary school of yours?"

# **Three**

Mel whirled around to find Vic Mazzotta standing in the doorway, wearing his usual scowl.

"What are you doing here at six o'clock in the morning?" she asked. He opened his mouth, but she raised her hand and cut him off. "No, don't tell me, let me guess: You woke up and said to yourself, 'Hey, I haven't pestered Mel in months, I think I'll go over there right now and see if I can get her all riled up.'"

Vic's lips twitched, which was as close to a smile as he ever ventured. He was built solid and was dressed casually in his usual khaki pants and a deep blue denim shirt, which made his thick head of gray hair seem silver in contrast. Even after all these years, Mel found it odd when she saw him without his white chef coat and toque.

Angie, Tate, and Joe looked from Mel to the strange man and back. They were waiting for an introduction, but Mel was too curious about Vic's sudden appearance to observe her good manners just now.

Vic strolled into the kitchen, looking as if he owned it. He leaned over the steel worktable and scrutinized her cupcakes.

"You call that a dessert?" he asked with a sneer. "I'd rather eat a clump of dirt with worms in it."

"That can be arranged," Mel said. Vic's gray eyes twinkled at her.

She saw Angie holding her pastry bag like a weapon. Realizing this could get ugly, Mel broke the tension with a laugh and threw her arms around Vic in a big hug.

"I've missed you, you old grouch," she said. She stepped back and looked at her friends. "This is Vic Mazzotta. Vic, these are my friends Angie, Tate, and Joe."

"I recognize you," Angie said to Vic. Her eyes were wide as she made the connection. "You're the chef on the show *World Chef*, the one who travels around the world trying foods from other cultures. Didn't you make an Italian chef cry over his meringues?"

"Yeah, that's how I want to be remembered, the tear maker. Maybe they'll use that for my epitaph," Vic said to Mel then he turned back to Angie. "Those chefs know what they're in for, and if they can't stand the heat with me, they need to get out of the kitchen."

"I'm sorry, how do you two know each other?" Tate asked.

"Vic was my least favorite cooking teacher at the institute," Mel said.

"Ha! She means her most brilliant maestro," Vic corrected her.

"I managed to drive him out," Mel said. "Shortly after I graduated, he went on to be a celebrity chef on the Food Channel. What brings you to town, Vic?"

"I'm judging the challenge to the chefs, pastry division,

at the Scottsdale Food Festival," he said. "When I heard you had entered, I had to come see how you were preparing yourself."

"Excellent," teased Mel. "Now I'm sure to win."

"Not if you try to serve me concoctions like that," he said.

"Try one," she said. "See if you can guess the mystery ingredient."

"Vic!" a voice called from the door. "What are you . . . oh, hello, Mel!"

"Grace!" Mel opened her arms and hugged the petite blonde woman who stepped into the kitchen. "It's so good to see you."

"Is this your bakery, Mel?" Grace asked. "It's lovely."

"No, it isn't," Vic argued. "It's too pedestrian for her. Mel, you could have your own cooking show. You could be a world-famous pâtissier. Why are you putzing around in a pokey little cupcake bakery?"

Angie frowned at him again, and Mel said quickly, "I like my bakery, and I don't have any desire to be famous. Besides, this way I'm near Mom."

"Hunh," Vic snorted, but he said nothing more. He had been friends with Mel's father, Charlie Cooper. They had shared a love of good cigars and fine wines, and when Charlie died ten years ago, Vic had been a surprising source of comfort for Mel in that he hadn't let her quit cooking school and had helped her to work through her grief in the kitchen.

"Well, I love your bakery," Grace said. She was dressed in her usual business suit—today's was a pretty shade of lilac—her makeup was perfect, and her hair was done in a cute blonde bob. She looked every inch the astute business manager that she was, having handled Vic's career for years. "I peeked through your front windows, and I noticed the retro decor. All pink and chrome with the black-and-white floor. It's terrific."

"Thanks," Mel said. Like yin and yang, Vic and Grace balanced one another. Where Vic was harsh, Grace was kind. Mel figured it was lucky for Vic he had Grace to sweeten his tartness, or someone might have stabbed him with a Ginsu by now.

"Well, I'll try a cupcake," Joe said. He sat at a stool at the table and took one off the tray.

Not to be outdone, Vic sat beside him and took one, too. The rest of them filled the remaining chairs, and Angie offered coffee all around, while Mel passed out forks.

Tate looked expectantly at the others, and Mel knew he was hoping to have stumped them with his choice of mystery ingredient.

Mel watched as Vic lowered his fork into the cupcake, taking an equal amount of cake and frosting. He studied the bite for a moment before putting it in his mouth.

Grace and Joe were quicker, and they both raised their eyebrows and exchanged a look that said "yum" louder than any words could.

Mel watched Vic. She knew from the surprised look on his face, which for Vic was a mere tightening of his jaw, when he tasted the burst of crystallized ginger hidden in the cream cheese frosting.

"Nice surprise," he said. "Sugared ginger. It complements the cake, which is very moist."

"So, what is my mystery ingredient?"

"Carrots. It's a carrot cake, right?" Joe asked. He had finished his first cupcake and was reaching for a second.

"Too obvious," Grace said. "It's sweeter than carrots."

Tate looked quite pleased to have stumped them. Angie

had her lips pressed together to keep from blabbing. She was not a very good secret keeper.

Vic, however, was not finished. He took a second bite of the cupcake and chewed thoughtfully.

"You could have gone with a spice cake, you know," he said. "But then your ginger cream cheese frosting would be too much."

"Exactly," Mel said.

"Parsnip," he said. "Three cups shredded and steamed."

Mel bowed her head in acknowledgment. Tate looked put out, but he really had no idea what he was up against. For all his egomaniacal bluster, Vic really was one of the greatest chefs in the country.

"Work on your presentation," Vic said as he snitched a walnut off another cupcake. "It underwhelms."

"Yes, sir." Mel gave him a smart salute, and again his lips twitched.

"And you could use a little of my secret ingredient," Vic said.

Mel let out an exasperated breath. "I would, but you refuse to tell anyone what it is."

"That's because you already know," he said.

"No, I don't. You always refuse to tell me," she argued. He just looked at her with one eyebrow raised.

"Mel, I've always said—" Vic began, but Mel interrupted him.

"Yeah, I know, you'll tell me your secret when you're dead." Mel rolled her eyes. "Come on, be a champ and tell me now."

"Nope. Come on, Grace," Vic said. "Don't I have an interview scheduled or something?"

Grace rose and took her cupcake with her. She waved to the group as she followed Vic out the door.

"It's delicious," she called. "I can't wait to see what you come up with next."

The door shut behind them, and Tate said, "I like her."

"Yeah, she's nice, but I'm surprised he could fit through the door with that ego of his," Angie said. "What can she possibly see in him?"

"Some women are drawn to famous men with giant egos," Tate said.

Angie gave him a quick glance, but his face was blank. Mel knew he was making a reference to Angie's relationship with Roach Malloy, but like Angie, she let it go.

"What's the deal with the secret ingredient?" Joe asked.

Mel smiled. "It's a running joke between me and Vic. When I was in school, I could never get my pastries to taste exactly like Vic's, and neither could any of the other students. We began to suspect that he withheld a seemingly insignificant but ultimately vital ingredient from his recipes, so that none of us could achieve his mastery, thus the secret ingredient."

"Well, that's rude," Angie said. "But with his ginormous ego, I could certainly see him doing that. He would want to stay the best."

Mel shrugged. "I just like to tease him about it. If he does keep his complete recipes to himself, that's his business. A good chef should be able to develop their own anyway."

With a round of hugs, Tate and Joe departed, and Mel and Angie set to work.

They spent the rest of the morning and well into the afternoon baking to restock their display case. One of their favorite customers, a pretty young girl named Tori Sampila, came in for her favorite four-pack of chocolate cupcakes topped with cookie dough buttercream frosting. Tori knew her cupcakes, and Mel always liked to get her opinion on the new flavors she was trying.

Tori pushed her long light brown hair over her shoulder as she bit into Mel's latest experiment, a peaches and cream concoction with peach-flavored cake topped with vanilla buttercream.

Tori's blue eyes met Mel's, and she asked, "Honestly?"

"Always," Mel said.

"Not your best," Tori said. Mel nodded. Tori was confirming what she'd suspected.

"The peach flavor is too faint, right?" Mel asked.

"Exactly," Tori said. "Make the peach stronger, and you'll have another winner."

"Thanks, hon," Mel said.

"Any time," Tori said. "And I mean any time."

With a wave, Tori clutched her four-pack and headed out the door, where her father Brad was waiting.

Mel did inventory. They were low on Tinkerbells and Moonlight Madness cupcakes as well as the Choco-Poms, which had proven to be a huge hit.

There were also several special orders to be filled. First, they had to finish making a huge cupcake tier for a retirement party for a lovely woman named Sharon who worked at the Phoenix Public Library. Then they had a specialty four-pack to decorate for a woman who was breaking up with her boyfriend. She wanted the breakup cupcakes to spell out, *I'm so over you*.

The woman was very pleased with them when she left, and Angie stared after her in wonder.

"Dump him with cupcakes," she said. "I think we may have a niche market there."

"I guess it sweetens the blow," Mel said.

"That was bad, as in artificial sweetener bad."

"Forgive me, I'm exhausted," Mel said. She put her head down on the counter.

"If we're going to be putting in these extra hours, prepping for the contest, then we have to hire some temporary help," Angie said. She was resting her chin on her hand on the counter, and by the look of it, she was keeping her eyes open through sheer force of will. "Is Marty available?"

"I already called him," Mel said. "He's on a cruise with Beatriz and won't be back for two weeks."

Marty Zelaznik was an older gentleman who had volunteered in the bakery before when they got into a time crunch. Well, more accurately when Angie had been spending more time with her boyfriend than in the shop. He had become a part-time employee, and up until his vacation, he could be depended upon to pick up several shifts every week.

"I'm glad that's working out for him," Angie said. Mel wasn't sure, but she thought she heard a note of jealousy in Angie's tone.

"Me, too," Mel said. "But fear not. I called Urban Technical High School, and they're sending over an intern to help us out in the afternoons. She should be popping in any time now."

"Perfect," Angie said. "Well done. That must be why you're the boss."

Mel could have listed a few other reasons, but the timer on her oven buzzed and she ducked into the kitchen to retrieve her latest batch of Cinnamon Sinners, a cinnamon mocha cupcake that she topped with a cinnamon buttercream frosting and Red Hots.

She was off-loading the cupcakes onto a wire cooling rack when she heard the string of bells on the front door jangle. She could hear voices, but it didn't sound like Angie's usual chipper tone with the customers. Mel knew she was tired, but that was no reason to be snippy.

The kitchen door swung open, and Angie stuck her head in. "Mel, can you come out here for a minute?"

"What's up?" Mel asked as she left the worktable and wiped her hands on her apron. "Cranky customer?"

"You'll see," Angie said.

Mel entered the bakery to find a large hulking teenage boy standing there. He wore his hair long and shaggy, and it looked as if it had been cut with dull scissors or finger-nail clippers. It hung over his eyes, making it impossible to see half of his face. The lower half that she could see was his mouth, with a lower lip that was pierced with multiple rings.

He was dressed all in black—black Vans, black jeans, and a black Ramones T-shirt. A chain hung from his back pocket to his front belt loop, and his hands were encased in fingerless black leather gloves.

"May I help you?" Mel asked. She tried to keep her voice even, as in showing no fear.

"I'm Oz, your intern," he growled.

# Four

"Excuse me?" Mel said.

"I'm Oz," he said.

"The great and powerful?" Angie asked.

His head swiveled on his neck in Angie's direction.

"Whoa, never heard that before," he said. His sarcasm was thicker than Mel's cream cheese frosting.

"I'm sorry. How can I help you, Oz?" Mel asked.

"This is Fairy Tale Cupcakes, right?" he asked. His voice was a low rumble and sounded like big-rig tires rolling on the Interstate. Mel watched his mouth move since she couldn't see his eyes.

"Yup, that's us," she said.

"Then I'm your intern," he said.

Mel wasn't sure, but his tone made it sound like he thought she might be dim.

"And you're from . . ."

"Urban Tech High School," he said with a sigh. "My counselor, Ms. Martin, sent me."

He handed her a form from the school, and sure enough, there was his name, his counselor's name, and Mel's bakery all filled out in very official-looking ink. His transcript was attached.

"Wouldn't you be happier at a guitar store or a tattoo parlor?" Angie asked him while Mel scanned the papers.

"No," he growled. "I like baking, but I'm not gay."

Mel and Angie both looked at him.

"Not that there's anything wrong with that," he added.

Mel glanced at the papers, noting he had taken several culinary classes at Urban Tech and his grades were excellent.

"Oz, could you wait here for just a minute?" Mel asked.

"Sure." He shoved his hands in his pockets and studied the cupcakes in the large display case.

"Angie, can I have a word?" Mel asked.

They sidled to the far end of the counter, neither of them eager to leave him unchaperoned in the bakery.

"He's going to scare the frosting off of our cupcakes," Angie whispered. "Not to mention our customers. What are we supposed to do with him?"

"Not exactly the cute cheerleader we were picturing, is he?"

"That would be a negative," Angie said.

"Would we be crazy to give him the job?" Mel asked.

Angie frowned. As a former teacher, this was a moral dilemma for her. She believed in giving all kids a chance, but they couldn't ignore the fact that Oz looked more like a bouncer than a baker, and there was no telling how their touristy customers would react to finding a sullen punk rocker behind the counter.

"'We all go a little mad sometimes. Haven't you?'" Angie asked.

"*Psycho*," a voice said from in front of the counter. "Nice."

Oz's pierced lips slid into a surprisingly charming Cheshire cat grin as he correctly identified the movie Angie had quoted.

Mel quirked up an eyebrow and studied him. "You like movies?"

"'You talking to me?'" he asked in a terrible New York accent.

Mel and Angie exchanged another look.

"*Taxi Driver*," they said together.

"It's a sign," Angie said. "I move that we give him a shot."

"I second that," Mel agreed. "Welcome to Fairy Tale Cupcakes, Oz."

Mel reached out a hand, and Oz grasped it and gave it a solid pump up and down. Then he did a complicated thing where he grasped her fingers, slid the back of his hand across the back of hers, and then pounded his fist on top of hers.

It made Mel feel uncoordinated and awkward, but Angie jumped right in. "Hey, teach me that!"

"Sure," he said, and he went through the same motions with Angie, who, Mel noticed, seemed to catch on much more quickly.

"What does *Oz* stand for?" Mel asked.

"It's my nickname," he said. "Short for Oscar Ruiz."

The bells jangled on the door, and several customers walked in. Angie motioned for Oz to come around the counter.

"I'll give him the down-and-dirty tour," she said. "And then you can figure out his hours."

"Give him an apron, too," Mel said.

"On it." Angie led him through the door behind the counter into the kitchen. "So, Oz, are you partial to blue or pink?"

"That depends," he said. "Are we talking hair dye or clothes?"

"Aprons," Angie said. "We're talking aprons."

"Nothing in black, huh?"

Angie looked him up and down. " 'You are a rumor, recognizable only as déjà vu, and dismissed just as quickly.' " She continued quoting the movie, watching Oz to see if he knew it. When she took a breath to finish, Oz joined in, " 'We're "them." We're "they." We are the Men in Black.' "

Oz's head bounced on his shoulders in a slow, approving nod, and he and Angie exchanged their complicated handshake once again.

Mel rolled her eyes. Leave it to them to get a movie junkie intern.

"Go." She shooed them into the back. Oz ambled ahead of Angie, and she turned at the kitchen door to face Mel.

"He knew the quote from *Men in Black*," Angie said. "I want to keep him. Heck, I want to adopt him."

"Then tell him he'd better be as good with a whisk as he is at shaking hands," Mel said. She gave Angie a push into the kitchen before turning to smile at their customers.

"Welcome to Fairy Tale Cupcakes," she said. "What can I get for you?"

"Don't you have anything besides cupcakes?"

# Five

The woman speaking was tall and thin, too thin, making her head look overly large for her body as it perched on her shoulders like a beach ball. It didn't help that her hair was dyed an unnatural shade of red, a cranberry hue with magenta highlights, and her face had seen so many nips and tucks it had developed an alarming sheen from being stretched too tight.

She was a standard-issue Scottsdale matron, one of the ones who had more money than sense. Mel had observed her type all her life. Sadly, these women seemed to be clinging more desperately to their youth than ever before, as if wrinkles and gray hair were a bad thing. Who had decided that? And why did all of these women buy into it?

"Well, we are a cupcake bakery," Mel said. "So, we pretty much stick to cupcakes."

The woman made a bad face, as if she'd just caught a whiff of sour milk.

"What's the problem, Audra?" the redhead's companion asked.

She was short and stout, dressed in an unfortunate leopard print. Her hair was big and blonde, and her fingernails were long and painted leprechaun green with little gold rhinestones glued on them.

"All they have is cupcakes," Audra whined. "Carrie, I wanted a nibble of something sweet, not a whole cupcake. How could I possibly eat a whole cupcake?"

The blonde let out a put-upon sigh. "Just buy a cupcake. Take your nibble and I'll eat the rest."

"Do you really think that's wise?" Audra asked, eyeing Carrie's middle with one eyebrow raised. It was not a nice look.

Carrie's eyes narrowed, and Mel glanced at the counter to make sure there were no sharp implements for the one named Carrie to use as weapons. She needn't have worried.

"Oh, my dear *older* sister," Carrie said, her voice sweeter than Mel's bin of sugar, "aren't you a love to worry about your younger, wrinkle-free baby sister?"

Audra's lips tightened—well, Mel thought they did. It was hard to be sure, given the immobility of her face.

"The only thing babyish about you is your fat rolls," Audra snapped.

Mel winced. That was a pretty low blow.

"Ooh!" Carrie gasped. "Listen, you bony-bottomed, knock-kneed twig—"

The bells on the door handle jangled again, and Mel was relieved that the arrival of more customers cut off Carrie's tirade and forced the two sisters to cease and desist their squabble.

Carrie pointed out the cupcakes she wanted, and Mel

packed up the six-pack of cupcakes for them and sighed with relief when they paid and left.

The newcomers were studying the menu board. They were a group of three, an older, sturdy-looking couple with a younger woman standing in between them. Mel turned to them with her usual welcome smile, but the older woman in the group glared at her.

"I don't see what's so special about these cupcakes," the woman said, obviously not caring whether Mel heard her or not.

"Mom, shh," the young woman said. She cast Mel an apologetic look.

"Why are we here again?" the man asked, but the woman hushed him.

From his vacant expression, Mel got the feeling he wasn't all there. The older woman gave him an irritated look as if he was being forgetful just to annoy her.

"May I help you?" Mel asked.

"Hi, my name is Polly Ramsey," the young woman said, and she held out her hand.

Mel shook her hand and guessed the young woman was in her early twenties. She wore jeans and a T-shirt, and her long light brown hair was scraped back in a tight ponytail at the crown of her head. She wore no makeup and had a pretty face, but her ears stuck out like handles, and Mel thought she might want to reconsider the ponytail.

"Hi, Polly. I'm Mel. It's nice to meet you."

"Hunh," the older woman grunted. She glanced around the bakery, obviously not liking anything she was seeing.

"How can I help you?" Mel asked.

"I just, uh, well, I wanted to . . ." Polly's face turned an alarming shade of red as she stammered to a halt.

Mel waited, figuring Polly would get there eventually.

"I'm in the challenge to the chefs, pastry division," she said. "In the food festival."

"Oh." Mel leaned on the counter and said, "So, you've come to check out the competition."

"As if she needs to," her mother scoffed with a sniff.

Polly gave her a pained look. "I'm sorry, my mother is a little biased about my skills."

"That's understandable," Mel said, pushing back up off the counter. "Although rudeness is not."

Polly's mother gave her a scathing look and spun on her heel and went to study the open cabinet in the corner that held all sorts of Fairy Tale Cupcake swag, such as T-shirts and coffee cups, featuring their atomic cupcake logo, newly designed by a fashion designer acquaintance of theirs, Alma Rodriguez, in a trade for cupcake deal.

The logo featured an aqua and pink cupcake with the swirls of an atom going around it. It really suited their fifties decor; even Alma had been pleased with her design.

"I'm sorry," Polly said. She looked painfully earnest, and Mel took pity on her.

"Don't worry about it," Mel said. "It's not your fault."

"I've never been in one of these competitions before," Polly said. "I'm afraid I'm in over my head, and I just wanted to meet someone else who was competing. I saw your name on the list, and I figured I'd pop in to say hello. Is that weird?"

"Nah, you're just looking for a friendly face. I felt like that when I started cooking school. I've never done one of these competitions either," Mel said. "So you're not alone. I take it you're a professional baker?"

"Not really. I run a cookie basket company out of my apartment. I started it a year ago, and it just took off."

"Impressive," Mel said.

"Yeah, then Mom entered me in this competition because she thinks it'll give the business a lot of publicity."

"It might," Mel said. "That's pretty much why we entered. Well, that and the ten-thousand-dollar prize."

"She thinks with Vic Mazzotta judging, I'll get on TV," Polly said. She looked mortified, and Mel felt sorry for her. It appeared Mrs. Ramsey was the "pushy stage mother" type.

Mel's own mother, Joyce, was nothing like that, for which Mel was extremely grateful. Joyce was happy as long as her kids were happy. Well, and as long as Mel kept dating Joe. Her mother always called him "dear Joe" and lived in constant fear that Mel was going to muck it up.

"Well, I don't know about any of that," Mel said. "But I do think it will be fun."

Polly looked doubtful.

Mel was about to give her another pep talk when Angie and Oz came back through the kitchen door.

"Nice," Oz said. "You've got a sweet Hobart mixer back there."

"Thanks," Mel said.

She glanced back at Polly, who was looking at Oz with huge eyes. Her mother came up behind her as if to protect her from the ogre from the kitchen.

"Polly, this is my staff," Mel said. "Angie DeLaura, my partner, and Oz Ruiz, our intern."

"You let *that* into your kitchen?" Mrs. Ramsey asked. She gave Oz a once-over that said she found him wanting.

Now Mel was annoyed. It was one thing to be rude to her; it was quite another to be rude to her staff.

"I don't really see how it's any of your business," she snapped.

"Yeah," Angie said. "Who are you anyway?"

"Polly's mother," Mel said. "Polly is in the challenge to the chefs, too."

"Well, Polly, unless you want to alienate everyone in the competition, you might want to muzzle your mother," Angie said and pointed at Mrs. Ramsey, who sucked in an outraged breath.

"I don't have to take that," Mrs. Ramsey huffed.

"No, you don't," Angie agreed. "You can leave. Now."

Polly looked down as if she hoped the black-and-white-tile floor had a built-in escape hatch. No such luck.

"I'd like a cupcake," Mr. Ramsey said. "A pink one."

"No," Mrs. Ramsey said. "You can't have one."

"What do you mean? Isn't that why we're here? To have cupcakes?" he asked.

"No, you dolt." Mrs. Ramsey grabbed her husband's arm none too gently and hustled him out the door.

He tried to dig in his rubber orthopedic heels, but she had a good grip on his arm and Mel could see the muscles bunch in her upper arm. She was no weakling. He gave her a mean stink eye but didn't make any more protests as she pushed him out the door.

"Sorry," Polly apologized again.

"No worries. See you at the festival, Polly," Mel said with a genial wave. Polly nodded and dashed after her parents.

The bells rang on the door once again, and Mel glanced up from the counter. What now?

She shouldn't have asked. Obviously, the rule of threes was in action here, as in three high-maintenance customers in a row. She glanced at the clock. It was only four o'clock; closing time at eight seemed eons away.

The tall black man who approached the counter gave

her a slow smile. It was the smile of a man who was used to getting his way.

"Dutch Johnson," she said. She didn't return the smile.

"Melanie Cooper." His smile became blinding.

Mel figured the reading on his charm-o-meter went right into the red zone as he approached the counter with a swagger that on a lesser man would look ridiculous. Dutch, however, made it look like the zoo had lost one of their big cats, as he walked in a gait that was purely predatory.

Both Angie and Oz stood frozen watching the stunningly handsome black man approach Mel. She had to admit he looked like something that had walked off the cover of a men's health magazine.

Muscles rippled under his purple silk dress shirt. He wore his hair so closely shaved to his head that it was impossible not to notice that even the shape of his head was attractive. When they were handing out good looks, Dutch had obviously gone back for thirds.

"So, how is my favorite classmate?" Dutch asked.

"Oh, please, I'm only your fave because I'm the only one who didn't sleep with you," she said.

"Yes, which damaged my self-esteem beyond repair," he said.

There was a twinkle in his eye, and Mel knew he was teasing her. The truth was he had never hit on Mel. She liked to think it was because he respected her culinary skills, but she suspected he was just not that into her. She'd had a relapse into her big-girl pants after her father had died and had been significantly larger back then.

"You look amazing," he said. "But then, you always did."

Mel squinted at him.

"What?" he asked, the picture of innocence.

"You're so full of it, I'm going to need a snow shovel to dig out of here tonight," she said.

"I'm hurt." He put his hands on his chest as if she had mortally wounded him.

"I'm sure," she countered. She glanced behind her, where Angie and Oz were still rooted to the spot.

"This is my partner, Angie, and our intern, Oz," Mel said. "Guys, this is Dutch Johnson. We went to cooking school together."

"Pleased to meet you," Dutch said. "I can see Mel isn't the only beauty in the Fairy Tale here."

Angie sagged a bit in the knees, and Oz quickly braced her with a hand at her elbow. She gave Dutch a weak smile.

It was harder to tell what Oz was thinking, given that his eyes were covered by his mop of hair, but since he was a teen male, the awe in his voice spoke volumes.

"How do you do that?" he asked, obviously referring to Dutch's ability to make women go limp

Dutch spread his hands wide. "It's a gift."

"Yeah," Mel snorted. "The gift that keeps on giving."

"If I didn't know better, I'd say you're unhappy with me," Dutch said.

"Not unhappy, just immune," Mel said. "I can't tell you how many girls I saw sobbing into their crème brûlée because of you. It was more effective than a vaccination."

"Huh." Dutch grunted, but Mel was pretty sure it was meant with respect.

Shaking her head as if pulling herself out of a trance, Angie stepped away from the counter. "Come on, Oz, I need to go inventory the walk-in cooler."

"But we did that yesterday," Mel said.

Angie gave her a flat stare. "Your point?"

Mel glanced between Angie and Dutch. Oh. "Don't have one."

"I thought not," Angie said.

They departed through the kitchen door, and Mel turned back to Dutch.

"So, I'm guessing you're not here just to catch up," Mel said. "What brings you by, Dutch?"

"What? A guy can't look up an old friend?"

Now it was Mel's turn to give the flat stare.

"All right, all right," he said. The veneer of charming rogue slid off him like a snake shedding its skin, and he gave her a straight face. "I'm one of the judges in the festival."

Mel's eyes widened. "The pastry division?"

He nodded.

"But you and Vic can't stand each other."

Dutch nodded.

"Awkward," Mel said.

"Little bit," Dutch said. "Which is why I need you."

# Six

"Does Vic know you're one of the judges?" Mel asked.

"I'm sure he must," Dutch said. "I was surprised he left *World Chef* to come and be a judge. But then I'm sure when he realized it was another opportunity to screw me over, he jumped at the chance."

"Dutch, be serious." Mel shook her head.

"I am. They were filming in India, so why would he leave the shoot early unless he had a reason?" The bitterness in Dutch's voice was as tart as Mel's lemon curd but lacked its subtle aftertaste.

"I sincerely doubt that Vic dislikes you so much that he would travel halfway around the world just to damage your career. If he left his cooking gig in Southeast Asia, it's because it was done."

Dutch snorted. "He had no qualms about forcing the network to pull the plug on my cooking show."

"He didn't force the network to sack you. You weren't

cooking," Mel argued. "You were being a poser, and Vic called you out on it."

A flash of anger sparked in his dark eyes, and Mel grimaced, afraid she'd gone too far. She didn't want to hurt his feelings, but she felt compelled to be honest.

"So he got to you, too," Dutch said. He spun away from the counter, anger in every line of his rigid body, then he turned back, looking defeated. "Even you believe the lies he spread about me."

"Dutch, I watched the show," Mel said. "What were you doing? You had all these celebrities on, and if I remember right, they were supposed to be cooking with you, but you didn't do much cooking. You did do a whole lot of dishing around the stove but not on plates. It was like watching a gossip show with recipes for cute appetizers."

Dutch opened his mouth to protest and then closed it again. Mel gave him points for knowing when he was beat.

"So, what if I was toying with being a talk show host?" he asked. "I could have been good."

"On the Food Channel, they're not really looking for the latest celebutante martini recipe," Mel said.

Dutch turned to look out the large front window. Mel studied his profile and watched his jaw clench and unclench.

"You know why Vic went after you," she said. "You have skills. You were one of the best in our class—"

"Present company excepted," he interrupted with a smirk.

Mel had been a better student than Dutch, that was true, but she forged on to make her point.

"It drove Vic crazy that you didn't live up to your full potential. He believed in you; that's why he was so hard on you."

Dutch shook his head. He didn't want to hear it.

"He was always jealous of me. He knew I was going to be a bigger star than he was, and he stopped it before it could happen."

"Is your ego really that big?" Mel snapped. She was out of patience. "Do you really think Vic cares if you're a star or not?"

Dutch turned back to her and shook his head as if this conversation had not gone the way he'd expected and he was giving up.

"Look, it doesn't matter, that's not why I'm here. I really do need you."

"Oh, so there *is* more to your visit than renewing our old friendship?"

Dutch gave her a small smile, and she was reassured that there were no hard feelings between them.

"Bertie Grassello is going to be judging the contest as well," Dutch said.

"Are you kidding me?" Mel asked. "Vic is going to have a stroke."

Bertie Grassello was another teacher from their days at the culinary institute. Both Mel and Dutch had studied with him as well as Vic. Dutch had been Bertie's favorite, while he seemed to merely tolerate Mel.

She had often suspected that Bertie disliked her because Vic favored her. Bertie opposed everything about Vic. It was no matter to Mel because, as far as she was concerned, Vic was the more talented of the two teachers and she learned more from him in a day than she did in a week of Bertie's classes.

"A stroke, huh?" Dutch asked. He grinned. It wasn't a nice smile.

"Yeah." Mel wouldn't be surprised if Vic popped a

blood vessel over this, because if Dutch and Vic disliked each other, then Vic and Bertie absolutely despised each other.

"Here's the thing: Bertie has some business in the works that could be very good for me, and I was hoping if the opportunity presented itself, you'd put in a good word with Bertie for me, you know, remind him of my skills and charisma."

"Should I work this into my challenge to the chefs presentation?" Mel asked. "Maybe deliver my dessert plated in a raspberry syrup that spells out your name with hearts around it?"

"You'd do that for me?" Dutch asked. "See? I knew you always liked me."

"Seriously, Dutch, why would Bertie listen to me? I wasn't his favorite, you were."

"Yes, but you are one of the best and the brightest of our class," he said. "And everyone, even Bertie, respects your opinion."

As if he'd flipped a switch, the charm was back on full force. Angie came trotting through the swinging doors, took one look at him, and turned back around and left.

"I like her," Dutch said.

"She has a boyfriend," Mel said.

"Ain't that always the way?"

"Listen, I can't make any promises, but if I see Bertie and the opportunity presents itself, I'll do my best to plug you," she said.

"You're a peach, Mel."

"Just remember that when you're judging the contest."

With a salute, Dutch headed out the door, and Mel felt herself collapse against the counter. Suddenly, the contest that had seemed like such a good idea was looming up like a storm cloud on the horizon, and she didn't have an umbrella.

"Long day?" Joe asked as he refilled Mel's wineglass.

"You could say that," Mel said. "Between cranky customers, crazy festival competitors, and judges, I'm done."

"How long does this thing last?" Joe asked as he stretched out beside her on the futon.

"Well, it starts with forty-four competitors, and they whittle us down each day until the last four remain."

"Wow," Joe said. "I think I'd rather try another serial murder case."

"It's going to be great publicity if we win."

"You'll win," he said. She loved the note of certainty in his voice. "You make the best cupcakes in the state. I feel bad for the poor shlubs going up against you."

Mel smiled. This was her favorite part of the day, curled up with Joe after a nice meal, flipping through the channels while they talked about their day. It just didn't get any better.

She had only had one significant relationship in her past, and that had been years ago when she was working as a marketing whiz in Los Angeles, before she pitched it all to go to culinary school. Her boyfriend had dumped her when she'd dropped out of the rat race.

Sometimes it frightened her how much she cared for Joe. It made her feel vulnerable in a way she had never experienced before. She truly didn't know how she would cope if their relationship didn't work out. She pushed the thought away as soon as it crept into her head. If her father's death ten years before had taught her anything, it was to live in the moment.

That being said, she wondered if Angie had heard from

Roach. Would their relationship die now that they were on separate continents? How would Angie handle it if it did go up in smoke?

"Whatcha thinking about?" Joe asked.

"Angie and Roach," she said.

"She still hasn't heard from him?" he asked.

"Not as of closing tonight," Mel said.

Joe was silent.

"Whatcha thinking about?" Mel asked his question back at him.

"That a good brother wouldn't be happy that his sister was about to get her heart broken," he said.

"Do you think Roach is going to dump her?" Mel asked.

"He's in Europe on tour with groupies launching themselves at him like sexy missiles," he said. "I find it hard to believe that he could resist for long."

"I hate that she might get hurt," Mel said.

"Me, too," he said. "But I'd also be relieved if she found someone more . . . stable."

"I don't want her to move to Los Angeles with him when he gets back," Mel said. "Selfish?"

"No, she's your best friend," Joe said. "It's perfectly understandable."

She yawned and burrowed closer into his warmth. He took the wine out of her hand and placed it on the table behind them. He wrapped his arms about her and held her close. Mel desperately wanted to stay awake, but she could feel the lethargy from weeks of getting up way too early seep into her bones. Joe kissed the top of her head, and Mel slid into sweet oblivion.

A high-pitched, ear-piercing wail jolted Mel out of her sleep. She jumped to her feet, fighting to clear her head while Joe did the same on the other side of the futon.

Finally the wailing stopped, and Mel blinked to find Angie holding an air horn up over her head.

"Angela Lucia DeLaura!" Joe yelled. "What the hell do you think you're doing?"

"You're late, Mel," Angie said. "I told you if you were late, I would take it upon myself to get you moving."

"How about knocking?" Joe asked. He was clutching his chest, looking like he was fending off a heart attack.

"Now where's the fun in that?" Angie asked. "Come on, Mel, it's our last day to prep before the big contest. We need to get our game on."

"Ugh," Mel grunted. "I'll be down in five."

"Okeydokey," Angie said. "But if you're not . . ."

She looked like she was going to give the horn another blast for good measure, but Mel snatched it out of her hands and said, "Don't even think about it!"

"Five minutes," Angie said. She must have sensed from the crazed look in Mel's eyes that it would be in her best interest to skedaddle.

The door shut behind her, and Mel turned back to Joe with a dark look. "Okay, I take it back. Los Angeles might not be far enough for her to move if she ever pulls a stunt like that again."

"Agreed," Joe said. "But I still think she can do better than Roach."

He was the middle of Angie's seven older bothers, and although he hadn't been superpleased with his baby sister's latest boyfriend, he'd been the most accepting of the brothers. In fact, Mel was pretty sure that the only reason Angie and Roach were even still dating was because he was away in Europe right now where the brothers didn't have access to him.

Mel grabbed her clothes out of the dresser in the corner and ducked into the bathroom. Once she was dressed, she gave her teeth a solid once-over and tried not to look at the clock, which read four forty. Good grief. No wonder she couldn't keep her eyes open past nine o'clock.

Tate was waiting with his usual brown bag. He looked wiped out, and Mel wondered if the past few weeks had been as hard on him as they'd been on her.

"One hour," he said. He handed Mel a steaming cup of coffee and disappeared into her office.

Mel peeped into the bag. After three weeks, she knew Tate must be running out of ideas, but this was going to be more of a challenge than she was up to this early in the morning.

"So, what do we have?" Angie asked.

"Sauerkraut," Mel said.

"What?" Angie asked.

Mel reached into the bag and pulled out a jar.

Angie curled a lip. "I dig it on a bratwurst but in a dessert? Not possible."

"You'd be surprised," Mel said.

"Clock's ticking," Angie said. "Let's do this."

Off the top of her head, Mel only knew one recipe that sauerkraut could be used in to make a delicious dessert. It was chocolate cake, but she also knew the judges would be expecting that. Given that she now knew three of the judges and one of her competitors besides Olivia, she figured she'd better pull out all of the stops on her creativity.

"Okay, here's what we're going to do," she said. Then she laid out her game plan for Angie, who grinned when she heard the whole idea.

"You are a culinary genius," Angie said in wonder.

They set to work, and an hour later when the buzzer went off and Tate popped out of the office, they had a tray of fabulous pastries, ready to be taste-tested.

The back door opened, and Mel glanced up expecting to find Joe, looking for his morning sweets fix. He had really taken to having fresh baked goods ready to sample first thing in the morning, even if they were made out of unexpected and downright bizarre ingredients. So far, she'd had really only suffered one failure, and that was when she'd tried to make a frosting out of barbeque sauce. It hadn't gone well.

But to her surprise, it wasn't Joe at the door, but Vic Mazzotta with a dark-haired young woman.

"Vic, what brings you here?" she asked. "No, don't tell me, let me guess: You came by to wish me luck."

"Luck?" Vic scoffed. "You'd better not need luck. You've got the skills that I taught you. Don't embarrass me and lose now, you hear?"

Mel rolled her eyes and held out her hand to the woman with him. "Hi, I'm Mel."

The woman took her hand, and Mel noticed she had a pretty face and generous curves but her eyes didn't meet Mel's. Instead, the woman glanced around the kitchen, and Mel got the sense she was cataloging the room with a mental cash register in her head sounding *ka-ching!* It was all Mel could do not to throw herself protectively in front of her Hobart mixer and Blodgett convection oven.

"This is Jordan Russell, my protégée," Vic said. "Say hello, Jordan."

"Hello, Jordan," the young woman joked as she let go of Mel's hand. "You have some amazing equipment for a bakery that is so new."

"I have a partner who is heavily invested," Mel said. "And cupcakes are all the rage. I'm pleased to say, we've been doing very well."

"I'd love to have a kitchen like this," Jordan said. She turned and gazed at Vic with adoring eyes. But just like she had assessed the kitchen around her, Mel got the feeling that Jordan's eyes glittered not for love of the considerably older man but because she viewed Vic as her own personal money bag.

"So, you're a chef, then?" Mel asked.

Jordan simpered, "Oh, no, I'm not formally educated in the cooking arts."

"She's learning from me," Vic said. "I found her working in a high-end grocery store in Manhattan, teaching customers how to make fifteen-minute gourmet meals."

Mel felt her smile get hard. What was Vic doing with a protégée who hadn't been to cooking school?

As if he read her thoughts, he said, "I hired her as a sort of personal assistant–intern type of thing."

Mel noticed that his gaze lingered on Jordan's figure when he said this, and she wondered when exactly *protégée* had become a euphemism for extramarital-activity partner. Poor Grace. Mel felt a flash of anger on her behalf. How could Vic be so stupid?

She glanced over at Tate and Angie. They were both looking at Vic as if he were a wriggly bug who'd crawled out from under a rock, and Mel knew she wasn't the only one to guess the truth about Jordan's true relationship to the Master Chef.

"Now what is this you're trying to pass off as an entry in the pastry division?" he asked. One of his bushy gray eyebrows was raised in his trademark derisive expression.

"Try it," Mel said. "You'll like it."

"Well, your plating is vastly improved from the last time." He stared at the tray of desserts as if trying to pick the best one. Finally, he settled on one and sat at the table. Jordan hovered behind him, and Mel had to fight the urge to elbow her out of the way, all the way out the door, in fact.

Vic had always had a mega-ego, but having this young little tart giving him massive doses of worship was only going to make it worse, way worse.

Vic forked up a bit of the dessert, and his lips twitched in surprise. Tate was watching him eagerly, and Mel knew he was hoping he wouldn't guess the mystery ingredient. Fat chance.

"Not a traditional use of sauerkraut as a dessert," Vic said. "You finely chopped the kraut and tucked it into a custard and then piped that into a puff pastry shell and topped it with warm cinnamon apples. The unimaginative generally bury it in a chocolate cake."

Mel saw Tate sag with disappointment, but Angie bolstered him by throwing an arm around his shoulders and giving him a squeeze.

Just then the back door opened, and Joe strode in with Grace, Vic's wife, right behind him. Mel glanced from Jordan to Grace and back. This could not be good.

"How did it go?" Joe asked Mel as he planted a kiss on her temple.

"You tell me," Mel said, and she gestured toward the table.

Joe pulled out the chair next to Vic's and helped himself.

"Vic, I have been looking all over for you," Grace said. "You have another TV interview scheduled for seven thirty. Really, Jordan, if you're going to be his personal assistant, you need to be more on top of his engagements."

Tate muttered something to Angie, who burst out laughing. She still had her arm around him, and he looked at her with such longing in his eyes, it was painful for Mel to watch.

Angie must have felt it, too, because she removed her arm and said, "I'd better go prep the front so we're ready to open."

Joe looked at her like she was nuts. "But you don't open for another three hours."

"So? I'll have you know there's a lot to do," Angie said. She hustled through the swinging door into the bakery.

Tate gave Mel a confused glance, and she knew he was trying to decide if Angie bolting away from him was a good thing or a bad thing. Then he smiled, making his decision clear.

"Don't blame Jordan for my being off schedule," Vic said to Grace. "I wanted her to meet Mel. It's good for her to meet the best of the best if she's going to get into this business."

Mel was oddly touched that he regarded her so highly. They'd had a rocky start when she was attending culinary school, mostly because like every other student at the culinary institute, she was dead scared of Vic. He was known for yelling at students if their cooking was below his exacting standards, and he made most of his students cry at one point or another.

Mel had never cried, however, and one day when she'd been whipping up a meringue, he'd gone to stick his finger in to test it, and she had whacked his hand with a spatula and snapped, "Don't mess with my meringue."

No student had ever dared to stand up to Vic before, and there had been a mutual respect between them ever since. After Mel graduated, Vic went on to stardom on the Food Channel, which from what she had seen had only worsened an already severe case of narcissism.

And now Vic was apparently cheating on his wife. Although Mel loved him dearly, she was disappointed that he was treating Grace so badly. Grace and Vic had been together for at least forty years. Mel couldn't fathom how he could step out on her now and with someone a third of his age no less. It was disturbing.

"Vic, the time," Grace said, and she tapped the face of her watch.

"All right, I'm coming," he said. "See you tomorrow, Mel. Do me proud."

He strode through the back door with Jordan on his heels, looking more like an adoring puppy than a woman in her mid-twenties.

"You know, if you'd tell me your secret ingredient, I'm sure I'd win," she called after him.

Vic laughed but didn't turn back and pony up the goods.

"See you at the competition, Mel," Grace said. She squeezed Mel's hand and added, "I know you'll do fabulously."

Mel watched her petite form leave the kitchen and only half noticed when Joe came to stand beside her. He was chewing, and through a mouthful he said, "These are your best yet."

Mel smiled at him. He was dressed for the office, and as always, her heart did a little cartwheel at how handsome he was.

"I'll call you later," he said. He snitched another pastry off the table, and Mel laughed.

As the door swung shut behind him, she turned to Tate and asked, "'But why would a man need more than one woman?'"

Without hesitation, he quoted the next line from *Moonstruck* right back at her, "'I don't know. Maybe because he fears death.'"

"Well, he should. If I were Grace, I'd kill him," Mel said.

Tate raised his eyebrows. "You can't even kill a housefly."

"Flies don't cheat on their wives of forty years," Mel said.

"Good point."

# Seven

"Stop eating the profits!" Angie slapped her brother Tony's hand as he reached into the glass display case.

"I need fuel if I'm going to man this bakery all by myself," he protested. He clutched his injured hand to his chest and gave her his best wounded look.

"Have a banana," Mel said. She handed him one from the bowl of fruit she kept in the kitchen as an alternative to a steady diet of sugar.

Tony took the banana with a put-upon sigh.

"Now what do you do if you get a special order while we're at the competition?" Angie asked.

"Take the person's name and number, and tell them you'll call them back," he said.

"Do you use any of the kitchen implements—yes, this includes the mixer—while we're gone?" Mel asked.

"I know, no touching the equipment," he said. "Gees, you two act like I'm an idiot."

"Oh, I'm sorry," Angie said. She didn't sound sorry at

all. She turned to Mel and said, "Silly me, I must have dreamt that the last time he covered the shop for us, he tried to modify the Hobart with a robotic arm that would frost cupcakes by itself."

"You have to admit, it would have been cool," Tony protested. He was the gadget geek of the DeLaura family and spent most of his days cooking up new and different electronic gizmos that he was sure would make him a fortune.

"Yeah, except we were cleaning up frosting for two days," Mel reminded him. "Don't touch my stuff."

"And Oz, our intern, is coming in later to help out," Angie said. "Be nice to him."

"All right. Go kick some baking butt already." Tony was tall and thin, and he hunkered down to hug them both. They squeezed him back, giving him one last warning look before they headed out the door.

The competition was being held outside at the Scottsdale Civic Center Mall, which was easy walking distance from the shop. But as they drew closer to the event, Mel was suddenly riddled with doubt. What if this plan for publicity backfired and she was bounced from the competition in round one? Olivia would probably announce it to the world with a billboard on the interstate. How would Mel live with the humiliation?

As they reached the grounds, she could see there were white-topped booths lining all twenty-one acres of the Scottsdale Civic Center Mall. Vendors including kitchen stores and local restaurants were all scurrying to unpack their assigned booths. The festival would be opening in just a few hours.

Colorful burgundy booths lined one of the pathways around the fountains. Mel knew from their packet of information that this was where the challenge to the chefs would be taking place.

"You know I always love attending the festival," Angie said as they paused to survey their work area. "But it's kind of weird to be in it."

"Agreed," Mel said.

"Melanie! Angela! Yoo-hoo!"

Mel looked behind her to see her mother, wearing a lime green polo shirt and matching sun visor, waving at her from the volunteers' booth.

They both waved back.

"I didn't know your mother was volunteering," Angie said.

"Neither did I," Mel said.

They crossed over to the booth, which was stuffed to the gills with women and men adorned in lime green. A stout woman with a clipboard, wearing bright orange lipstick with her lime green uniform, was addressing the group.

"Now, for every shift you work, you get ten free tasting coupons."

Mel sidled over to her mother's side. "Who is that?"

"That's Millicent Penny," Joyce whispered. "She's in charge of the volunteers."

"What are you doing here, Mom?" Mel asked.

"Ginny thought it might be fun for us to volunteer," Joyce said. "She's over there behind Millicent."

Mel glanced over the crowd. Sure enough, there was her mother's best friend, Ginny Lobo. She was a tiny little thing with platinum hair and huge blue eyes. Ginny had come from poverty and married up when she snagged Monty Lobo.

Now she was as rich as all get-out, but her elevator had gotten stuck somewhere between floors, and she spent a lot of time and money trying to convince the world that she was the love child of Elvis Presley and Marilyn Monroe.

She caught sight of Mel and Angie and gave them a little finger wave over Millicent's head. She was sipping on a bright pink water bottle that Mel would have bet her last cupcake did not have water in it.

"Why would you want to do this?"

Joyce's face flamed red under her green visor. She had recently taken to streaking her naturally blonde hair with copper, and now it matched the color in her cheeks.

"Ginny thought I might . . ." she mumbled with her head turned to the side, making it impossible for Mel to hear her.

"I'm sorry, I didn't catch that," Mel said.

"Me either," Angie chimed in.

"Now remember, people, you are the face of the festival. You must be smiles, smiles, smiles!" Millicent called out.

Joyce ducked her head and repeated herself, but Mel still couldn't hear her over Millicent bellowing out the roll call for the volunteers.

"What?" Mel yelled. "I still can't hear you."

"Meet a man!" Joyce yelled in return. "Ginny thought I might meet a man here."

Millicent had stopped calling the roll right as Joyce had shouted. Now the horde of volunteers swiveled their heads to look at them.

"Oh, nuts," Joyce said. Now her face flamed even brighter than her hair.

One of the male volunteers stepped forward. Beneath his lime green shirt, he wore pink and green checkered polyester pants with a wide white belt and matching white shoes. He gave Joyce the once-over and then shifted his dentures in his mouth and winked at her.

"No need to look any further, lovely lady, I do like a spicy redhead."

"Oh, gross! Do you want me to punch him in the face for you?" Angie asked Joyce.

"Oh, heavens no," Joyce said. "You just can't go around punching people, Angela."

"Really? How unfortunate." Angie leaned toward the paunchy oldster with the bad comb over and smacked her left palm with her right fist. He backed up in a hurry.

Mel blew out a breath. She couldn't shake the feeling that having her mother and Ginny volunteering here was going to be a titanic disaster.

"People!" Millicent clapped as she addressed the group. "It is time to man your stations." She fluttered her hands at them, and the group dispersed.

"We need to go check in," Mel said to Angie. "Mom, try to stay out of trouble. You, too, Ginny!"

Ginny lifted her mouth from the straw in her plastic cup and yelled, "Aw, don't be a party pooper, Mel!"

Mel opened her mouth to protest, but Angie half carried and half dragged her away. "Come on, we're going to be late."

"She just called me a party pooper!" Mel protested. She tried to turn back and give Ginny a good zap of stink eye, but Angie pulled her inexorably forward.

"Now is not the time," Angie said.

"You think she's right, don't you?" Mel asked.

"Are you kidding? Heck no, you're more fun than a barrel of monkeys," Angie said.

"A barrel of monkeys?" Mel repeated. "That's the best you could do. How old are we, five?"

"Hey, monkeys are fun and they're cute," Angie said.

"They are not cute; they're known for throwing their own poo," Mel argued.

"That could be cute, depending upon the target," Angie countered.

"Cute? Who's cute, or are you talking about me again?"

Mel spun around to find Dutch walking behind them.

Angie sucked in a small breath and said, "I'll go sign us in."

Dutch watched her go with a small smile on his lips.

"Stay away from my sous-chef," Mel said. "She's vulnerable right now."

Dutch raised his eyebrows in an interested look, and Mel could have kicked her own backside. What an idiot she was. Here the shark was circling the water, and she pointed out the blood to him, you know, in case he missed it.

"I thought you said she had a boyfriend," he said.

"He's away on business," Mel said. She didn't dare mention that Angie was dating a rock star for fear that this might make her even more enticing to Dutch.

He studied her and then shrugged.

"The first round starts in an hour, you ready?" he asked.

"As I'll ever be," she said. "It's hard to prep when you don't know what the mystery ingredient is."

"You've been practicing, haven't you?"

"Of course. I'm a pro," she said. There was no need to mention it had been at Angie and Tate's prodding.

"Good, I'm counting on you to win," he said.

Mel gave him a quick glance. "What do you mean?"

He gave her a careless shrug. "Nothing. I'm just hoping for the best for you."

He turned and walked away. He looked like the consummate superstar in his powder blue dress shirt with the sleeves rolled back to his elbows, his crisply creased coffee brown dress slacks, and brown Archdale loafers with the perforated skull and crossbones on the toes. His outfit probably cost more than Mel spent on clothes in a year.

She glanced down and took in her pink Converse One Stars and olive cargo pants. Thankfully, she and Angie were wearing white chef coats, and they'd don their pleated toques before they started cooking. Mel had figured she only needed to look like a pro from the waist up.

She felt her cell phone in the lower right pocket of her pants vibrate. She had shut off its usual *Gone with the Wind* ringtone so as not to be disturbed during the competition.

She pulled out her phone and checked the display window. It read *Fairy Tale Cupcakes*. Oh, no!

"Hello?" she answered.

"So, I was thinking what you're really missing here is a punk rock cupcake."

"Oz?"

"Yep, it's me," he said. "You've got too much pink here. You need some balance. Punk rock cupcakes would be the way to go. It could be a niche market."

"Because cupcakes aren't enough of a niche?" Mel pinched the bridge of her nose between her thumb and her pointer finger.

"I'm thinking black icing."

"You're calling me with this now?" she asked. "I saw the bakery name pop up on my phone, and I thought it was Tony calling to tell me the place was on fire."

"How could it be on fire when you won't let me use the oven?" he asked.

"Oz, you and Tony are babysitting the shop until we get back," Mel said. "There's usually a lot of foot traffic because of the festival. Are you sure you two can handle this?"

"Two of us?" he asked. "I have a DeLaura brother, and the T-man is hanging out."

"T-man?" Mel asked.

"Tate," Oz explained. "He's kind of cool when he loses the suit."

"He's okay," Mel said, feeling cranky. "Aren't you a little early for your shift? I thought you had school in the morning."

"Early release day," he said. "So, picture this: a dark chocolate cupcake with smooth white frosting, possibly a fondant, with a black fondant skull on it."

"Halloween isn't for six months," she said.

"Okay, I can see where it might appear seasonal," he said. "How about we spell out *Black Flag* or the *Ramones*?"

Mel was watching Angie sign in when all of a sudden Olivia Puckett appeared beside Angie and hip-checked her out of the way.

"Oz, I'm kind of busy here," Mel said.

"It's cool, just think about it," he said.

"Right, don't use the oven or the mixer," Mel said. "Keep Tony from eating everything, and call me if there's trouble!"

She snapped her phone shut and hurried over to the table, where Angie looked like she was going to launch herself at Olivia. Mel slid into the gap between them and smiled at the registration lady, who was looking decidedly alarmed.

# Eight

"Problem?" Mel asked Angie.

"Not yet," Angie said. She glared over Mel's shoulder at Olivia.

"I'm going to frost your cute little butt right out of round one," Olivia growled as she sauntered by Mel.

"We'll see," Mel said.

She refused to take the bait, mostly because if the situation escalated, she'd have a hard time controlling Angie and her temper. Angie was known to swing first and talk later, which was why she'd had her own personal desk in the detention room in middle school. Mel couldn't afford to lose her assistant chef this close to competition time.

"Challenge to the chefs competitors, please report to the conference room," the registration woman called through a microphone, which let loose a shriek of piercing feedback, making Mel jump.

Once the competitors had all packed into the room to don their chef clothes, a skinny woman with a big head, sporting a highly teased hairdo of vibrant red hair, addressed the group.

"I am Felicity Parnassus. I am the chairwoman of this year's festival."

She paused as if to give them a chance to applaud. There was a smattering of claps, and she nodded her head in acknowledgment. Angie caught Mel's gaze and rolled her eyes. Mel looked away before she laughed.

"Welcome, chefs," she said. "Now we need to quickly go over the rules. You will wait onstage in your kitchens while our host announces the mystery ingredient. You will then have an opportunity to gather your mystery ingredient off of the cart we wheel out. That is your only chance. Back onstage at your designated station, you will find it fully stocked with all of the kitchen staples you'll require, such as flour, milk, sugar, and eggs. Also, assigned to your station will be your designated runner. This is your runner for the duration of the competition. It will be their duty to acquire whatever special items you need to make your culinary creations from the pantry that we are maintaining in the corner of the conference room. This is where we will be keeping unusual spices and other possible ingredients.

"The judges will be in attendance for the duration of the contest, and while they will be judging you primarily on creativity, presentation, and taste, they will also be watching to see how you manage your kitchen. Professionalism is always appreciated. The contest will begin in half an hour. I suggest you go familiarize yourself with your kitchens."

As they made their way out of the conference room back to the festival, Mel felt her stomach clench. She was nervous. She couldn't believe it. She was never nervous about cooking. She always looked at it like an adventure.

But she'd never had scads of free publicity and ten thousand dollars riding on it before.

"What's the matter?" Angie asked. "You look a little sweaty and pasty."

"Do I? It must be something I ate," Mel said.

"Hi, Mel!" Polly Ramsey darted in front of her. "Isn't this exciting? It's actually starting."

Mel frowned at her. She was a kid running a cookie business out of her apartment, and she didn't look nervous at all.

"Angie, you remember Polly—she came by the bakery the other day?"

"Oh, yeah, you're the one with the Sherman Tank for a mom," Angie said.

Polly had the grace to look embarrassed. "I'm sorry about that. I did take your advice," she said. "I banned her from coming here until the finals, assuming I make the finals. Truly, I'm just happy to be a part of all this."

She gestured around at the hordes of people now filling the walkways, the vendors hawking their wares, and the general happy chaos that filled the place.

Mel felt her shoulders drop. Polly was right. This was supposed to be a fun event, not do or die. Sheesh. She had to get her priorities straight.

"Come on," she said with a smile. "Let's go find our stations."

Mel and Angie found themselves in a well-appointed spot with plenty of shade. The day was beginning to heat up, and Mel was grateful for the cool breeze that blew across the grounds, keeping the desert sun from becoming oppressive.

The challenge to the chefs, pastry division, had been divided into two groups of twenty-two. Mel was relieved that they were in the first group as the second group had to go cool their heels in a conference room nearby so as not to be tipped off to the mystery ingredient.

Mel and Angie studied their mini-kitchen, and Mel felt reasonably sure she could function in it. She was used to baking in bulk, so it would be weird to use the mini-appliances that they'd been supplied with, but then they only had to cook for the four judges—Bertie Grassello, Dutch Johnson, Vic Mazzotta, and Candace Levinson, who was an editor with *Food and Wine* magazine.

Spectators gathered to watch as their host arrived with a large white plastic box. Mel and Angie exchanged a look.

"If it's eels, I am so out of here," Angie said.

"It's not going to be eels," Mel said. "At least, I don't think so."

Their host, celebrity chef Johnny Pepper, bounded onto stage, exploding like a firecracker and drawing the crowd to him like moths to his flame.

"Are y'all ready?" he addressed the crowd with his charming Southern drawl and engaged them in guessing what the mystery ingredient could be. As he shouted back and forth with the gathering throng, Mel took the opportunity to study him.

He had spiked, bleached blond hair that shone almost white in the midday sun, a nose ring, and a sleeve of tattoos running up both of his arms. He wore combat boots and fatigues under a black chef's coat that sported flames shooting up from the bottom hem. He looked too punk rock for the kitchen, and Mel suspected Oz would love him.

Johnny was a veteran of the Food Channel and had made his fame and fortune by being a badass grill man. His face was now on everything from charcoal briquettes to bottles of BBQ sauce. He was as close to a rock star as a chef could get.

Angie leaned next to her and said, "Is it just me or is he hot?"

"*En fuego,*" Mel confirmed.

As if he heard them, Johnny glanced over at their station and gave them a wicked grin.

"Dutch better watch it," Angie said. "I think Johnny could eclipse even him."

Mel had to agree. She pulled her gaze away from Johnny and glanced at the crowd. She saw Grace Mazzotta wedged between a family and a young couple. Grace was standing up on her toes and scanning the faces of the people around her as if looking for someone. Mel glanced over at the judges' booth to see Dutch and Bertie and a woman taking their seats, but there was no sign of Vic.

She frowned. She didn't see Jordan either. Was Vic off dallying with his bimbo protégée? Mel felt a hot spike of anger rush through her. If Vic wanted to be a two-timing lowlife, that was his choice, but here was Grace, his counterbalance of kindness, and she deserved to be treated better than this.

"I'll be right back," Mel said.

"But . . ." Angie began, but Mel shook her off.

She slipped off the dais, feeling Olivia's gaze upon her as she went. She really wished the other baker had been put into the second round.

"Grace," Mel called to her friend. "Are you all right?"

"Oh, Mel, hi there." Grace gave her a beaming smile.

Mel reached past the young couple and pulled Grace toward her. "You look like you're about to be trampled."

"Oh, no. I'm fine, dear. Shouldn't you be up there listening to your instructions?"

"My partner has it under control," Mel said.

"Well, then you've chosen well," Grace said. She went back to scanning the crowd. "Now, if I could just find Vic."

"He's not here?" Mel asked.

"If he is," Grace said. "I can't find him."

"Grace, is everything okay?" Mel asked. It was as close as she could get to saying that she thought Vic was cheating on her.

Grace turned to look at her. Her eyes crinkled in the corners, and she tipped her head in understanding. "All marriages weather storms, even when they're named Jordan."

Mel scanned Grace's face. It was still a pretty face, softened just a little bit with wrinkles and the toll of gravity. She was in awe of the acceptance in Grace's eyes. If Joe ever pulled a stunt like this, why she'd . . .

A flash of movement near the stage caught Mel's attention.

"Speak of the devil," she said.

Jordan was coming toward them. Her long dark hair was pulled back in a casual knot at the back of her head. She wore jeans and a plum-colored blouse, which was wrinkled as if she had just thrown it on.

A close glance at her face and Mel could see her lips were clamped tightly together, and she was without makeup, which seemed out of character for a young woman who appeared to get by on her looks.

"Jordan," Grace called out to her, and the young woman whipped her head in their direction. She didn't look pleased to see them. "Have you seen Vic?"

"No! I'm his intern, not his keeper," the young woman snapped, and then she plowed past them back into the crowd.

Mel frowned, but Grace patted her arm.

"Vic is just going through a phase. It'll pass. It always does, and I'll still be here for him."

"But aren't you . . ." Mel's voice trailed off, realizing that this might be none of her business.

"Angry?" Grace guessed and then shook her head. "To what purpose? Vic is my best friend. He'll figure it out. He just needs some time and understanding."

"Or a swift kick in the patoot," Mel suggested.

Grace tipped back her head and gave a delighted laugh. "No wonder you've always been Vic's favorite. You're not afraid of him at all, are you?"

"Not even a little," Mel said. "And I am more than willing to offer my size nines to do the kicking."

"I'll keep that in mind," Grace said with a chuckle. "Now get up there before you're disqualified. I'm sure Vic will turn up any minute; he always does."

Mel gave her a quick hug and squeezed her way back up onto the dais.

"And your mystery ingredient is . . ." The host paused for dramatic effect, while reaching into the plastic box, and then yelled, "Parsnips!"

Angie turned to Mel and said, "Oh, yeah!"

Mel nodded, and they exchanged the complicated handshake Oz had taught them but not nearly as coolly as he did it.

"I wouldn't celebrate yet if I were you," Olivia said from across the kitchen.

"You think you can beat us?" Angie taunted her.

Olivia curled her lip, and her sous-chef mimicked her hands-on-hips stance of intimidation.

"I could beat you with my whisk tied behind my back," she said.

"Isn't that how you usually cook?" Mel asked. "Or maybe it just tastes that way."

Olivia snarled, and Angie spun Mel away from her before it got physical.

"Game face," Angie ordered, and Mel nodded.

On Johnny's count, they had to run to the cart and collect their parsnips. This was no time for squabbling with Olivia. They could save that for later, after they whipped her meringue in this competition.

# Nine

It was almost too easy, which made Mel nervous.

Their runner was an elderly woman named Joanie. She was short and skinny with gray hair that hung in a long ponytail down her back. She wore thick glasses, giving her a birdlike appearance, which was only enhanced by the two vivid circles of rouge she wore on her cheeks and the cherry red lipstick she wore on her lips, although her ability to color within the lines was questionable at best.

She moved pretty quickly for a woman who looked to be shoving eighty back pretty hard. When Mel asked her to get them some candied ginger, Joanie took off for the special pantry with her head ducked low and her steps quick like the determined march of a badger.

"I think she's going to work out," Angie said.

"She is a spritely little thing," Mel agreed.

Angie pointed over her shoulder in the direction of Olivia's station and said, "I'm not sure, but I think Puckett's runner just peed his pants."

Mel glanced over to see Olivia sweating profusely while dressing down her sous-chef and her runner, as if she were starring in an episode of *Hell's Kitchen*.

"Lunatic," Angie scoffed, and she went back to monitoring the cupcakes.

Mel watched Dutch as he strolled amongst the different stations, pausing to watch the pastry chefs in action. She ignored him and set to work on her cream cheese frosting.

The sound of a bowl shattering brought her attention up, and she glanced over to see Polly Ramsey, flushed with embarrassment, as Dutch grinned down at her.

Polly's father was standing in her kitchen with her, and Mel was surprised to see him there. He hadn't struck her as being too much on the ball when he'd been in the shop, but maybe that was because Polly's mother seemed to suck all of the air out of the room with her stage-mother histrionics.

Mel watched him for a moment and noted that he seemed to move about the kitchenette as if he knew exactly what he was doing. When Dutch lingered with Polly, her father shooed him away, showing an awareness Mel wouldn't have guessed he possessed.

"Score another victory for Dutch," a voice said from behind Mel.

She turned to find Bertie Grassello standing there.

"Hi, Bertie," she said. "How are you?"

Bertie Grasello had been Mel's least favorite professor at the culinary institute. He was a poser, and she had no patience for him.

Instead of working on his craft, he worked at making himself look like James Beard. Tall and stocky, he shaved his head bald and sported a gray mustache neatly trimmed over his upper lip. But that was where the resemblance ended.

While James Beard had been one of the key persons responsible for giving America a gourmet food identity, Bertie Grassello was a publicity hound always looking for his next close-up.

"Looks like Vic couldn't be bothered to show up," he said. "That's a pity—for you."

"What's that supposed to mean?" Mel asked.

"Oh, come on, you know you're favored to win. Vic has all but guaranteed it. I saw your face when they announced the mystery ingredient was parsnips. You knew already, didn't you? He told you, didn't he?"

"He most certainly did not!" Mel said. She saw several people glance their way, and she lowered her voice. "If you have any evidence of wrongdoing, by all means bring it forward; otherwise, I suggest you shut it."

Bertie stiffened. "Still Vic's girl, aren't you?"

"Always," Mel spat. She forgot her annoyance with Vic as she defended him to his archrival. Maybe Vic was behaving like a jackass lately, but that did not mean Bertie could talk trash about him.

"Well, we'll see how far that gets you in this competition," he said. "Did you know I've been hired to replace Vic on his television show? I just got the offer this morning, and of course, my manager accepted. I imagine we'll have to negotiate a few things like salary and my expense account, but you're looking at the new host of *World Chef*."

Mel blinked in surprise. She hadn't heard. Vic was leaving his show? Why hadn't he said anything? Did he even know?

"Yeah, apparently, good old Vic has been phoning it in, especially during his recent Southeast Asia tour. His viewership numbers are down. I think he should have paid more attention to his program and less to his protégée, if you know what I mean."

It galled Mel that she did know.

"So, the network was looking for someone with a little more pizzazz, and they chose me. My star is on the rise," Bertie said as he stuck his finger in her cream cheese frosting. "You might consider being nice to me."

He walked away licking his finger, and Mel had to fight to keep from launching the entire bowl of frosting at his head. Jerk!

She wanted to talk to Vic, and she wanted to talk to him now. She scanned the booths, but she didn't see him anywhere.

She caught sight of Grace, standing below the dais talking to the festival chairwoman, Felicity Parnassus. Grace looked as if she were on the verge of tears, and Mel felt another spurt of anger toward her mentor.

How could Vic be so callous and stupid? It made her want to find him just so she could shake some sense into him or kick his butt around the festival grounds for a few laps.

Felicity looked none too pleased, and she stormed away from Grace, leaving her biting her lip and looking worried. Mel was about to jump down and find out what was going on when Angie rushed to her side.

"Cupcakes are out of the oven and in the cooler," she said. "The clock is ticking, Mel. Come on. Focus!"

Mel glanced back at Grace, who looked as if she was pulling it together. Then she thought of Vic, who would murder her if she messed this up.

"Okay, I'm with you," she said.

Joanie had delivered the ginger, and they quickly mixed it into the frosting. Using pastry bags with open tips, they piped frosting onto the cooled cupcakes in large swirls and then placed a toasted walnut on top. Sensitive to Vic's opinion that their presentation had underwhelmed last time, Mel melted some caramel and drizzled it across the plate before placing a cupcake in the center, very artsy.

An air horn went off, and all of the chefs were ordered to step back from their stations. Angie had just placed the last cupcake onto a plate, and she and Mel stepped back together.

Out of the corner of her eye, Mel saw Polly look crestfallen, as if she just hadn't been ready yet. She also saw one of the volunteers shoo Olivia back from her table to keep her from continuing now that the siren had sounded.

Angie looped an arm around Mel's neck and gave her a big squeeze. They were both hot and sweaty, but Mel felt as if they had done their best and now it was in the judges' hands.

The panel of judges had taken their seats at the table under the canopy adjacent to the dais. Professional waiters were now in charge of serving the judges the competitors' offerings.

Bertie and Dutch were both seated as well as a woman Mel did not recognize but assumed was the editor from *Food and Wine* magazine. There was also an empty seat, which indicated that Vic had yet to show up. Mel watched as Felicity Parnassus escorted Jordan Russell, Vic's protégée, to the empty seat.

"Where the heck is Vic?" Angie asked Mel.

"No idea," Mel said.

"They are not having that bimbo fill in for him, are they?" Angie said.

"Looks like it," Mel said. She frowned as she watched the brunette toss her hair over her shoulder and smile coquettishly at the photographer who was snapping a picture for the local newspaper.

"You know, this is so typical," Mel scoffed. "It's always beauty before ability. If anyone should be taking Vic's place, it's Grace. They met in cooking school, you know, and she was really talented. If she hadn't put her career on hold to manage Vic's, I'm sure she'd be famous in her own right."

"There she is." Angie pointed. "Should we go keep her company?"

Mel followed the direction of Angie's gaze and saw Grace huddled with one of the festival officials beside the stage. She was nodding at him while holding her cell phone to her ear.

"She looks busy," Mel said. "I can imagine the fallout from this is going to be huge. From what Bertie Grassello told me, Vic is already on the outs with the network. I can't imagine what he's thinking not showing up in time for this."

Mel and Angie trooped off the stage with the rest of their competitors. Because there would be two sessions to today's cooking competition, the results would not be in until after the next group.

"So, how did it go?" Tate asked as he popped up in between them.

"You're never going to believe what the mystery ingredient was," Angie said.

"Eels?" he asked.

"Ew, no," Angie said. "Parsnips."

"No way," he said.

"Way," Angie countered.

"Well, you two should have this sealed up, then," he said. "Hey, maybe I've missed my true calling. Maybe I should be a mystery-ingredient food scout for cooking competitions."

"I think you're looking at a bit of a dip in salary," Angie said. "Hey, what are you doing here anyway? Aren't you supposed to be at the bakery, helping Tony and Oz?"

"Your brother Sal took my shift for me. They all look stunning in the pink aprons, by the way. You might want to consider giving them those for Christmas," he said.

Mel and Angie chuckled as they tried to picture the brothers in the pink bib aprons that the bakery was known for.

"Besides, I can't miss this. I have a vested interest. So, where's your buddy Vic?"

Mel was watching as the judges sampled the first round of parsnip-based desserts.

"I don't know. He never showed up."

"That's odd, isn't it?" he asked.

"Well, Vic's always been a tad arrogant," Mel said. "He may have thought they'd wait for him."

"A tad?" Angie asked. "That's like saying a habanero pepper is a little hot."

"Okay, so he's an egomaniacal, narcissistic butthead. Still, he was very good to me after my dad died, and I'm fond of him."

"Understood," Tate said. "Do you two want to stay here or go do some sampling while the judges get through all of those desserts?"

"Let's go sampling," Angie said.

Mel realized she was starving, so she let them pull her in the direction of the rest of the festival.

The first thing that struck her was the smell. The perfume of mesquite smoke from a grill blended with another booth's Mexicali lattes, causing Mel to salivate. There were more than fifty restaurants represented, and as participants in the challenge to the chefs, she and Angie had free tasting coupons to use at any booth they chose.

"It's past lunchtime," Angie said. "I feel the need for something solid in my belly."

"How about a Southwestern burger?" Tate asked. He was consulting the list of restaurants. "The Barrio Bistro makes a juicy burger with jalapeño cheddar and guacamole."

"Lead the way," Angie said. "And we'd better wash them down with margaritas. My nerves are shot."

They wound their way through the booths. More than forty thousand people would be visiting the festival during the week, and Mel had a feeling that most of them were here right now.

They passed a stage with a Native American group performing. The steady beat of the drum gave rhythm to the hoop dancers, and Mel paused to watch for a moment before Angie grabbed her arm and dragged her along.

"Later," she said. "I'm so hungry I could eat overcooked Brussels sprouts."

They stopped at the margarita booth first. Mel ordered three, which Tate graciously paid for since he had a wallet and Mel and Angie had only their looks to get by on, which after toiling in the competition for an intense hour, were not up to getting them anything for free.

Mel was trying not to think about how their cupcake had stacked up against some of the other desserts. It wasn't that she was competitive; it was just that she really wanted to beat Olivia into the ground, repeatedly.

While they were waiting, the bartender barked at his bar back that he needed more ice. Mel tried not to let her impatience show, but she was hot and cranky, and a frosty beverage would have really hit the spot.

"I always pick the bad one," Angie muttered. "Always. Here I pick the bar that has no ice, at the grocery store, I choose the line with the oldster who writes a check, and on the highway, I get in the lane with the texter in it. You name it, I am a slowpoke magnet."

"I'm sorry, ma'am," the bartender said. His badge read *Daniel.*

"No, it's not you, Dan, it's me," Angie said.

"She's just a little wiped out from competing this morning," Tate said. "Challenge to the chefs, you know."

"Nice," the bartender said. "Good luck." Then he glanced behind him and yelled, "Pete, what's the holdup? I have people waiting here."

"It's the door," Pete snapped. "It's stuck."

Mel glanced over the bar to see Pete yanking on the back door of what appeared to be a refrigerated trailer.

"Excuse me, our store of ice is in there," the bartender said, and he jogged over to where Pete was still trying to yank open the door of one of several trailers.

The bartender pushed him aside, braced his foot against the side of the trailer, and pulled with all of his might. The door wouldn't budge.

"Maybe we should go someplace else," Angie said. "This could take a while."

"I don't know," Mel said. "Our barman seems determined."

She gestured back to the trailer, and they watched as Daniel got a crowbar from a nearby truck and wedged it into the door. Both he and Pete pushed on the crowbar, and with a loud crack, the door popped open and out came a tumble of ice and a body.

Pete shrieked like a girly-girl, while Dan let loose a string of curses that could have barbequed meat without flame.

Mel glanced at the body and felt all of the blood drain from her face as she recognized the burly build and thick head of gray hair. Vic!

# Ten

Tate pulled his phone out of his pocket as Mel ran forward to check on Vic. His skin was as white as paper, and his lips were tinged with blue. He was, not surprisingly, ice-cold to the touch. She pressed her ear to his chest. He wasn't breathing, and she couldn't hear a heartbeat.

Mel knelt beside him and cradled his head in her lap, thinking, *No, Vic, no!*

It couldn't end like this. Vic Mazzotta was larger than life. He couldn't be dead. She couldn't accept that, because if he was, she was losing not just her mentor but also her friend.

The crowd, alerted to the drama by Pete's shriek, pressed forward, but Angie spread her arms wide and pushed them back.

"Give the man some room!" she shouted.

Dan and Tate joined her, and together they made a human chain that was impossible to breach.

One of the volunteers from the festival came running along with several of the festival's security staff.

Tate sent one security man to greet the paramedics who were on their way and told the volunteer to get over to the challenge to the chefs' staging area and bring Grace Mazzotta there immediately.

The rest of the security team fanned out to help keep the way clear for the paramedics while one of them joined Mel on the ground, where she cradled Vic.

"I'm trained in CPR and first aid," the young man said. He laid his ear on Vic's chest, and Mel had to fight the urge to shove him away even as she knew he might be Vic's best chance.

He checked Vic's airway and his pulse. Mel studied the security guard's face and felt alarm pulse through her at the grim set to his features.

Three paramedics with a stretcher pushed through just then, and the young man stepped back, allowing them to get through.

"He's not breathing, and there's no pulse," the security man said.

The one who looked to be the senior paramedic nodded and looked at Mel. She realized that she was still sitting in the mound of ice. As a female paramedic knelt beside her to take her place, the man in charge held out his hand to her and pulled her to her feet.

"It won't help him for you to get frostbite," he said. His voice was kind, and Mel felt Tate reach out and pull her close.

The crowd was silent as the men went to work. The paramedics looked as grim as the security man who had tried to help. Mel felt her throat close up. She didn't want to be here. She didn't want to watch this.

A soft cry sounded from the crowd, and Mel turned to see Grace Mazzotta escorted by the volunteer. Her eyes were huge and her body was aquiver.

"Vic?" she asked. Her voice was barely more than a whisper.

The paramedics had placed Vic on the stretcher. Mel noticed that they had no equipment hooked up to him. They began to wheel him through the crowd, looking more like pallbearers than emergency medical technicians.

The head of security stood with Grace. He caught her arm when she looked like she might go down in a heap. She watched as they wheeled her husband past, and Mel could only describe the look on her face with one word, *shattered*.

◦ ◦ ◦

"How did it go?" Oz asked as they trooped back into the bakery a few hours later.

Mel didn't answer. She supposed it was rude to leave the poor kid hanging, but she was beyond basic manners at the moment.

She heard Angie telling him about the day's events in hushed tones, and she heard Oz's shocked exclamations of disbelief.

She sat on a stool at the steel worktable in the kitchen, feeling equal amounts of shock and regret. How could Vic be dead? She had been so angry with him. She hated that her last thoughts of him had been ones where she wanted to kick his patoot.

"Hey, Mel, how are you doing?"

Tate shouldered his way in through the swinging door and gazed at her with such empathy that she burst into tears.

She folded her arms on the table, laid her head down, and wept. Tate stepped forward and put his large, warm hand on her shoulder.

"Let it out," he said as his hand ran up and down her back. Mel did as she was told, and although she cried for what seemed like a very long time, she knew there would be more tears to follow.

When her father had died ten years ago, she had discovered that grief had a bottomless quality to it. Every time she had thought she'd hit the bottom, she discovered that another labyrinth of pain lay beneath the last just waiting for her to fall into it.

"Come here," Tate said when her tears had subsided into hiccupping snuffles.

He helped her to sit up and dabbed at her face with his handkerchief. Mel let out a wobbly sigh, and he pulled her into his arms in a bear hug that threatened to squish her ribs.

Mel laid her head on his shoulder and soaked in the comfort of his warmth. She knew she would never forget the hardened coldness of Vic's body, whether from being frozen or from rigor mortis, she didn't know, but it gave her the shivers all the same.

The kitchen door swung open, and Angie strode into the room. Her eyes went wide as she took in the sight of Mel in Tate's arms.

"Oh, sorry, didn't mean to interrupt." She turned and dashed back into the bakery.

"No, Angie, wait!" Mel stepped away from Tate. But it was too late. She was gone.

"Oh, damn," she said. She turned to look at Tate.

He was watching the door swing on its hinges, as if trying to figure out what had just happened. Then he turned to Mel and shrugged.

"You're my oldest friend," he said. "Of course I'm going to hug you and let you cry on me when you just discovered your mentor frozen to death."

"But Angie may have gotten the wrong idea," she said.

"Then she's an idiot," he said. "A lovable idiot, but an idiot nonetheless."

"I need to call Uncle Stan," Mel said. "Maybe he'll have some information. I don't want to bother Grace."

"Are you sure you're up for that?" Tate asked.

"Yeah, it's better to know," Mel said. She patted his arm. "Thanks for helping me through this. You're a good friend."

"'It's an insane world, but in it there is one sanity, the loyalty of old friends.'"

Mel reached up and patted his cheek. *"Ben Hur.* Good one."

Tate looked pleased with himself. He watched as she went into her closet-sized office and shut the door. She knew she should probably go and talk to Angie, but really, what could she say?

Angie had been convinced since they were kids that Tate carried a torch for Mel. It was ridiculous, since Mel had always loved Tate like the older brother she'd never wanted, but Angie refused to believe it.

The irony was, of course, that Tate was in love with Angie but hadn't gotten up the courage to tell her yet. Sometimes Mel felt like she was watching a train wreck in slow motion, and she wondered what would be left of the three of them when the collision finally happened.

She shrugged off these thoughts and picked up her office phone. Uncle Stan was a veteran detective with the Scottsdale Police Department, and since south Scottsdale was his beat, she knew he would have heard about the body at the festival by now.

He answered on the third ring. "Cooper, here."

"Hi, Uncle Stan," Mel said. "Did you hear—"

"About the Food Channel guy in the freezer? Yeah, I got tapped for the case. I was just heading over to the medical examiner's," he said. "Why?"

"Uncle Stan, it was Vic Mazzotta," she paused. "He was a friend of Dad's and mine."

Uncle Stan was quiet for a couple of beats. Then he cleared his throat. "Ah, hell."

"He was my teacher at the institute," Mel said. "He was the one who wouldn't let me quit after Dad died."

She heard Stan blow out a rough breath. "I'm sorry, Mel, this has to be brutal for you."

"Yeah, especially since I was there when they found him," she agreed.

"What?" he asked. He sounded as though he was flipping through some paper. "I have a bartender named Daniel and a bar back called Pete listed as first on the scene."

"Well, yeah," Mel said. "Tate, Angie, and I were there getting margaritas . . ."

"At what time?" he asked. He had his cop voice on, which meant he didn't want to hear any whining or excuses.

"Oh, I guess about one o'clock," she said.

"In the afternoon?" he asked. He sounded incredulous. "Little early in the day for a cocktail, don't you think?"

"I had just finished competing, and I was hot," she said.

"I hear lemonade is mighty refreshing."

"Last time I checked my ID, I was of age," Mel said. "Now moving on, the door to the refrigerator truck was stuck, and Dan and Pete had to pry it off and out came Vic."

"Nasty business," Stan said. "Freezing a man to death."

"Was he murdered? Oh my god," Mel's voice trailed off.

"No, no, I don't know anything for sure," Stan said quickly. "That's just speculation on my part. Listen, I'm headed over to the medical examiner's now. I'll call you when I know more, and Mel, I really am sorry."

"Thanks, Uncle Stan," she said. She hung up the phone and glanced up to find Angie standing there, wringing the bottom of her pink apron in her hands.

"Are you all right?" Angie asked.

"I've been better," Mel said with a sigh.

"I'm sorry about earlier," Angie said. "I didn't mean to make things awkward."

"You didn't," Mel said. "Tate and I are just friends, you know."

"Not my business," Angie said. She raised her hands as if Mel were holding a gun on her, and Mel shook her head. When it came to who was the bigger fathead, she was hard pressed to choose between Tate or Angie.

"Except that I'm dating your brother Joe," Mel said. "So, yeah, it is your business."

"So, did Uncle Stan have any information about Vic?" Angie asked, clearly changing the subject.

"He's on his way to the ME's right now," Mel said. "He seemed to think Vic was frozen to death."

"On purpose?" Angie asked.

"Well, it seems unlikely that he fell into the freezer trailer by accident," Mel said.

"Then he was . . ."

"Murdered."

# Eleven

Mel didn't hear back from Uncle Stan that night. She assumed it was because he didn't have anything to report. This was not conducive to sleep, and a little after midnight, she slipped out from beneath Joe's protective arm and crept down to the bakery.

She rarely had insomnia, but when she did, it required the elixir of a batch of Moonlight Madness cupcakes. This was her go-to cupcake, a chocolate cupcake with vanilla buttercream rolled in shredded coconut and topped with an unwrapped Hershey's Kiss.

She set to work, losing herself in the whir of her pink KitchenAid mixer and the smell of baking cupcakes. She was not at all surprised when there was a knock on the back door.

She glanced through the window. There was Angie. Her long brown hair was sporting a fine case of bed head, and she was wearing her black Sewers T-shirt over her pajama bottoms. She looked as if she hadn't slept a wink. Mel unlocked the door, and Angie barreled inside.

"I can't sleep," she said.

"Looks like it's contagious."

"Moonlight Madness?" Angie asked, and Mel nodded. "Yay, I was hoping you'd be making those."

The cupcakes were cool enough to frost, and they both set to work with a rubber spatula and a bowl of shredded coconut. While they topped them with unwrapped Hershey's Kisses, neither one of them mentioned that it was a "one for the cupcake and two for me" sort of deal.

When the last cupcake was finished, Angie looked at Mel and said, "What do you think will happen to the challenge to the chefs?"

"I don't know," Mel said. "I think they have to finish it. Bake-Rite cake flour is sponsoring it, and I heard they put a lot of money into advertising, not to mention the ten-thousand-dollar grand prize. I can't think they'll be happy if the festival committee cancels it. Probably, they'll just keep Jordan as a substitute judge."

"Do you want to withdraw?" Angie asked, and Mel appreciated that she was leaving it up to her.

"I don't know," she sighed. "I can't imagine staying in, but I'm afraid Vic will haunt me if I back out now."

"He'd make a fearsome ghost," Angie said.

"Indeed," Mel agreed. A sob bubbled up, and she tried to swallow it down.

"It's okay," Angie said. "I know how important he was to you."

She stood up and circled the table and hugged Mel in her strong arms. Mel hugged her back fiercely. At the moment, she felt as if she were being buffeted about on a rough sea and her friends were her life preservers.

The back door opened, and Mel knew who it was before she turned around. It was hard to say whether it was her sadness or the smell of the fresh-baked cupcakes that had drawn him to the kitchen, but either way, she heard him whisper, "How's she doing?"

"She's tough. She'll be okay," Angie said as she stepped back and studied Mel's face as if to confirm what she'd just said.

"I'm right here, you know," Mel said, but her voice was teasing.

"I know, but I didn't want to break up any cathartic keening," Joe said. He took Angie's place and pulled Mel into his arms.

"I think I've dried out for the moment," she said. She hugged him tight, just like she had Angie. She wanted the people closest to her to feel how much she loved them. Vic's death was a sad reminder that she didn't tell the people she cared for often enough how very much she did love them.

"I know Vic wasn't perfect," she said. "Far from it, but he was always there for me, always. It's hard to think of my life without Vic Mazzotta in it."

"I know," Joe said. "I'll help you through this any way I can."

"Me, too," Angie said.

"Well, right now you can help me eat these cupcakes," Mel said, pushing out of his embrace. "The cooler is full, and I have no idea what I'm going to do with all of these."

"Say no more. I am the man for the job," he said.

He took a seat and chose two cupcakes. Mel and Angie did the same.

"So, I'm thinking I should go and see Grace," Mel said. "I mean, she's got to be devastated. Vic was her whole life."

"Really?" Angie asked. "Even though he was cheating on her?"

"We don't know that," Mel said.

Angie gave her a flat stare.

"Okay, we do know that," she said. "But I talked to her about it, and she wasn't even mad. She seemed to think it was just inevitable, and she was waiting it out."

"Bully for her," Angie said. "I'd wait it out—in the state penitentiary after I shot the miserable louse in the privates."

Joe glanced at her across the table. "This is not information I want to hear."

"Sorry, sometimes I forget you're an officer of the court," Angie said. "Still, how can she put up with that?"

"You are assuming that she did put up with it," Joe said. "We don't know how Vic ended up in that freezer, and spouses are frequently—"

"Grace did not murder Vic," Mel interrupted. "I know it. She loved him, despite his character flaws. Besides, she's not a killer. I know her and she's not."

Angie and Joe exchanged a glance, but Mel didn't back down. She knew Grace. They didn't. As far as she was concerned, that made it case closed, and she was going to tell Uncle Stan and anyone else who cared to listen the same thing.

\` ／ ＼ ／ \`

When Mel and Angie arrived at the festival the next day, they were greeted by two bright-eyed volunteers. Well, one bright-eyed volunteer and one tipsy one—Mel's mother, Joyce, and her best buddy, Ginny.

"Oh, honey, how are you?" Joyce asked as she pulled Mel into a crusher hug.

"I'm fine," Mel said, hugging her mother back just as tightly.

Joyce had checked on her the day before, but Mel was happy to see her again today. Her brother, Charlie, who lived in Flagstaff, had called repeatedly, and Mel had to admit that having her small family circle the wagons for her made her feel much more secure.

"We were shocked, just shocked, to hear about the dead guy in the freezer," Ginny said. She patted Mel's arm while taking a long sip from her water bottle. "And then we heard he was your old professor—didn't see that one coming."

"Thanks, Ginny." Mel turned back to her mother. "Have you seen Grace?"

"No," Joyce said. "And we're under strict orders from Millicent to say nothing about the incident."

"Incident?" Angie asked. "Since when is a dead man just an incident?"

"When it's a dead man who might turn off forty thousand festival visitors," Ginny answered.

"Ah," Angie said.

"Any word on what they're doing about the challenge to the chefs?" Mel asked.

"Business as usual," Joyce said. "Because of yesterday's chaos, they've put up a leader board, you know like in golf, so if you made it to the next round, you're on it."

Mel stared at her, and Joyce gave her a ghost of a smile. Then as if she couldn't stand the suspense, she jumped up and down and said, "You're in the lead!"

"We're what?" Mel asked.

"In the lead, numero uno, tip-top," Ginny said.

"I have to see this," Angie said. She grabbed Mel's arm and said, "Come on."

They skirted the booths where restaurants were in the midst of setting up for the day and cut across the lawn. Mel couldn't help glancing at where the bar had been yesterday.

She noticed the trailer that Vic had been found in was gone, and she wondered if the police had impounded it.

They reached the stretch of the mall where their cooking dais was situated, and sure enough, mounted above the cooking area was a huge billboard and Fairy Tale Cupcakes was at the top.

"I'll be damned," Mel said. "Look at that."

She quickly perused the board and noticed that Confections was listed third after Polly's Cookies.

Angie pumped her fist and let out a very unsportsmanlike whoop. Given the circumstances with Vic, Mel couldn't get that enthused, but she did feel a surge of satisfaction that was impossible to deny.

"Don't get too used to it," a voice snarled from behind them. "This is just the first cut."

Mel whirled around to find Olivia and her sous-chef glaring at them. She wondered if Olivia had any other look or if she suffered from an advanced case of permascowl.

"Oh, I don't think it's for us to get used to," Angie said. "I'd say that's more your problem, 'cause we're number one and we're planning to stay there."

"Hunh," Olivia grunted. "That's going to be kind of hard now that your little judge buddy is dead."

Mel felt a blast of white-hot anger light her up from the inside with the explosive force of gunpowder. Olivia did not deserve to even utter Vic's name, never mind be dismissive of his death.

"Shut up," she said. There must have been something in her tone because both Angie and Olivia's sous-chef looked at her in surprise. "A man is dead—show some respect."

Olivia shrugged. "What do I care? I didn't know him. I wasn't his little pet."

Mel moved before it was a conscious thought. She fisted

Olivia's blue chef coat in her left hand while her right formed a fist.

"I said show some respect," she said through gritted teeth. "What part of that don't you understand?"

A flash of fear lit Olivia's eyes, and her sous-chef stood behind her flapping her arms uselessly as if she thought she should defend her boss, but she didn't want to be the one to take the pounding herself.

"Hey, would you look at that?" a voice asked. Mel glanced over her shoulder to see that the pert and perky Polly Ramsey had joined them. She was looking at her number two spot and appeared very chuffed about it.

"Wow, do you see my name?" she asked. "Look, I'm up there with you!"

Polly set off to get a closer look at the board, and they all watched her go before anyone moved.

Mel relaxed her grip on Olivia's coat and smoothed the creases with her palm as she said, "I think we understand each other now."

"Oh, I understand," Olivia spat. "Now *you* understand I'm going to pound you, just so we're clear."

Angie stepped forward, but Mel stopped her with a hand on her elbow.

"May the best chef win," Mel said.

"Don't worry, I will," Olivia said, and she stormed away from the dais.

"Mel, so help me, if you withdraw us from this competition because of Vic, I will understand, but oh, I will be so disappointed."

"I'm not going to withdraw us," she said. "After all, this may be the best place to find out more about Vic's death."

"No, no, no!" Angie protested. "We are not getting involved in this, absolutely not."

# Twelve

"We already are involved," Mel said. "Vic was my friend, and we're the ones who found his body. How much more involved can we get?"

"That's one way to look at it," Angie agreed.

Mel had started to walk around the grounds, and Angie fell into step beside her. They had to duck and weave as workers were hauling carts, setting up for the day's events.

"Or we could focus on making mincemeat out of Olivia in the competition and save the whole murder thing for the police."

"Absolutely," Mel agreed. Her eyes scanned the gathering crowd. "Olivia's going down, but if along the way I happen to gather information that I think will help Uncle Stan, I'm going to pass it on to him."

"But that's not our purpose," Angie said, looking concerned. "That's secondary. Mel, hear me, 'There's one thing I want you to do for me. Win. Win!'"

Mel turned to look at her and frowned.

"Did you really just quote *Rocky II* to me?"

"It helped, didn't it?"

Mel shook her head and walked away.

"Oh, come on, it had to help a little," Angie protested. Then because Mel didn't acknowledge her, Angie started humming the *Rocky* theme song behind her. She jogged around Mel, doing her best Rocky impression, which was pretty bad. Mel couldn't help cracking a small smile.

"All right, all right," she said. "I get it. You want to win. I promise I won't let anything get in the way of that."

Angie stopped jogging and hugged her. "And I will do anything I can to help you gather information."

Mel gave a nod and glanced at her cell phone. They had only a half hour until they were to report to the dais for today's culinary competition. She wondered if Grace would be here or if she'd stay holed up in her hotel room. Mel was betting on the latter.

"I'm going to run a quick errand," she said. "Meet me at the stage in twenty minutes."

"Where are you going?"

"I want to ask our host what he thinks about Vic ending up in a freezer," Mel said.

"Johnny? You're going to talk to Johnny Pepper?" Angie gaped. "You said you were going to gather information; you didn't say you were on a suicide mission."

"Why is it a suicide mission?" Mel asked.

"Have you seen Johnny's show?" Angie asked. "That man is crazy. He actually learned how to eat fire. How do you know he won't shish kebab you?"

"I'll be fine. I'm just going to see what I can find out," Mel said. "Don't worry. I'll be subtle."

"Joe is going to be so unhappy about this."

"I don't see any reason why Joe would have to worry his pretty little head, do you?"

"No," Angie said with a resigned sigh. "Fine, I'll go see if I can chat up Pete and Dan from the bar yesterday. Maybe they heard something."

"Twenty minutes," Mel said, and she hurried off to the conference hall they had met in yesterday. Johnny Pepper had a dressing room in it all to himself. She was hoping he was there now, prepping for today's competition.

She blew through the conference room, where her fellow competitors were caffeinating and carbing up on the free coffee and muffins that had been put out for them.

She saw Polly, who waved at her, but Mel stayed in motion while she waved back, not stopping until she reached Johnny's door. She raised her fist to knock, but the sounds of shouting made her pause and press her ear to the door.

"She's not qualified!" a Southern drawl as thick as molasses sounded through the door.

"Who cares?" a voice snapped back. It sounded familiar, but Mel couldn't place it. "She's a damn sight better looking than that miserable old—"

"Watch it," the drawl said again. "You're talking about my friend."

"Whatever," the voice argued. "You can't replace her now. She's already been photographed as the replacement judge, and like it or not, she's going to be a real boost to our ratings."

"Even though she doesn't know a garlic press from an egg slicer?"

"She doesn't need to. She's representing the everyman palate."

"Oh, spare me." The drawl sounded disgusted. "Are we through?"

"For now," the voice said.

"Good, then clear out," Johnny said. "I need some prep time."

Before Mel could step back, the door was yanked open, and she found herself face to face with Dutch.

"Mel, what a surprise," he said.

He was dressed in his usual creased slacks and dress shirt, but she noticed that he didn't look as calm as usual. In fact, his shaved head was beaded with sweat, and he didn't even bother to put on the charm.

"What are you doing here?" he asked.

"I just came by to see Johnny," she said.

"I didn't know you two knew each other."

"Well, now you do," Johnny said. "If you'll excuse us?"

Dutch glanced between them and gave Mel an inquisitive look before he reluctantly departed.

"Always a pleasure," Mel called after him. She stepped inside the room and closed the door.

"Melanie Cooper, right?" Johnny asked.

"That's me," she said. She clasped his outstretched hand and was surprised to find it rough with calluses. Johnny Pepper hadn't always been a celebrity.

"I saw your work yesterday," he said. "Impressive."

"Thanks," she said. "And thanks for chasing Dutch off."

"No worries. He's an idiot—charming, but an idiot."

He turned and grabbed two water bottles out of a mini-fridge and then handed her one. "It's going to be hot out there; you'd better drink up."

Mel unscrewed the top and took a sip. She was stalling for time, because now that she was here, she really didn't know what to say.

"I accidentally, no, I take that back," she said. "I was eavesdropping at your door—"

Johnny interrupted her with a bark of laughter that was as abrupt as the spikes of his blond hair.

"Now I know why Vic liked you so much. You're a straight shooter," he said. "You know, he talked about you all the time."

Mel felt her throat get tight, but with a grimace, she pushed it away.

Johnny gave her a sympathetic look. "It was a crushing blow to lose Vic. He was a pain in the rear, but I liked him and I respected him. The man was larger than life."

Mel nodded. She took a sip of water, trying to loosen her throat. "Can I ask you what Dutch was so mad about?"

"Oh, that." Johnny looked unhappy. "Bake-Rite cake flour, the sponsor, isn't thrilled with having Jordan Russell take Vic's place, a bit of a drop in prestige, and he wants me to support Jordan as Vic's replacement."

"Dutch is okay with her?" Mel asked.

Johnny raised his eyebrows, and Mel got the feeling there was something between Dutch and Jordan that Johnny wasn't too happy about. Rather than put him in an awkward position, she decided to let it lie for now.

"Listen," she said, "I came to talk to you because Bertie Grassello told me yesterday that Vic had been let go by the network. You're employed by the same network; can you tell me if it's true?"

Johnny hesitated, and Mel couldn't tell if it was because he didn't know the answer or he wasn't sure how much he should say.

Finally, he blew out a breath and said, "Yeah, it's true. For the record, I hate to be the one to confirm this for you."

Mel realized that it was his loyalty to his friend that made him hesitate. Knowing that Mel had been Vic's favorite student, he didn't want to do anything that would diminish Vic in her eyes. She decided that she liked Johnny Pepper.

"It's okay," she said. "I loved him, but I wasn't blind to his faults."

Johnny looked relieved. "He had a few."

"More like a hundred," Mel said, and Johnny grinned.

"I'm going to miss the old bastard," he said.

"Me, too," she said.

There was a sharp rap on the door.

"Ten minutes, Johnny!"

"Got it!" he yelled back.

Mel stepped toward the door. "Thanks for your time, Johnny. I appreciate the information."

"Anytime," he said. "If you want to catch dinner sometime and talk, just let me know."

Mel met his gaze and noticed that his eyes were a green-blue hazel like her own. They also had a spark of interest in them that she couldn't ignore. For a nanosecond, she was tempted to accept his offer. It wasn't often that she met a man with whom she had so much in common. But then she remembered Joe, and it was a no-brainer. She belonged with Joe, period.

"Thanks," she said. "I'll keep that in mind. See you on the stage."

She shut the door behind her, and no sooner had she stepped into the main conference room than a ruckus erupted, the cause being a volcanic-looking Olivia Puckett.

"See?" she shrieked. "See? She's cheating! She's getting the mystery ingredient information from Johnny Pepper. I demand that you remove Fairy Tale Cupcakes from the competition!"

# Thirteen

Mel glanced up to find a red-faced Olivia pointing at her with one meaty finger while a glowering Felicity Parnassus stood beside her. It took Mel a moment to recognize Felicity as her hair was a completely different shade today. Mel was sure her hair had been fiery red yesterday, but today it was platinum blonde; however, the same stick figure and too-big head gave away that it was indeed Felicity.

"What?" she asked.

"Is this true?" Felicity asked. "Are you cheating, Ms. Cooper?"

"Are you serious?" she asked. "I was in there talking about Vic Mazzotta as he happened to be special to both Johnny Pepper and me."

The door behind her popped open, and Johnny stuck his head out. "Problem out here?"

"And I want him fired, too!" Olivia declared. "Cheater!"

Johnny's dark eyebrows lowered in a squint as if he were sighting Olivia for a blast from a canon.

"What did you say?" he asked. His voice for all its Southern charm sounded as lethal as a rattlesnake's bite.

"You told her the mystery ingredient, didn't you?" Olivia asked. "Admit it!"

"Given that I am not told the ingredient until I reach the cooking area, that's impossible," he said. He glanced at Felicity. "You know that."

Mel looked at Felicity, who was busily looking anywhere but at Johnny.

"Quite right," she muttered. "Silly of me, really. Well, now that I've done my duty, shall we get on with it?"

She glared at Olivia and swept past her to the exit. Olivia flounced after her as if she'd like to take up her cause again, but Mel had a feeling Felicity would not be so eager to listen to her this time.

"Thanks, Johnny," Mel said.

"No problem," he said. "You'd better hurry. We start in five."

Mel waved and ran out of the building toward the cooking dais. She hoped Angie was already there.

"What took you so long?" Angie hissed as Mel skidded into the kitchen beside her.

"I got held up by Puckett," Mel said.

"Oh, well at least you look happier than she does." Angie glanced over to where Olivia stood. Her chest was heaving, and her expression was twisted as if she were having bad thoughts about what she could do with some of her sharper cooking implements.

"Yeah, she accused me of trying to get the mystery ingredient out of Johnny," Mel said. "She even called in Felicity Parnassus."

"No!" Angie gasped.

"Yes," Mel countered. "Luckily, as Johnny pointed out,

even he doesn't know the mystery ingredient until he steps on the stage and they hand him the box."

"The woman is becoming unglued," Angie said. "How far will she go to beat us?"

Mel turned her head and studied her friend. Angie's brown eyes widened as she realized what she'd said. They turned to look at Olivia, who was rattling around in her kitchen, looking like she wanted to mince someone. Mel had a pretty good idea whom she would pick.

"Nah," she said. "Olivia wouldn't murder Vic to get to me. That's crazy talk."

"Is it?" Angie asked. "Think about it. She knows you're Vic's favorite student; heck, everyone does. It's not like he made it a secret. She was furious that he was one of the judges. She may have whacked him just to make sure you'd lose."

"That's mental," Mel said.

"Yeah, we're talking about Olivia. Do you know anyone else who fits the description of nutso like she does?"

Mel had to admit, Olivia had cornered the market on crazy, but a murderer? She had to give it a solid maybe.

She was about to say as much when Johnny Pepper leapt onto the stage in front of them, holding yet another large box. It was crunch time now, because this was no longer just a challenge to the chefs competition.

Mel wanted to know who killed Vic, and the best way to do it was to be here where his killer had struck. She couldn't afford to be bounced from the competition and lose access to all of the players. With that thought in mind, she pushed aside all of her questions and focused on what was in the box.

With his usual flourish, Johnny worked the crowd, and finally when they were whipped into a frenzy of curiosity, he pulled the lid off the box and announced, "And the mystery ingredient is . . ."

Mel and Angie were riveted as he reached into the box and pulled out a bottle of dark beer.

"A stout!" Johnny held the bottle aloft, and Mel heard the crowd go wild.

This was not one of the ingredients Tate had tested them with; still, she had an idea. With eight of their competitors gone, it would be easier to get to the ingredients they needed. Mel told Angie to go for the dark stouts, a chocolate if she saw any, and they waited with tingly anticipation for Johnny's count.

"Go!" he yelled, and the chefs mobbed the cart. Mel and Angie each managed to snag some excellent choices, and when they got back to their kitchen, Mel was in full chef mode.

"Joanie," she called their runner. "This is what I need."

Joanie repeated the items to make sure she understood them and bolted off in the direction of the supply cupboard. Mel and Angie stood next to each other and talked with their hands shielding their mouths like two baseball players devising a play on a ball field just in case any of the other chefs were watching.

They broke apart and started cooking. Mel could feel the eyes of other chefs on them as she and Angie worked like a well-oiled machine. Joanie hurried back with a bag of ingredients. She stood at the side, ready to make another dash if she was needed, but Mel was feeling very confident.

"Hey, Angie and Mel, say cheese!"

They glanced up to see a pack of Angie's brothers and their families standing in the crowd, holding up signs that read, WE LOVE FAIRY TALE CUPCAKES!

"Oh my god," Angie said. "This is as bad as the time

they showed up shirtless with body paint and sounded off an air horn when Principal Harris said my name at high school graduation. Shoot me."

"I can't, I need you," Mel said. "Hey, at least this time they have their shirts on."

"Given that they stood out of order and spelled my name Nagie instead of Angie, I'm pretty sure they've abandoned the body paint idea for life." Angie said. "At least I hope so."

Mel smiled and wrapped an arm around her as they mugged for her brother Paulie's camera. Then they pulled Joanie in and made her pose, too.

The halfway buzzer sounded, and Mel pulled their dessert out of the oven. It was going to need to be cooled down, so she popped it into the mini-fridge and set about getting the plates ready. She wanted these to look as professional as possible.

The judges wandered amongst their stations; mercifully none of them stopped to chat with her. She didn't know if it was because she was a blur of busyness today or if they were respecting her grief over Vic. She suspected it was the blur factor, which was fine with her. She could rally a smile for the family but not for anyone else.

She and Angie finished plating with five minutes to spare. She was delighted to see the other chefs pushing it right to the last second. Olivia in particular seemed to be huffing and puffing her way to the finish line.

Of course, then Mel was riddled with doubt. What if her recipe was so simplistic that the others blew it away? Maybe she should tweak it. She stepped toward her finished desserts, but Angie pulled her back.

"No, it's perfect," she said as if she had read Mel's mind. "Don't change a thing."

Mel nodded. Angie was right. The final buzzer sounded, and they sagged with relief. It was good to have no more time to second-guess her work.

They took off their toques and their chef coats and stepped down from the dais.

"Do you want to watch the judging today?" Angie asked. "We're down from forty-four to thirty-six. Tomorrow will be the top twenty-eight."

"I don't know," Mel said. "I think it will be too nerve-wracking."

Angie nodded. Just then the tidal wave of DeLauras engulfed them, and Mel lost sight of Angie while they were both soundly hugged and patted on the back by several of her brothers.

"So, what was that thing you made?" Ray asked. "It looked amazing."

Mel smiled at him. Ray had a sweet tooth that rivaled even Joe's, which was saying something.

"It was a chocolate stout brownie torte," she said.

"Oh, man," Sal said. "I think I'm drooling. Was there any left?"

"As if we'd give it to you," Angie teased Sal, the car salesman of the family.

"Hey, I'm the oldest," Dom said. "I think I've earned it."

"I'm the baby," Al said. "If anyone gets the leftovers, it's me."

And on and on they went. Mel debated calling Joe to let him know what he was missing, but she figured he'd probably lived through enough DeLaura family squabbles of his own.

She glanced up at the stage. The judges had taken their seats, and the professional wait staff was scurrying forward with the first of the desserts to be sampled. With thirty-six entries to judge, it was going to take a while. Her gaze stopped on Jordan, and she couldn't help the hitch in her chest that told her it should be Vic sitting there.

Mel eased her way out of the DeLaura group hug and scooted around the dais. She had a sudden longing to go and visit Grace.

She hadn't seen her since they'd taken Vic's body away, and Mel knew that no matter what Vic had done, Grace would be mourning him. And right now, she really wanted to be with someone who understood the complicated loss that was losing Vic.

She knew the judges were all staying at the Hotel Valley Ho on Indian School Road on the south end of Old Town Scottsdale. The hotel had enjoyed its heyday in the fifties, when cocktail hours and lounges were all the rage and its guests included stars such as Humphrey Bogart, Betty Grable, and Jimmy Durante. It was said that when Jimmy Durante couldn't sleep, he went down to the lounge and played piano. Mel loved that image.

Sadly, the hotel had fallen in popularity over the years. But recently, with the returning trend of the martini and cocktail hour, the new owner of the hotel had decided to renovate and remodel the resort while preserving its history and its unique charm. It now hosted the most popular pool to see and be seen at, and celebrities such as Johnny Pepper were bringing it back to its former glory.

Mel slipped off the festival grounds. She supposed she could walk to the hotel, but she didn't know how long she could be gone before Angie and the others noticed her absence. She cut across Brown Avenue and hurried to the back of her bakery, where she kept her bike chained up.

She supposed she should pop in and check on Tony, but since she didn't see any people crawling out of the bakery retching or flames shooting out of the windows, she assumed all was well.

She hopped on her Schwinn Cruiser and pedaled through Old Town, turning north on Scottsdale Road and west on Indian School Road. It only took her a few minutes to get to 68th Street, where the Hotel Valley Ho was located.

She road right up to the valet and hopped off her bike. He raised his eyebrows as she handed it to him.

"Watch that for me, will ya?" she asked as she slapped a tip in his hand and marched through the front doors, which were open.

She turned left and stopped at the large wooden desk, taking in the rounded furniture and geometric patterns that filled the waiting area to the right.

The desk person, who introduced himself as Doug, offered to ring Grace's room for her. Mel didn't know her room number, and she didn't want to barge in on Grace if she wasn't up to company.

Doug spoke softly into the phone, and then looked at Mel and said, "She says to come right up. Would you care for an escort?"

"No, no thank you," Mel said.

Doug gave her directions, and Mel left the swank lobby behind as she headed for the elevator. Grace's room was a tower suite on an upper floor with a view of the pool and Camelback Mountain. Mel wasn't surprised. Vic always demanded a room with a view. She knocked on the door, and it was a few moments before Grace answered.

When she pulled open the door, Mel hardly recognized her friend. Grace was always well put together, even in times of stress. She favored neutral colors of black, brown, and beige, but she always looked professional right down to her shiny black pumps. Not today, however.

Grace was wearing one of the fluffy hotel robes. Her hair was matted, her face was pale, and dark circles surrounded her eyes. She gestured for Mel to come in and then said, "Come on, I'm not allowed to smoke inside."

Mel followed her through the room, past the bright-colored retro furniture and large square bed with the long roll pillow, out onto the terrace. It overlooked the meticulously groomed grounds and was decorated in the same retro style.

A pitcher of iced tea and two glasses sat on a small square table, along with an ashtray that was holding a half-smoked cigarette. Mel watched a wisp of smoke stream from the cigarette tip, while condensation ran along the side of the glass pitcher. Grace sat down heavily in one of the round wicker chairs next to the table.

"Do you mind?" she asked, pointing to the ashtray.

"No, go ahead," Mel said. She sat in the other wicker chair, which made her feel like she was sitting in half of an eggshell. Too bad she felt more like an old bird than a spring chicken.

"I haven't smoked in thirteen years," Grace said.

"Well, if not now, when?" Mel asked.

Grace squinted at her through a plume of blue smoke and then turned to look out over the pool, where tourists were laughing and splashing under the glorious Arizona sun.

"I take it you've heard what they're saying?" Grace asked.

"No," Mel said. "I've been sadly out of the information loop."

"The rumor is that Vic killed himself."

# Fourteen

It wasn't true. Mel pedaled faster as if she could out-run the horrible rumor that Grace had told her. Vic did not take his own life. She knew this like she knew the pattern of faint freckles on her own nose.

She had spent an hour with Grace, refuting the rumor. Why would Vic kill himself? The consensus was that he was depressed after losing his show to his rival.

So he shut himself in a freezer? Mel didn't buy it. Over-dosing on pills, leaping from a tall building, even dumping a toaster in his bathtub, she could see Vic doing if he were the type to take his own life, which he wasn't. But locking himself in a freezer? He was way too flamboyant for that, and when pressed, even Grace agreed that the freezer was unlikely.

Mel had spent the better part of the hour convincing Grace that he hadn't done it, that it was just speculation on the part of the food world, who loved juicy gossip almost as much as a juicy steak. Mel could believe he'd had a few too many margaritas and had fallen into the trailer before she could believe that he had willingly chosen such a chilly end.

Grace seemed a little better after Mel left. She'd had some tea, and Mel had ordered her a small meal from room service. It arrived right as she was leaving, and Mel was pleased to see Grace eat a little bit before she left.

She parked her bike back behind the bakery and again was relieved to see that the bakery seemed to be doing just fine. There was no punk rock blaring from the interior or gang tagging covering the building. She'd have to thank Tony later for being such a trooper.

She raced back to the festival, using her VIP credentials to get through the gate. The smell of food permeated the air, and people were swarming the various booths to taste a little of this and a little of that. Mel could see the leader board over the crowd, but it was the same as yesterday, so either they were holding their own, or the results had yet to be announced.

She made her way to the margarita stand, hoping to find Dan or Pete. She had a nagging question that she wanted to ask them before she forgot.

The after-lunch crowd had formed a line going around the bar. She sidled up the side of it and peeked over the shoulder of a rather large and sweaty man to see who was tending the bar. Crouched over, filling a plastic margarita glass with ice, was Dan.

He caught sight of Mel and she waved. "Remember me?"

"Kind of hard to forget you after yesterday," he said. He didn't look overly happy to see her, and Mel couldn't blame him. He'd probably forever associate her and Angie with a dead guy in his freezer.

"I've got a question for you," she said. "Got a minute?"

"If you can talk while I work," he said. He gestured with his ice scoop toward the line, and Mel nodded.

"That freezer trailer," she said. "Do you know how long it was parked there?"

Dan was pouring mix and tequila two fisted into the glass. "It was here when we came to set up in the morning. When it arrived? I don't know. You'd have to ask one of the festival officials if they know."

Mel nodded.

"Anything else?" he asked as he gave the man his drink.

"That's for you," the customer said as he handed Dan a tip.

Dan rang the bell over the bar and stuffed the tip in a big jar perched behind the booze bottles on the back of the bar.

"The trailer," Mel asked. "If you did get locked inside by accident, is there a way to open the door from the inside?"

"Oh, yeah," he said. "They have a door handle on the inside for safety, you know? I've locked myself in there a couple of times, and I can tell you for the few seconds you're scrambling to find the door handle in the dark, it's damn scary."

Mel winced.

"Oh, sorry," he said. "I forgot he was your friend. I'm really sorry."

"It's okay," she said. "You've been a big help."

She felt him watch her go, and she dove back into the crowd before she humiliated herself by bursting into tears.

She knew if there had been a way out of that freezer, Vic would have found it unless for some reason he couldn't. There was no way Vic committed suicide. It just wasn't who he was. Someone put him in that freezer, someone who wanted him to die.

She was walking blindly through the restaurant booths, not seeing or caring what was happening around her. She paused by one of the large fountains that surrounded the mall and watched a white swan glide by.

"Mel," a voice called from behind her, and she turned to see her Uncle Stan barreling toward her with two plates loaded with food.

As always, there was a split second when she saw him that he looked just like her dad. The Cooper men shared the same portly build, round face, and thinning hair, which was something she really enjoyed teasing her brother, Charlie, about.

"Your mother said to find you and feed you," Uncle Stan said as he thrust a plate at her.

"Thanks," she said. Even though she wasn't hungry, there was some amazing-looking food on her plate that required her to taste-test it at the very least.

They found a vacant bench and sat down by the quiet man-made pond, while they tucked into their food.

After a few moments, Uncle Stan said, "Did you get some of this?"

Mel looked at his plate. "The falafel? Oh, yeah. Good stuff."

"Flawhatal?" Uncle Stan asked.

"Falafel," Mel said. "It's believed to originate from Egypt and is made from ground chickpeas."

"Wow, I'm going to have to get more of it," he said. He wiped his mouth with a napkin and asked, "So, how you doing?"

Subtle Uncle Stan was not.

"Honestly?" she asked, and he nodded. "Not good."

"Want to talk about it?"

"Vic Mazzotta did not kill himself," she said.

Stan let out a long, drawn-out sigh. "I was hoping you wouldn't hear about that."

"Why?" she asked.

"Because I knew it would crush you," he said. He shifted on the bench. "The worst part of suicide is the people left behind."

"He didn't—" Mel began, but Uncle Stan interrupted.

"Mel, you don't know that," he said.

"Yes, I do," she said. "I knew Vic. He didn't kill himself."

"His career was in ruins, his young girlfriend had just dumped him—"

"What?"

"Oh, you didn't know about that?" he asked. He looked like he wanted to take it back, but of course, he couldn't. "According to Ms. Russell, she broke it off with him that morning."

"She's lying," Mel said.

Uncle Stan gave her a hard stare. "Something you care to share?"

"No, I just know," she said.

"Well, just knowing doesn't do me any good," he said.

"But why would he choose to freeze to death?" Mel asked. "This is Vic; he does things *big*. He doesn't slink away and hide in a freezer box."

Uncle Stan stared thoughtfully over the crowd. "Between you and me, I'm not convinced that it was suicide either."

"Really? Because I've got to tell you I think it was murder," Mel said. "Vic had a lot of enemies."

"So I've gathered," Uncle Stan said. "Gee, I wonder why. Let's see, he was cheating on his wife, he screwed over the sponsor of his show by refusing to use their prod-

ucts, he humiliated his former colleague on the air, you
know, the same one who just got hired to take his job, he
ruined the career of a young up-and-comer by calling him
out on live TV, oh, and he promised his cute little intern
stardom in return for being his girlfriend. Yeah, small
wonder I'm thinking murder is more likely."

"He wasn't all that bad," Mel said.

Uncle Stan just looked at her.

"He was a friend of Dad's," she said.

"So you've said, but your dad was known for taking in
strays," he said. "It wouldn't surprise me if Vic was one of
his rescue cases."

It was true. Mel remembered the day her mother had to
put her foot down and made her father stop taking in every
stray animal he found. At one point, they had four dogs,
five cats, two tortoises, a bunny, and an assortment of birds
and fish. Mel and her brother sometimes joked that when
their dad passed, he hadn't gone to the rainbow bridge to
meet all of their deceased pets, but had been picked up by
the rainbow ark.

"I don't care," Mel said. "All I know is that after Dad
passed away, Vic was the one who pushed me to finish
cooking school. Without him, I wouldn't have graduated, I
wouldn't have the bakery, I wouldn't have the life I love so
well. I owe him."

Uncle Stan looped an arm around Mel's shoulders and
gave her half of his usual bear hug.

"Well, it's a good thing for him he did one thing right in
his life—he took care of you," Uncle Stan said. "We'll find
out what happened to him, Mel, I promise."

"Thanks, Uncle Stan." She leaned against him for just
the briefest moment in an attempt to absorb some of his
strength.

When they broke apart, Uncle Stan took their plates to a nearby trash can and came back and kissed Mel on the forehead.

"Be good," he said. "I'll be in touch."

Mel nodded. As she watched him slip back into the crowd, she thought about what he had said. After hearing Vic's list of wrongs, she believed someone was mad enough at him to kill him.

She knew about Grace and Dutch and Bertie. They were all old news. But she didn't know about his sponsor, nor did she know anything about Jordan Russell. The young wannabe Food Channel star seemed as good a place as any to start.

# Fifteen

Mel figured the judging should be done by now. She wandered back toward the staging area, partly to check their status on the leader board but mostly to check out Jordan Russell.

The judges were just finishing up. Mel wasn't sure whose offering was the last concoction of the day, but both Dutch and Bertie grimaced during the tasting. The *Food and Wine* critic delicately spit hers out in a napkin, and Jordan took one sniff of it and then pushed it away. She was not about to let anything so vile pass her collagen-puffed lips.

Mel stood studying her. She was young, yes. She was pretty, yes. But what had Vic seen in her besides that? There were scores of pretty young things in cooking school. What had made Vic single her out as his protégée?

She wasn't even a real cook by her own admission. Was she just riding Vic's coattails to fame and glory on the Food Channel? How did Vic's sudden demise affect her rise? Given that she had taken his place, it didn't appear to be an adverse turn of events for her.

While Mel watched, Jordan tossed her thick dark hair over her shoulder and gave Dutch Johnson, who was seated beside her, a decidedly flirty look. Interesting move on her part, given that her lover had just been murdered. But then, Johnny had all but admitted that there was something going on between Jordan and Dutch.

While the other judges were dressed in professional-looking blazers and sports coats, Jordan had decided this was the place to wear a hot pink halter top and a black ruffled miniskirt. She looked like she was ready to go dance the merengue.

"Melanie, it's impolite to stare."

Mel turned to find her mother standing beside her. There was no sign of her friend Ginny.

"Where's Laverne?" she asked.

"Who?" Joyce frowned at her.

"Your BFF," Mel said. "The Laverne to your Shirley?"

"Oh, Ginny, well, she got a little overheated, and her husband, Monty, came and picked her up."

"Overheated or shnockered?" Mel asked.

"It would be indelicate for me to be more specific," Joyce said.

Mel smiled. Even in her vibrant green shirt and matching visor, Joyce Cooper was every inch a lady. It was one of the things Mel most admired about her mother. She never swore, she always looked her best, and her glass was always half full even when it was empty.

"I love you, Mom."

"I love you, too," Joyce said. "Now why were you staring at the brunette at the judges' table?"

"Her name is Jordan Russell, and she is . . . was Vic Mazzotta's girlfriend," Mel said.

"Oh, dear, I didn't know he and Grace had divorced."

"They didn't."

Joyce stared at the brunette and frowned. She took it personally when younger women made off with older women's husbands. "I bet those are fake."

"Well spotted," Mel said. "I'm pretty sure the whole package is fake."

"What's fake?" Angie asked as she joined them.

"Jordan Russell."

"Hunh," Angie grunted. "I heard Olivia complimenting her outfit earlier. What do you want to bet she marks Olivia higher than us?"

"That's fine," Mel said. "I don't want her vote."

"Are you kidding me?" Angie said. "I will worship her heinous fashion sense if it keeps us ahead of Olivia."

"You're obsessed," Mel said.

"No, I'm competitive," Angie said. "Now if you'll excuse me, I'm going to go suck up."

Joyce and Mel watched as she approached the judges' table. They had finished the taste testing and turned in their score cards and were now calling it a day.

Three of the four judges had grudges against Vic. Maybe Angie wasn't so far off the mark to get in their good graces.

"I'm going to join Angie," Mel said to Joyce. "I'll call you later."

"Good idea. Try to make nice with them. After all, you could use that prize money for the bakery."

"Oh, I'll make nice," Mel said. "Very nice."

If Joyce heard a hint of sarcasm in Mel's voice, she chose to ignore it.

Mel found Angie standing with Dutch looking tongue-tied and nervous.

"Nice concoction you pulled out today," he said to Mel. "Using the stout in a brownie was brilliant, but serving it in a crunchy chocolate shell with a thin layer of chocolate mousse and topped with whipped cream really added texture and complexity. Well done."

"Thank you."

Mel bowed her head in acknowledgment. Dutch might be wrapped up in his desire to be a celebrity, but the man still knew his way around a kitchen and the praise was not to be taken lightly.

"Your partner here tells me that you're dating her older brother, an assistant district attorney?"

"I am," Mel said.

"Funny, I always figured you'd go for a foodie type, you know, a restaurant owner or a food critic or a TV celebrity chef."

He glanced meaningfully at Johnny Pepper, who was chatting up a few contestants and contest officials, and then back at Mel. She knew he was trying to determine if her visit to Johnny's dressing room had been personal or professional. Too bad it was none of his biz.

"Nah, you know the old saying, 'Too many cooks in the kitchen spoil the stew.'"

"Only if it's one like that one," Dutch said. He pointed over his shoulder with his thumb to where Olivia had the *Food and Wine* critic cornered in the judges' booth like a bug in a Venus flytrap.

"Someone should really go rescue her," Mel said.

She and Angie both looked at Dutch.

"Oh, no," he said. "She'll suck me into her crazy vortex,

and I'll never get out. She got me and Bertie yesterday, and we thought we'd never escape."

"What time yesterday?" Mel asked.

"After the competition," he said. "Why do you think we bolted out of the booth today?"

"Like rats off a sinking ship?" Mel asked.

"Now, is that nice?" he countered.

"Sorry, I'm a little surly since my mentor was found dead in a freezer."

"I'm sorry about that," Dutch said. He met her gaze, and he ran a strong hand over his shaved head. It was a nervous gesture that Mel remembered from their cooking school days. "Listen, Vic and I had our differences, but I didn't wish him dead."

"Really?" she asked.

She could feel Angie's eyes boring into the side of her skull, trying to get her to shut up, but she had to know. Did Dutch have something to do with Vic's murder?

He blew out a breath. "I can't believe you just asked me that." He gave her a look full of recrimination, but Mel lifted her chin defiantly.

"I'm planning on asking everyone who had an issue with Vic the same thing," she said.

He stepped close, leaned over her, and said, "Then you'd better watch your back."

Mel could feel Angie bristle beside her, but before she could question Dutch further, an arm looped around Mel's waist and jerked her back. She turned and found Joe standing behind her.

"So, how's it going, Cupcake?" he asked.

She turned back around to see that Dutch had stepped back with a smirk. "I can see you're in good hands. Later."

Without waiting to be introduced to Joe, he disappeared

into the crowd, and Mel wondered if it was the fact that Joe was the assistant DA that had him in full retreat.

"Was it something I said?" Joe asked. He kissed the spot just below Mel's ear, and she felt her entire body shiver.

"I do not like that guy," Angie said. "He's as charming as all get-out but about as trustworthy as a toothy alligator."

"Funny, I had the same impression, especially since he seemed to have my girl in his sights," Joe said. "So who is he?"

"One of the judges for the competition," Mel said. "He's also an old classmate of mine, who just happened to have a big falling-out with Vic."

Joe raised his eyebrows. "You don't think . . ."

"I don't know," she said.

"Good, then let's leave it to the police," he said.

Mel was about to open her mouth to protest. She wasn't sure she liked his bossy tone, but Angie interrupted her.

"Hey, look!" Angie cried. "They're putting up the winners on the leader board!"

# Sixteen

Mel wasn't sure what she'd been expecting—okay, maybe she had been expecting them to remain on top, where in her humble opinion they belonged. That didn't prove to be the case, however.

As Fairy Tale Cupcakes slid down to second, a chortle from behind her announced the presence of the new leader on the board. Instinctively, Mel and Joe both grabbed one of Angie's arms, pinning her between them before she did anything that would get them disqualified.

Olivia and her sous-chef pranced by them chanting, "We're number one, you're number two, we're going to beat the whoopee out of you."

"Just let me go kick her in the pants," Angie pleaded. "Please just one swift kick in the derriere and I'm good, I swear."

"No!" Mel and Joe said at the same time.

"She'll press assault charges," Joe said. "And then you'll be out for good."

Angie closed her eyes and drew in a deep breath through her nose, held it, and then released it slowly. Mel and Joe waited patiently while she did this several times until the crazy light in her brown eyes dimmed.

"Okay, I'm good," she said.

Mel and Joe exchanged a glance before they released her.

"I need to see what she beat us with," Angie said. "I'll be right back."

Mel watched to make sure Angie went to the judges' table to see the tally sheets. Mel wouldn't put it past her to chase Olivia out of the festival. But true to her word, Angie was up at the table overlooking the critiques.

A crestfallen Polly walked over to Mel and said, "I really thought I nailed it, but look, I slid into fourth."

Molly's Moonpies had taken the number three spot. They were located in Phoenix, and Mel wondered what they'd done to knock Polly down on the board. Obviously, they were a competitor to watch.

"I hate her," Angie said as she stomped back over.

"I'm sorry," Polly said with wide eyes.

"Oh, no, not you," Angie said. "Olivia Puckett."

"Oh, yeah, she is unpleasant," Polly said.

"Check this out: She beat us with Guinness pudding with whiskey sauce," Angie said. "That's just a bunch of baloney. There is no way that was better than ours. She just liquored those judges up."

"You don't think she's corrupt enough to buy off the judges, do you?" Joe asked. He had on his district attorney bad face.

Mel and Angie just looked at him. Olivia had been a rock in their shoe since the day they'd opened Fairy Tale Cupcakes. It was hard to say what lengths she'd go to in order to win.

"Well, that's really low," Polly fumed.

"That's nothing for Olivia," Angie said.

"Listen, I have to get back to the office," Joe said. "If you turn up anything that warrants looking into, call me."

Mel kissed his cheek. "I love having a crime-fighting attorney for a boyfriend," she said, and he grinned at her, looking embarrassed but pleased.

They watched Joe leave, and Polly said, "Well, I'd better get back to my apartment so I can have another night of insomnia while I try to guess what they'll throw at us next."

"Hey, this is supposed to be fun," Mel reminded her.

"It was until I slid down the board," Polly said. With a wave, she took off, striding through the tourists.

"So, now what?" Angie asked.

"Now we go back and see how Tony and Oz are doing," Mel said.

They left the mall, crossing Brown Avenue into Old Town Scottsdale. They passed Mick at the tattoo parlor and Christine at the salon, both of whom looked busy with customers. When they arrived at the bakery, the patio tables outside were full of people chomping cupcakes, and there was a line going out the door.

"This can't be good," Mel said. "Why are there so many people here when the festival is going on down the street?"

They picked up their pace and hurried to the entrance. No one would budge from their spot in line, however, even with Angie glowering at them, so they had to circle the building and enter through the kitchen door in the back.

The kitchen was as immaculate as they'd left it. But Mel could hear the sound of music coming from the bakery. She strode forward and pushed through the swinging doors.

A large jukebox now sat at the end of the room, and

Elvis's voice was being emitted through its speakers, adding a lively vibe to the place. Oz was manning the counter, and two of Angie's brothers, Al and Tony, were waiting and bussing tables.

Mel scanned the crowd. It was a solid mix of tourist families, kids just out of school, and seniors. It was actually hard to hear Elvis over the laughter and chatter that filled the room.

"Oz," she called, but he was busy taking an order and didn't hear her.

"Oz!" Angie's bark was louder, and he turned to see who was calling him.

"Hey!" he called. "How did it go? How did you do?"

"Not as good as this," Mel said. She grabbed an apron and tied it on. It was obviously a time for all hands on deck.

"I know, this is crazy, right?" Oz asked.

"Where did the jukebox come from?" she asked.

"Yeah, well, it was dead in here this morning, so me and Tony got to talking and decided you needed some tunes to liven up the joint," he said. "I mean you're all fifties decor, but you have no music. That's just wrong."

"Let me get this straight," Angie said as she tied on an apron as well. "My brothers and you thought a jukebox would draw people in, and you were right?"

Oz opened his arms wide. "Check the evidence."

Mel looked at Angie. "How could we have missed that?"

"We were sort of busy making cupcakes," Angie said. "You know, product."

"Where did the jukebox come from?" Mel asked. "Or more accurately, who do I owe and how much?"

"Oh, I don't know," Oz said. "I'm just the idea man. Tony actually hooked us up with one. He knows a guy."

"I hate it when 'they know a guy,'" Angie said. "That's how I got my first bike, my first computer, you name it. It always has some mysterious point of origin, like it fell off the back of a truck somewhere."

"Well, since I'm dating the assistant DA, we'll have to make sure it's legit," Mel said. "Let's get this crowd served, and then we'll pry the info out of Tony."

They set to work boxing up four-packs and twelve-packs and single servings. Mel and Angie grooved to the jukebox, but the best music was the ring of the cash register every time it opened. Success sounded sweet indeed.

When Angie flipped the sign on the door and turned the dead bolt for the night, Tony shut off the jukebox, and they all trooped into the kitchen for a restorative cupcake and a glass of cold milk.

Tony crossed his arms on the steel table top and rested his head. "Is it always this busy?"

"No," Mel and Angie said together.

"It was the King," Oz said. "He brings them in."

Mel couldn't argue, since the King had crooned the day away and the people had kept coming and coming.

"How much for the jukebox?" Mel asked.

"Consider it a gift," Tony said.

Mel glanced at Angie, who shrugged.

"It'll pay for all of the cupcakes he mooches," Angie said as she gave Tony a second Caramel Crunch Cupcake. It was one of Mel's newest experiments, a buttery cupcake frosted with vanilla buttercream drizzled with melted caramel and sprinkled with candied pecans. Tony's eyes glazed as he took in the treat before him.

"I can get you anything you need," he promised before tucking into the luscious little cake.

"Oh, Angie, a package arrived for you," Al said. "I signed for it and put it in the office."

Angie gave him a quizzical look and disappeared into the office. Mel could hear her grunt as she ripped open the box. There was silence for a moment, and then she heard Angie say, "Aw."

Curious, Mel went to the door to find Angie cradling a wooden cuckoo clock in her arms and clutching a note.

"It says, 'I'm cuckoo about you,'" Angie said. "Isn't that sweet?"

"It's something," Mel said. "So I take it you've been hearing from Roach more regularly?"

"Every day," Angie gushed. "He felt really badly that I was worried, but he was having some band issues."

Noting the bliss on her face, Mel couldn't deny Angie her happiness. Tate obviously wasn't doing anything to forward his cause, so how could Mel hope that Angie would choose him when he wouldn't even get himself in the running?

When the brothers had eaten their fill and trooped out, Angie and Mel set to work replenishing the edible stock. Tinkerbells, Death by Chocolates, and Blonde Bombshells were needed, as well as Kiss Me Cupcakes and Orange Dreamsicles.

It took several hours, and by the time they had frosted the last batch and put them in the walk-in cooler, Mel was pie-eyed tired and Angie didn't look much better.

They said good night with a hug at the foot of the stairs that led up to Mel's apartment. Angie, carrying her cuckoo clock, turned to cross the alley to the parking lot beyond when a cry ripped through the quiet evening, making the hair on the back of Mel's neck stand up.

"What was that?" Angie asked as she spun back around.

"It sounded like someone being stabbed."

"Where did it come from?"

"The Dumpster," Mel said.

They both hesitated. The piercing howl sounded again.

"I am going to be so unhappy if there is somebody in there," Angie said.

"No one is in there," Mel said. "Still, we should check it."

They eased their way toward the large metal box. It smelled like most Dumpsters, a rank combination of decaying food and sour milk.

Angie put her clock down, and they each grabbed a corner of the lid.

"On three?" Angie asked and Mel nodded.

"One, two, three." Together they flung open the heavy metal lid and jumped back.

A streetlight illuminated the inside of the Dumpster. The trash had been picked up the day before so the bin was empty except for the smell, which was strong enough to take a corporeal form, and a few pink boxes of cupcakes that had been too old to be donated to the local shelter.

A scuttling sound came from beneath the boxes and they both jumped back.

"It's probably a rat," Angie said. "A rat with rabies."

"Let's just be sure," Mel said. "I'm going to get my flashlight."

"No need." Angie scrambled for her keys, where she had a penlight on her key ring. She pressed a button and a weak light shone into the Dumpster.

At first there was no movement. Then a tail appeared. It was a white tail with a black tip.

"That's no rat tail."

They leaned over the edge, trying to get a closer look. White haunches followed the tail and then a white back.

Whatever it was, it was trying to drag something out of one of their tossed-out cupcake boxes. Shoulders appeared, followed by a head sporting the biggest ears Mel had ever seen. With a great, growling grunt, the animal braced its legs and pulled.

And just like that, a tiny white kitten went rolling back, feet over ears, while the chocolate and vanilla cupcake it had been trying to get sailed over its head and hit the side of the bin with a splat and then sank to the bottom with a thud.

The kitten glared up in the direction of the light and blinked as if it was their fault that it had lost its cupcake.

"Oh, my," Angie said. "He's so tiny."

Mel glanced down at the little scrap of fur. He was pure white except for one spot of black fur that circled his right eye and the black tip of his tail.

"He looks like a pirate wearing an eye patch," she said.

"I'm surprised he wasn't going for your rum cupcakes," Angie agreed with a laugh.

"What are you doing in there, silly?" Mel asked him, but he just ignored her and licked his chest fur. "I'm going to try to fish him out."

"Better you than me," Angie said. She waved her hand in front of her nose. "I'll hold the light."

"Here, little fella," Mel spoke softly as she hoisted herself up on the edge of the bin. She had been afraid he'd scamper away, but no. He looked merely impatient as if wondering how long exactly it was going to take her to get him out of his predicament.

Mel leaned forward and stretched out her hands. She tried to ignore the metal digging into her hips and the stench that assaulted her nose.

The kitten stretched up to meet her, for which Mel was

grateful. She scooped him up with one hand and clutched him close to her chest as she rose back out of the bin and pushed off the edge, landing on unsteady feet.

The kitten was purring loudly, and he rubbed his head against her. She bent forward to put him on the ground, and he hooked his little claws into her shirt and dangled. Mel straightened back up and tried to unhook him.

"Uh-oh," Angie said. "Looks like he likes you."

"No," Mel said. She cradled him in her hands. "He's just hoping I have some food on me." She looked at the fur ball and said, "I don't."

She tried to put him down again, but he was having none of it.

"Listen, buster," she said. She tried to sound stern, but he just purred louder.

"He's clinging to you like a barnacle, aren't you, Captain Jack?" Angie asked. She reached out and rubbed under his chin, causing him to purr even louder.

"Excuse me?" Mel asked.

"You know, *Pirates of the Caribbean*, Captain Jack Sparrow," Angie said. "You did say he looks like a pirate."

"Captain Jack doesn't have an eye patch," Mel said.

"No, but the way this little guy was taking on a cupcake bigger than him, he has the same devil-may-care charm, don't you, Captain Jack?" Angie asked as she rubbed his little head. He purred and stretched out for more.

"Do not name him," Mel said. "Someone is probably desperate to find him. I'm sure he belongs to someone."

"He looks skinny and he has no collar," Angie said. "I'm thinking he's been abandoned."

Mel looked at the pitiful ball of fluff in her hands. He couldn't weigh more than three pounds, and he looked to be only a few months old. How could someone have abandoned him?

"Well, I'll take care of him tonight, and tomorrow after the competition we can hang up some signs and see if anyone claims him."

"Okeydokey," Angie said. "Good night, Captain Jack."

"And stop calling him that," Mel called after her.

Angie kept walking, completely ignoring her.

"Come on," Mel said. "But don't get any ideas. I want to be clear that this is just for tonight."

She unlocked her apartment, and this time the kitten let her put him down. She went to the pantry and foraged until she found a can of tuna. Then she put half of the can into a bowl and filled another bowl with fresh water. She placed the bowls in an unused corner of her small kitchen and watched as Captain Jack, er, rather as the cat chowed down with a hunger that appeared insatiable. Finally, when he had all but licked the painted flowers off the bowl, he drank some water and flopped down on the floor and began to groom.

"Make yourself at home," Mel said. "But only for tonight."

She found a long rectangular Tupperware tub and shredded some scrap paper. It was a makeshift litter box at best, but it would do until she could pick up the real deal tomorrow. Next, she found a fleecy blanket and folded it into a bed for him. She put it on the floor by her futon. As she turned out the light and slumped into the mattress, relieved to finally call an end to this day, she felt gentle tugs on her blanket and was not at all surprised that Captain Jack had managed to climb up onto her bed. He gave a jaw-popping yawn and kneaded the covers until they were just to his liking, and then he promptly fell asleep beside her.

Mel wondered how Joe felt about cats but then pushed the thought away. It didn't matter because Captain Jack was not staying.

# Seventeen

Mel woke up to find Captain Jack had wound himself into a tight ball and nestled himself right under her chin. His purr was a calming noise, and she stroked his fur and marveled at how soft he was.

She carefully climbed out of the bed so as not to disturb him. It bothered her to think of how long he may have been out on the street.

She had a few hours before she had to be at the festival. She decided it might be a good idea to see if she could talk to Jordan Russell. Uncle Stan had said she broke up with Vic the morning that he died. Something about that struck Mel as being awfully convenient.

Mel had not liked the woman when she met her. Jordan had struck her as cold and calculating, and the thing that really gnawed at her was that she couldn't figure what Jordan would have to gain by breaking up with Vic.

She couldn't have known that they would make her a guest judge, could she? Unless Dutch had somehow managed to make that happen, but how? They could have asked any number of famous Phoenix chefs, such as Mark Tarbell or Tammie Coe. No, that had to have been a lucky happenstance for Jordan.

Mel mulled over the possibilities while she showered and dressed. Captain Jack hadn't moved, so she put more tuna in his bowl and refreshed his water before she slipped out the back door. Since Jordan was Vic's protégée, she was betting that Jordan was staying at the Hotel Valley Ho, too.

She was just unlocking her bike when Angie pedaled up beside her on her purple mountain bike. Unlike Mel's utilitarian cruiser, Angie's bike was tricked out with a rear bag and custom fenders, and Angie looked the part as well in her black bicycling outfit and bright yellow helmet with a mirror attachment.

"How's Captain Jack?" she asked.

"Snoring," Mel said. "On my bed."

"So, it's just like having Joe there," Angie teased. She unstrapped her helmet and shook her hair out. The April morning was already heating up, and a sheen of sweat coated her hair where her helmet had been.

"Just so you know, he's not allergic to cats," Angie said.

"Not that it matters since Captain Jack isn't staying," Mel said. "He needs a real home with kids and a dog to annoy."

"I can hook you up with a dog," Angie offered.

"No!" Mel said. It came out more forcefully than she'd intended, and Angie smirked.

"Oh, shut it," Mel said.

"Fine," Angie said. "I was going to bike down to the Dutch Brothers Coffee Shop on Scottsdale Road and then window-shop a bit. You game?"

"Is that why you're taking your bike?" Mel asked. "To keep from buying anything too big?"

"I find it curbs the spending if I can't get it home," Angie agreed. "You want to tag along?"

"Nah," Mel said. "I have an errand to run."

Angie stared at her. "You're not taking Captain Jack to the pound, are you?"

"On my bike?" Mel asked. She thought it spoke well of her that she didn't add *duh* to the question.

"Sorry, that was dumb," Angie acknowledged. "It's just that I'd hate to see the wee fur ball get put down."

"You could always adopt him," Mel said.

"Can't." Angie shook her head. "Not until I know if I'm staying."

Angie didn't talk much about the fact that Roach had asked her to move to Los Angeles with him, but Mel knew she was considering it. Mel found that if she didn't think about it, it kept her from panicking.

"Well, he's very sweet and cuddly," Mel said. "I'm sure someone will adopt him."

"So, what's the errand, then?" Angie asked.

"It's nothing," Mel said. "Just a little thing, no big deal."

Angie stared at her. "Great, then I'll go with you."

"You don't have to do that," Mel said.

"But I want to," Angie insisted. "It'll be fun. But you have to wear your helmet."

Mel never wore her helmet. It was hot and sweaty and made her short blonde hair stick to her head, which made her look like a dude. She hated it.

"Safety before beauty," Angie said. Mel took one look at the stubborn set to her jaw, and she knew that not only was she stuck with Angie for the ride, she was also going to have to wear the stupid helmet. She was not happy.

She stomped up the first three steps to her apartment and then remembered the kitten was sleeping, so she jogged quietly up the rest and eased through the front door.

Captain Jack burrowed deeper into the blanket when she entered, and she smiled at his fuzzy white body lost amidst the lilac comforter on her bed. She didn't want to disturb him, so she quietly opened her closet door and dug out her bicycle helmet, which was buried beneath a pair of cowboy boots and a tennis racket.

She slipped back out and locked the door behind her. Angie had put her helmet back on, and Mel envied the wave of dark brown hair that ran out from under the helmet and over the shoulders. Angie never looked like a dude when she took her helmet off.

"Where to?" Angie asked, and Mel climbed onto her bike.

"Hotel Valley Ho," Mel said.

"Cool, we can grab breakfast at their café," Angie said.

"Yeah, that sounds good," Mel said. Perfect. She could leave Angie in the café while she hunted down Jordan for a little chat.

It took only minutes to arrive at the hotel. The parking valet did not recognize Mel—she blamed the helmet—but was fine with letting them leave their bikes near the main entrance.

"Come on," Angie said. "I'm starving."

They arrived at the café, and Angie asked the hostess for a table outside that overlooked the pool.

"I haven't been poolside since last summer. Remember when Tate and Christie were here all of the time?" Angie asked.

"Vaguely," Mel said. She was checking out the people

beginning to fill up the funky lounge chairs around the pool. She wondered if maybe Jordan was out there.

"Just think if Christie hadn't been murdered, Tate would be married by now," Angie said.

Mel pulled her attention from the pool and stared at Angie. "What?"

"Tate would be married by now," Angie said. "Weird, huh?"

"Welcome to Café Zuzu," the waitress greeted them. "Can I start you with some coffee?"

"Two, please," Mel said.

"Coming up," the waitress said and left them.

"Angie, what are you talking about?" Mel asked.

Angie shrugged. "Nothing. I guess it just hit me how different our lives would be if Christie and Tate had gotten married."

Mel blew out a breath. When Tate's fiancée had been murdered six months ago, it had been a turning point for the three of them and the friendship they had maintained for more than twenty years.

"What do you think would be different?" Mel asked.

"Well, Tate would be married, for one thing," Angie said.

"Does that bother you? After all, you probably still would have met Roach and started to date him," Mel said.

She wondered if Angie could sense that she was fishing. Angie was holding off on making a decision about moving in with Roach until he was back from his tour. Mel wondered how much of her hesitation stemmed from the fact that she had always been and most likely still was in love with Tate.

"It doesn't bother me," Angie said. "I'm just acknowledging what might have been. What looks good to you?"

She scanned the menu in front of her, clearly wanting to change the subject. Mel was not feeling that accommodating, however.

"Angie, are you still in love with Tate?" she asked.

"I . . ." Angie looked up at Mel, and her brown eyes were troubled.

Mel felt as if Tate were breathing down her neck. This was what he needed to know to get off his butt and tell her how he felt. Because, of course, being a man, he had figured out only after Angie had met someone else that he was in love with her.

But now they were hitting critical. If they were going to keep Angie from moving to L.A., then Tate had to screw up the courage to tell her how he felt. Mel knew that if she told Tate that Angie still had feelings for him, it would motivate him to do the same.

"Well, lookey here," a voice broke into their conversation like a fist through glass. "What are you two doing here when you've got your third challenge coming up today?"

"We *were* enjoying a peaceful breakfast," Angie said with a scowl. She didn't like Bertie since they had dropped on the leader board.

Bertie Grassello ignored her and pulled out a chair.

"Well, since you're on a downward trajectory, maybe it's no matter," he said.

"We're not worried," Mel said. "We've got a few more rounds to go. We'll be all right."

"Assuming you don't get cut," Bertie said.

Mel thought she heard a gloating note in his tone. She wasn't surprised. Bertie had always despised anything and everything that was Vic's, including his favorite student.

"We won't get cut," Angie growled at him.

The waitress stopped by, and Angie ordered the three-cheese egg sandwich while Mel ordered Zuzu's breakfast casserole, both of which would give them enough protein and carbs to get through the next round.

"I hope you're not thinking of scoring us low just because of old grudges," Mel said. "I'd hate to have to complain to the festival officials when you're about to begin your new television show."

Bertie's face turned a sickly shade of gray. "What are you playing at?"

"Nothing," Mel shrugged. "Just that it would be a shame to have bad publicity, about you being biased against your predecessor's favorite student, for instance, accompanying the launch of your show. Don't you think?"

"Are you threatening me?" Bertie asked. His voice was just above a hiss.

"Do I have to?" Mel asked.

"You'd better watch yourself, little missy." Bertie reared back from the table like a walrus on the beach. The metal legs of his chair scraped harshly against the concrete patio. "You don't have Vic to pave the way for you anymore."

"You did not just call her 'little missy'!" Angie snapped. "What decade are you living in, you big gas bag?"

"How dare you!" Bertie blustered, and Angie roared out of her seat.

"Oh, I dare," she said. She looked like she was about to launch herself at him, so Mel swiftly rose from her seat and hooked Bertie by the elbow.

"She's got a bit of a temper," Mel said. "If I were you, I'd get out of her line of fire."

She spun Bertie around and gave him a solid push toward the exit. He stomped into the café without looking back.

"What a jerk," Angie fumed. "Do you think he'll get us kicked out of the competition?"

Mel thought about it for a second. "No, he's too smart. He knows I'm not kidding about the bad press. If he doesn't judge us fairly, I will ruin his television debut with bad press."

"Would you really?" Angie asked, looking impressed.

"For Vic, yeah, I would," Mel said.

Angie snagged a newspaper from a nearby table and began to peruse the headlines.

Mel glanced over her head at the pool and saw the oh-so-buxom form of Jordan Russell being led to one of the cabanas by a pool attendant. She appeared to be alone.

Now was Mel's chance. She said, "I'm going to the restroom. I'll be right back."

"I'll save your seat," Angie said, not looking up.

Mel headed toward the restroom and waited for a few moments until a family, two weary parents with young children, passed her on their way to the pool.

As the father swiped his card to open the pool gate, Mel stepped forward and offered to hold it open as the parents shuttled the kids, bags of toys, and floatation devices into the pool area. Mel took a quick look around and then stepped into the pool area.

When she glanced back, Angie was immersed in the day's crossword puzzle, and Mel hoped that she would be back before she was missed. She loved Angie to pieces, but her temper would not help Mel with questioning Jordan.

She checked her phone. They still had a few hours until the competition, which was probably why Jordan was out sunning herself like a turtle on a log. Why not? Her old lover was dead. She had to keep up her healthy glow so she could reel in the next big, fat fish.

Mel supposed she was being unfair to Jordan, but she really didn't care. Yes, Vic was responsible for their affair, too, but still she found she blamed the younger woman more.

It was very old school of her. Blame the other woman and not the man, but with Vic being dead, it made it difficult for her to be as mad at him as she would like, so it was all getting channeled onto Jordan.

Mel strolled along the wall of cabanas until she reached the one she believed was Jordan's. Each cabana was made up of three thick concrete walls with a long, hanging white curtain that closed across the front for privacy. There really wasn't a place to knock, so she wondered how exactly she was supposed to announce her presence.

She decided to clear her throat when she heard voices coming from the small enclosure. She had thought Jordan was alone. In a panic, she slipped into the vacant cabana next to Jordan's and held her breath.

"Do you really think it's wise to be drinking before the competition today?" a male voice asked.

"Oh, please," Jordan's voice sounded irritated. "My nerves are shot. If a mimosa will get me through the next hellish few hours, than I'll drink one. Shoot, I'll drink three if I have to."

"There are other ways to work out your tension," the man said.

Mel recognized the voice. It oozed charm like an oil slick on water. Dutch was in there with Jordan. She remembered overhearing his fierce defense of her to Johnny Pepper and how Johnny seemed to think there was something going on there.

"Don't be pushy," Jordan whined. "No one likes a pushy male."

"You used to like it when I pushed," he said. His double meaning made Mel want to gag, and he sounded petulant, like a child denied his favorite plaything.

"Oh, don't be like that," Jordan said. Her voice had changed from whiny to soothing. "It's going to be good between us again, baby, I promise. I just can't get Vic's death out of my mind."

Mel froze. Was Jordan actually choked up about Vic's death? It seemed unlikely, but she couldn't deny the note of distress in Jordan's voice.

"What if someone finds out—" she began, but Dutch interrupted.

"Don't go there, Jordan. We promised we wouldn't talk about it."

"But I can't help thinking about it," Jordan protested. "Look at me. I can't sleep. I can't eat. I've got circles under my eyes, and I think I'm getting dehydrated. My skin is a mess."

"You always look beautiful to me," he said.

Mel heard a shuffling noise and the distinct sound of two people kissing. She felt her face grow warm. Okay, now would be the time to announce herself, but she really wanted to hear if they'd say more. She had a feeling there was much left unsaid in their conversation, and maybe a part of it had something to do with Vic's murder.

After all, if Jordan and Dutch were involved, that gave them a real motive to have killed Vic. Or did it?

Maybe Jordan had broken up with Vic the morning before he died like she said, and now she had the guilts.

"Listen, baby, as long as we play it cool, no one is going to find out about what we did," Dutch whispered, and Mel felt a chill ripple down her spine.

That was it! They had done something. She made to step out of her hiding spot and confront them, but just then, she heard her name being shouted.

"Mel, is that you?"

She whipped her head around to see Grace heading toward her. Oh, no! Mel did not want to be found eavesdropping by Jordan and Dutch. She scuttled out of her hiding spot and rushed across the pool area, heading Grace off before she got any closer.

"Hi, Grace," she said in a low voice. "Angie and I were just having breakfast at the café. Care to join us?"

"Well, I—" Grace started to refuse, but Mel ignored her and looped an arm through hers and dragged her out of the pool area toward the outside dining tables.

"Angie, look who I've invited to join us," Mel called.

Angie looked up from her half-eaten plate of food. Her face was a sickly shade of gray, and her eyes were fuzzy as they tried to focus on them.

"Hi, Grace," she said. Then she slid from her chair onto the ground in a heap.

# Eighteen

"Angie!" Mel cried. There was a painful grunt from beneath the table. Mel turned to Grace and yelled, "Get help now!"

Mel dove under the table. Angie was slumped on the hard concrete, clutching her chest.

"I think I'm having a heart attack," she said. "Oh, no, I'm going to throw up."

Her eyes rolled back into her head, and she slumped into unconsciousness. The hostess for the café crawled under the table with Mel.

"An ambulance is on the way," she said. "Let's get her out from under there."

"Angie, can you hear me?" Mel called anxiously. "Angie?"

Together they half lifted, half dragged Angie out from under the table. Mel pressed her fingers to Angie's wrist. Her pulse was slow and irregular.

"They have to hurry," she said to the hostess.

"I'll go meet them outside and bring them right here," she promised.

Grace crouched down beside Mel and frowned at Angie with worry. "Oh, dear, the poor thing."

"What's taking them so long?" Mel yelled. "Does anyone have a car? I'll drive her to the hospital myself."

Just then three burly EMTs stormed into the café. Two set to work, taking Angie's vitals. They worked efficiently, which would have relieved Mel if they hadn't looked so worried. The third one turned to Mel.

"Were you with her? What happened?"

"I was with her," Mel said. "But then I went to the pool area. I was only gone for a few minutes, twenty maybe, but when I came back, she fell to the floor. She said she thought she was having a heart attack, then she thought she was going to be sick to her stomach."

"Does she have a history of heart disease or any other illnesses?" he asked.

"No, Angie has nothing. She's the strongest person I know," Mel said. Her voice cracked, and she felt her throat constrict.

She watched as Angie was quickly strapped onto a stretcher, and the three men prepared to whisk her out the door. Mel ran after them, determined to ride with them. She wasn't going to let Angie out of her sight, not for one second.

It was a short ride to Scottsdale Osborn Hospital, situated just down the street from the hotel. Mel hugged the side of the ambulance while the siren wailed and the lights flashed and they tore through intersections on their way to the emergency room.

With the skill of those trained to function in a crisis, the paramedics burst out of the back of the ambulance and hustled Angie on her stretcher inside. They didn't wait to fill out paperwork but sped into a glassed-in room at the end of the ward, where a doctor was waiting. Mel went to follow, but one of the paramedics held her off.

"You're going to need to wait here, ma'am," he said.

"But—" Mel protested.

"We'll do everything we can," he said and then shut the door.

If Mel could have clawed her way through the glass window to get to her friend, she would have. Instead she stared helplessly into a room while a team worked on Angie. With every head shake between the masked personnel, she felt her body spasm in terror.

Angie was her best friend. Mel couldn't even picture a day that didn't have Angie in it. A sob bubbled up, but she forced it away. This was Angie. She was tough. She was young. She was going to be fine.

Mel wiped away a tear that had spilled down her cheek. She had to let the DeLauras know what was going on. Keeping an eye on the activity in the room, she pulled out her cell phone and called Joe.

He answered on the third ring. "Hey, Cupcake, are you ready for your competition today?"

"Joe, it's Angie," she said. Her voice wavered, but she forged on. "She's in the hospital, Scottsdale Osborn, I don't know what's wrong."

Joe was silent for a second. "Car accident?"

"No, we were at breakfast and she was fine and then she was on the floor. She thought she was having a heart attack, and her pulse got really faint."

"I'll be right there," he said. "It's going to be okay."

Mel shut her phone wondering which of them he was trying to convince.

Next she called Tate. He was in a meeting, so she left a message with Mrs. Gurney, his secretary, letting him know where she was and why. She didn't want to panic him, but she didn't want to have to keep calling him either. She felt like all of her energy needed to be channeled to the pale woman supine on the other side of the glass.

Angie had been Mel's anchor for so long that just the sight of her lying flattened in the next room made Mel feel cut adrift, which invited in a whole lot of panic.

Why didn't Angie wake up? Why were the doctors just hovering over her? Couldn't they tell what was wrong? As if sensing Mel's stare, one of the doctor's glanced up and met her gaze. Mel did not like the perplexed look in his sharp brown eyes.

He must have said something, because the next thing she knew, the curtain was drawn shut, blocking out her view. Mel tried to protest, she even banged on the glass, but the curtain remained closed.

"Mel!" It was Tate. He was running toward her with his tie askew and looking frantic. Somehow, it took the edge off Mel's panic to have someone to soothe.

"Tate, thanks for coming," she said and gave him a big hug.

"What's going on? Mrs. Gurney interrupted my meeting, saying she thought I'd want to know you were here with Angie. What's happening?"

"I don't know," Mel said. "Angie got really sick at breakfast, and now she's behind the curtain in that glass room."

Mel felt her voice crack. She didn't know how much longer she could go without knowing what was happening.

"Well, let's find out, then," Tate said.

He strode over to the door of the room and opened it as

if he had every right to do so. Again, Mel was reminded that in the privileged world Tate had grown up in, they operated by a different set of rules, one of which was that virtually no door was ever closed to him.

The staff in the room looked over as he pulled the curtain open. Mel recognized the electrocardiogram that was hooked up to Angie. Her father had had to have that when his own ticker had started to go kaput. It scared Mel more than any other piece of equipment in the room. Could Angie really have had a heart attack?

A nurse blocked them from coming any closer. "I'm sorry," she said. "You can't be in here right now."

"Please just tell us if she's all right," Mel said.

"Are you related?" the nurse asked.

"I'm her husband," Tate said. "And this is her sister . . . in-law."

Mel didn't even blink at the whopper of a lie as it flowed out of Tate's mouth as smooth as royal icing.

The doctor Mel had seen earlier left Angie's side and approached them. "Let's step outside for just a moment."

He turned to the nurse and said, "We need to start the gastric lavage and doses of potassium chloride."

"Yes, doctor, I'll begin the prep," the nurse said and turned back to Angie.

Mel and Tate followed the doctor into the hallway. He lowered his mask, and Mel could see that he was young—she guessed him to be about their age, maybe a bit older in his mid- to late thirties.

"I'm Dr. Patel," he said. His voice had just the trace of an accent, and his warm brown eyes were full of sympathy, a sympathy Mel did not want to see. "I'm sorry, Mr. . . ."

"Harper, Tate Harper," he said.

"Mr. Harper, it seems your wife has been poisoned," Dr. Patel said.

Tate hissed in a breath and went rigid. "Is it treatable? Will she be all right?"

Mel studied the doctor's face. He looked grim, and she felt every muscle in her body tighten in fear. Angie could not die. She would not accept that.

"It is a particularly nasty poison, reminiscent of *Digitalis purpurea*, commonly known as foxglove, but that's not it. In fact, I'm having a hell of time trying to figure out what it is exactly. The symptoms she's exhibiting are giving us an idea of how to treat her, but I'm afraid without a conclusive diagnosis of the poison, or the amount of the poison she ingested, it's going to be touch-and-go. I'm sorry."

"Doctor, we're ready," the nurse said as she popped her head out of the doorway.

"Excuse me," he said. "I'll update you on her condition as soon as I can."

The door shut behind him, and Mel and Tate reached blindly for one another in a terrified hug. The sobs Mel had been holding inside exploded from her, making her body shake as she leaked snot and tears all over Tate's shoulder.

"I'm sorry," she said as she stepped back.

She looked blindly around for a tissue, but Tate was ahead of her and grabbed a paper towel from a dispenser on the wall over a nearby sink.

"It's okay," Tate said. "It's an old suit."

He handed her the towel, and Mel blew her nose. She glanced at him through watery eyes and could see he was struggling to keep it together.

He had gone a unique shade of gray, and his eyes were red. He looked to be pushing back some tears of his own.

"Mel!" a shout sounded down the hall, and Mel turned to see Joe running toward her with the entire pack of De-Laura brothers right behind him. Seven grown men all looking as if they'd rip the building apart brick by brick, if they had to, to get to their baby sister. No wonder Angie loved them so.

"Oh, man, I don't know what to say," she said.

"It's all right," Tate said. "I got it."

"Where is she?" Sal demanded.

"Yeah, what's happening?" Tony asked.

"She's in there," Tate said. "Dr. Patel says it appears that she's been poisoned."

"Poisoned?" Al echoed. "Like food poisoning?"

"No," Tate answered.

Joe reached out and pulled Mel into his arms as if he was trying to comfort her and get strength from her all at the same time. Mel buried her face against his solid warmth and said, "Oh, Joe, I'm so scared."

"It's going to be okay." He soothed her by running his hand up and down her back. "Angie is the strongest person I know. She'll pull through."

"I want to go in there," Dom said. "I'm her brother. I should be allowed in there."

"Yeah, well, I'm her husband, and they wouldn't let me in," Tate said.

The brothers all turned as one to stare at him. He shrugged. "I had to say something so they'd tell me what was happening."

The brothers nodded. The group was silent.

"Seven of us and not one of us is a doctor?" Joe asked. "That was an oversight."

"Did anyone call Mom and Dad?" Ray asked.

They all exchanged blank looks.

"I'll call," Dom said. "I'm the oldest. It's my responsibility."

He left with Al, the baby, tagging along behind him. The rest of the group stood awkwardly in the hallway until a nurse showed them to a waiting room just three doors down.

The room was more of an oversized closet than anything else. Utilitarian carpet on the floor and beige upholstery on wood-framed chairs filled the small room. A corner table held an in-house phone, a lamp, and a stack of well-thumbed magazines.

"I'll let Dr. Patel know where you are," the nurse said. "He'll be with you as soon as he can."

They all nodded numbly. There weren't enough seats in the room, so Mel and Joe stood in the doorway. She preferred that. She wanted to know the minute the door opened.

"Can you tell me what happened today?" Joe asked.

"I was headed over to Café Zuzu, and Angie decided to bike over with me. We ordered breakfast, but I saw Jordan Russell and decided to say hello."

"Vic's protégée?" Joe asked. "I didn't think you were overly fond of her."

"True. Honestly, I wanted to ask her some questions about Vic," Mel said. She glanced at Joe's face to see what he made of this, but he said nothing. "I ran into Grace by the pool and invited her to join Angie and me, but then Angie got sick and now we're here."

"Any idea what the poison was?" Joe asked.

They were standing close together, and Mel appreciated that Joe was keeping his voice neutral, sounding almost conversational, despite the horrible news she was conveying.

"No, the doctor said it was similar to foxglove, but he didn't seem to think that was it."

"I have a contact in poison control that we used as an expert witness on a case a few years ago," he said. "I think I'll give him a call."

Mel nodded. "Do it now, right away, please. If they can identify the poison, then the doctor will have a much better idea of how to treat her."

"All right," Joe said. "I'll need to call my office to get the number. I'll be just a minute. Will you be okay?"

Mel gestured to the waiting room with the four remaining DeLaura bothers and Tate. "I'll be fine."

Joe kissed her forehead and strode away.

Mel couldn't sit, so she began pacing, back and forth, up and down the hallway. No one came from the room with Angie. The clock felt as if it were moving backwards. Mel was sure she was going to lose her mind with worry.

After her third pass, Tate got up and joined her. Together they walked back and forth, up and down, and on their second pass, Tony joined them. And so it went until six of them were striding shoulder to shoulder up and down the hallway.

A few of the staff looked at them but said nothing. On their fifth pass, Mel glanced up and saw them, Maria and Dominick DeLaura Senior, hurrying down the hall toward them.

Maria was clutching her rosary beads, and Dominick Senior's thick gray hair was disheveled, as if he'd raked his hands through it repeatedly, a gesture Mel knew that each of his sons had inherited and used when they were stressed.

Dom and Al bookended their parents, as if to bolster them emotionally and physically as they led the way to Angie's room.

Maria was an older version of Angie, with the same warm brown eyes and striking features, the same compact figure that was soft but not pudgy. Her hair was short and gray, and she wore jean capri pants and tennies with a pink sweatshirt. There was a streak of dirt on her knee, and Mel would have bet money that she had been in her garden when they got Dom's call. Maria had a gift for plants and was the only person Mel had ever known who'd actually grown a tree from an avocado pit.

Maria looked strained but not panicked. Having raised eight children, she had done her share of time in the emergency room. She nodded at the cluster of them, and Mel knew it meant a lot to her that the whole family was here.

Dom Senior moved more slowly than his wife, having recently had hip replacement surgery. Still there was fire in the stout Italian man's eyes when he asked, "Where is she?"

"In there," Mel said.

Maria and Dom exchanged a look and then stiffened their spines, and as one, they pushed through the door into the room where Angie was being treated.

Mel heard a protest, but then Dom Senior spoke and there was no more argument. Dom was a large man, standing well above six feet. His sturdy build and harsh features, topped by a bushy gray mustache and matching eyebrows, gave anyone who considered arguing with him a moment's pause.

Mel craned her neck, trying to see over the DeLauras' heads, but no luck. The circle of medical staff surrounding Angie blocked any view she might have gotten, and the door closed before she could get even a glimpse of her friend. One glance at the crew around her, and she noticed she wasn't the only one trying to get a peek.

"Oh, to hell with this," Tate said. He looked half crazy with worry. "I'm her husband. I'm going in."

No one stopped him, and he slipped through the door right behind her parents.

Mel looked up to see Joe striding back down the hall toward them. It was at a time like this, when her whole planet was thrown into chaos, that she really appreciated the sense of order Joe brought to any situation.

From his blue striped tie and crisp dress shirt to his shiny wingtips, Joe looked every inch the man in charge. It occurred to Mel that someday he probably would be the chief district attorney or maybe even the attorney general for the state. Where would she fit in his life then?

She shook her head. Now was not the time for unsubstantiated panic about her relationship, and she suspected she was only going there because thinking of Angie was becoming unbearable.

"Any news?" Joe asked as he slid into her side and scooped her close with one arm about her waist.

"Not yet," Mel said. "But your parents are in there."

"How did they look?" he asked.

"Scared."

"Where's Tate?" he asked.

"He's in there, too," she said. "Given that he's her husband and all."

"You know he's in love with her," Joe said.

Mel turned to study him. His voice had sounded odd, as if he were trying to sound more casual than he felt. Did Joe worry about her relationship with Tate? He had never said anything before.

She was about to open her mouth to explain that she knew how both Tate and Angie felt, the fatheads, but the swinging door opened and all thought fled from Mel's mind as she braced herself for any news.

Tate was the first to step out followed by Dr. Patel.

Looking limp, Tate looked at Mel and nodded. "She's going to be all right."

Cheers erupted from the DeLaura brothers, and Joe snatched Mel up into his arms and hugged her tight enough to crack a rib. He set her down and joined the huddle of brothers as they pounded one another on the back. Mel could see them all making surreptitious wipes across their eyes to hide their tears of relief.

Tate opened his arms and she hugged him close. They hadn't lost Angie. She was going to be okay. Maria and Dom Senior came out of the room and joined their sons, then Maria reached out and pulled Angie and Tate into the group.

"You're family, both of you," she said in a voice gruff with emotion as tears streamed down her cheeks. "Don't ever forget it."

Mel and Tate exchanged a glance and joined in the hugging. It felt good after the strain of the past two hours to pull these people she had known since she was a child close and hug them.

Dr. Patel glanced at their group, looking relieved. Mel imagined having both Tate and Dom Senior hovering would make even the best doctor nervous.

"Are you Mel?" Dr. Patel asked.

"Yes," she answered.

"She's asking for you," he said.

"You can talk for just a minute, but then I'm moving her up to the ICU," he said.

"All right," Mel said.

She squeezed Joe's hand as she broke away from the group and went into the room. They had changed Angie's clothes, and she was wearing one of the hospital johnnies that opened in the back and flattered no one.

Her dark hair fanned out across the pillow, but her normally olive skin tone now looked to be a sickly shade of gray against the white sheets. She was hooked up to several machines, one of which was the electrocardiogram.

"How are you feeling?"

"Are you kidding?" Angie asked through dry lips. "'My life is as good as an Abba song. It's as good as "Dancing Queen."'"

"Seriously?" Mel asked on a snort that turned into a choked sob. "You're quoting *Muriel's Wedding* to me now?"

Angie opened her mouth as if she was about to sing. Mel held up her hand to stop her. "No, save your strength. Is there anything you need, or is there something I can get you?"

"I want my jammies," Angie said. "The blue ones with the cupcakes all over them."

"Done."

"What time is it?" Angie asked.

"I don't know," Mel said. "It must be past noon."

Angie's eyes went round. "What are you doing here?"

She arched her back as if she would sit up, but she didn't have the strength, and the nurse nearby caught her and pushed her back down.

"Oh, no you don't," the nurse said. "You are to stay put."

"Mel, you have to get down to the festival," Angie said. "You have to compete today, you can't forfeit."

Mel hadn't even thought about the festival. With Angie so ill, the contest had less than no importance for her.

She waved her hand. "Angie, I don't care about that stupid competition. The only thing that matters to me is that you're okay."

"Really?" Angie asked. "Well, I care. So I am telling you as your best friend and business partner that you need to get your butt down there. Pronto."

"Angie, I really don't think—" Mel began, but Angie interrupted her.

"Obviously," Angie said. She grabbed Mel's hand as they began to wheel her out of the room, forcing Mel to walk with her or be dragged. "Because if you were thinking, you'd realize that whoever poisoned me is trying to stop us from winning the competition, and you should be down there at the festival figuring out who it was."

The rolling bed was rounding a corner, and Mel couldn't hang on. Angie's fingers slipped through her grasp, but she heard Angie call out, "Start with Olivia!"

# Nineteen

"I'm not going," Mel said. "I'm not leaving her. I'm sure it was just the aftereffects of the poison making her think someone from the competition tried to poison her. I mean, that's paranoid, right?"

Joe was silent. The entire family had moved up to one of the ICU waiting rooms. Only two people were allowed in at a time to see Angie, so they were taking turns.

Sal, Dom, and Ray were the only DeLaura brothers with families of their own, and their wives and children soon joined the vigil.

Dom's little girl looked just like him with a sturdy build, chocolate brown eyes, and thick black curls. Given the strength of the DeLaura DNA, it meant she also looked just like Angie. She was as cute as could be, and Mel could hardly stand to look at her.

"Mel, I think Angie might be right," Joe said. "My friend at poison control was stunned by what I described, and he said a substance that was so obscure with such a short reaction time was most likely a deliberate poisoning."

"Oh my god."

Joe took her hand in his and squeezed her fingers hard as if bracing her for more bad news.

"And Mel, I have to be honest, I don't think the poison was meant for Angie. I think it was meant for you."

"What? Why?"

"Because you're the baking genius behind the team that is Fairy Tale Cupcakes," he said. "If this is a competitor, it makes sense that they'd go after you."

"The prize is ten thousand dollars," Mel said. "Yeah, it's a lot but certainly not worth murdering the competition."

"That would be true if it was just ten thousand dollars that you are competing for, but it isn't. This is a very prestigious competition with a lot of cash, *and* the competitors all know that the Food Channel is always looking for new and fresh talent. Winning this would be a coup for anyone who had dreams of Food Channel stardom."

"I just don't see it," Mel said.

"We'll have to agree to disagree," he said. "But I do think Angie is right. We need to get down there."

"We?" Mel asked.

"You don't think I'm letting you out of my sight, do you?"

"I don't want to leave her," Mel argued.

"I'll be here," Tate said as he joined them. "I'm not leaving her, and I'll call you if there is anything, even a case of hiccups, to report."

"I—"

"Go," Tate said. "It's the best thing you can do for her. She'll rest easier if she knows you've gone. Besides, with this crew waiting, you won't get in to see her for at least a few more hours."

"So, it's settled," Joe said. "Excellent."

Mel did not like the dark expression that shadowed his features. With his jaw set and his brow lowered, he looked like he wanted to do some damage.

"You know the contest started fifteen minutes ago. We've probably already been disqualified."

"Well, let's go see if we can talk some sense into those judges."

Scottsdale Osborn Hospital was across the street from the San Francisco Giants Stadium, well, their spring training stadium. Mel's father had taken her and her brother, Charlie, every year to spring training games. Mel had always loved the red brick and green trim, and she could never pass it without thinking of her dad and missing him. Today it seemed particularly poignant.

As if sensing her distress, Joe laced his fingers with hers as they crossed the street and strode past the ball park and the Civic Center Library to the festival grounds.

Mel flashed her VIP badge at the perky volunteer. Joe just gave her his best dimpled smile, and the flustered woman let them in without hesitation.

"How do you do that?" Mel asked. "It's like a super-power."

Joe grinned at her and she shook her head. The man could charm a girl right out of her apron with a smile like that.

She felt her stomach knot up with a sick feeling of dread as they approached the challenge to the chefs staging area. She tried to brace herself for the gloating satisfaction she would see on Olivia's mug, because no matter how you looked at it, Mel was late and she was pretty positive that alone put her out of the competition. There was no way she could make a dessert out of whatever ingredient they'd hit them with when there was only a half an hour left to go and she didn't have her sous-chef.

The staging area was in its usual full-throttle chaos as Mel and Joe approached. The judges were circling, and Mel watched as Dutch stopped by what was usually her station. Today it was occupied by someone else. Naturally, since she and Angie hadn't shown up, it had been given to a different competitor.

Mel squinted at the booth. A large man with a very bad haircut was slicing and dicing and sending Joanie, their runner, off the stage to fetch something. Oh, man, they even gave their runner away? That seemed cold.

Joanie was pounding down the stairs and jogging past Mel when she stopped and gaped at her. "What are you doing here?"

"Well, I just thought I'd—"

"Get up there," Joanie interrupted her and gave her a shove toward the stage. "He needs you, the boy is in way over his head, but he's fighting to keep you alive. Now git!"

Mel looked back at the station. Recognition zapped her like a knife in a toaster. "Oz? Is that Oz?"

She turned a wide-eyed glance at Joe, who looked equally surprised and a lot impressed. "Well, go help him!"

Mel gave Joe a quick kiss and ran up the steps onto the stage.

"Oz!" Mel called. "I can't believe you, what possessed you to attempt this?"

"Tony called the bakery and told me about Angie, and I didn't know what else to do to help out. I know how important it is to her to beat that cow," he said with a glare over at Olivia.

"Oz, I . . . you . . . you're awesome."

"Thanks, but are you going to help me here or what?

The clock is ticking louder than Dick Clark's New Year's Eve countdown, and I'm starting to panic," he said.

It was true. His round face was beaded up with sweat, and his chef's coat was too tight and looked the worse for wear.

"I'm in!" Mel jumped into the kitchenette beside him.

"Oh, thank the culinary gods!" Oz sagged against his cutting board.

"All right, what's the mystery ingredient, and what are you cooking with it?" she asked.

"You ready for this?" Oz asked. He held up a string of red chili peppers. "Are we having fun yet?"

Mel broke into a grin. "Oh, yeah, we are. What's your plan?"

The timer buzzed on the oven, and Oz hustled over to it. He took out a pan of cupcakes and popped them in the cooler. "Well, we're called Fairy Tale Cupcakes, so I figured I'd make the chocolate chili cupcakes my *abuela* made when I was a kid."

"Oh, Oz!" Mel grabbed his face and planted a kiss on his shaggy head. For a nanosecond his eyes appeared from between the hanks of the hair that usually hung over them, and they were wide with surprise. "It's perfect, you know that, right?"

He flushed with pleasure and began to stammer, "B-But now I'm stuck. I don't have the skills to plate these."

"I'm your sous-chef," Mel said. "I'll work on the plating. You just finish what you started."

Oz blew out a breath. "Okay. Hey, how is Angie?"

Mel smiled at him. "Well, after this, she's going to demand that we give you a raise."

"But I'm interning. You're not paying me anything," he said.

"We're going to have to rethink that," Mel said. "Now, let's do this."

Oz snapped back into action. The boy had skills—of that, there was no question. His cupcakes had cooled, and he was carefully unwrapping them. In a pot on his small stove top he had melted a chocolate candy coating. Mel watch as he used a long wooden skewer, stabbed the top of a cupcake, and dipped it into the chocolate. He moved quickly, dipping each one and placing them carefully on wax paper.

When he removed the wooden skewer, Mel carefully placed a whole chili from the strand onto the top of the cupcake. When they were done, Oz put them into their small refrigerator to set the chocolate.

Mel helped herself to the leftover chocolate candy and set to making intricate swirls of chocolate on the dessert plate and then sprinkling tiny amounts of chili flakes amidst the whirls and curlicues.

The warning bell sounded. They had one minute to go. Oz pulled out the cupcakes with their hardened chocolate shells and placed one onto each plate. They looked amazing.

They exchanged a high-five and a half hug just as the alarm sounded for the end of the competition.

There were a couple of cupcakes leftover, and Mel was dying to see how Oz's cupcake tasted. Even if they were lousy, she was so proud of him for jumping in to help, she boxed the leftovers and couldn't wait to bring one up to Angie to show her.

The servers took away their entries, and Mel and Oz departed the staging area. Joe was waiting and he asked, "How did it go?"

Mel opened the box to show him, and his eyes got their usual sugar-crazed glaze on them.

"Are those chocolate chili?" he asked.

"Uh-huh," Mel answered. He reached for the box, but she smacked his hand away.

"I'm saving these for Angie. Oz, I want you to take the rest of the day off," she said. "You went above and beyond. I can't wait to tell your guidance counselor about how you saved the day. Hey, how did you get them to let you compete for us anyway?"

"I found Angie's VIP tags at the shop," he said. "So, I had those, and then some crazy blonde lady threatened to have her husband shut the festival down if I wasn't allowed to represent the bakery."

"Ginny," Mel said. "Huh, I'll have to thank her."

"I want to sleep for two years," Oz said. "How do you people do this? God, they're going to judge those cupcakes. What if they're a bust? I can't stand to watch."

"Go," Mel ordered. "They're going to be great. I know it. You saved us, Oz."

He flipped her a lopsided grin and loped off through the crowd toward the exit.

"You're really not going to let me try one?" Joe asked.

"Well, maybe one, back at the shop. I have to see if the bakery is okay. I'm going to keep it closed today. I want to get back to the hospital and check on Angie."

"Tony just called to report. She's still in the ICU, but she's doing fine," Joe said. "I didn't tell him about Oz. I thought you might want to share that story."

Mel smiled. "It is a good one."

Together they clasped hands and made their way back to Old Town. Mel noted that Oz had put a sign on the door saying that because of a family emergency the bakery would be closed. The doors were locked, the lights were off, and all seemed calm. She really had to hire that boy on permanently.

"Hungry?" she asked as they climbed the stairs to her apartment.

"Are you offering me a cupcake?" he asked.

"How about a chicken sandwich and then a cupcake?" She unlocked her door and pushed it open.

"O . . . ah!" Joe's answer turned into a yelp as a white ball of fury flew out of the open door and latched on to his pant leg.

"Captain Jack!" Mel shoved the cupcakes into Joe's arms and unhooked the kitten from the fabric of his pants. "Oh, dear, I'm sorry, little guy. I forgot about you."

Joe looked at her over the box. "New boyfriend?"

"Angie and I found him in the Dumpster last night trying to eat a cupcake that was bigger than him," Mel said. She held the white ball of furious fur under her chin and tried to soothe him. "It's okay, buddy, you're all right. I've got you."

Captain Jack began to purr, and Mel felt him nuzzle her. It appeared he had decided he liked her, or maybe he had just scared himself silly and was willing to take comfort where he could get it.

"Captain Jack?" Joe asked.

"Angie named him because of his black eye spot. It looks like a pirate's patch."

"So, we're talking *Pirates of the Caribbean*'s Jack Sparrow?"

"Exactly," Mel said.

"But Jack doesn't have an eye patch."

"Yeah, tell your sister that."

Joe followed her into the apartment with a little wince.

"Are you okay?" she asked.

"I don't know," he said. "He gashed me pretty badly. I think I'm bleeding."

"Oh, let me get you some Neosporin and a Band-Aid," Mel said.

She turned to go to the bathroom, but Joe stopped her by grabbing the back of her jeans and pulling her back.

"I really think a kiss and a cupcake will do the trick," he said with a grin.

"Oh, you big faker," she said. "You have cupcakes on the brain. Here, he can kiss you."

She held out Captain Jack to him, and Joe gave her a wary look before he took him. "He's not going to shred me, is he?"

"No, but he may try to steal your cupcake."

Joe lifted the kitten until they were nose to nose. "Apparently, we need to come to an understanding," he said. "The cupcakes and the girl are mine. I'll share but remember more mine than yours, got it?"

Captain Jack gave him a squinty stink eye and then promptly began to lick his own shoulder.

"I'm just guessing here, but I think this little pirate is plotting to have me thrown off of his ship."

Mel laughed as she quickly made them each a chicken sandwich on toasted sour dough with lettuce and tomato and a light smear of mayonnaise. She then poured Captain Jack a small saucer of milk and gave him some diced-up chicken of his own, placing it on the floor in his corner of the kitchen.

"No wonder he attacked me," Joe said. "You feed him like this and he's never going to leave."

"Would that be such a bad thing?" she asked.

Joe looked at the kitten and then at her and back at Captain Jack, who seemed to sense that his future swung in the balance. He looked up at Joe and gave a very loud belch for such a tiny cat. Joe burst out laughing.

"He really is a Captain Jack," he said. "I'm game if you are."

Mel smiled. "We have a pet."

Joe took a bite of his sandwich. "It'll be good practice for us."

"Practice?"

"You know, for having kids," he said.

# Twenty

Mel sucked in a gulp of air and a piece of bread lodged in her throat, making her choke. It wasn't the "delicate clearing of the throat" choking; it was a full-on hacking like she was going to die before she got the bread dislodged with several whacks on the back from Joe.

"You okay?" he asked.

"Fine," she answered, her voice tight. She took a long sip of water, trying to ease the raked feeling of her esophagus. It only helped a little. "Wrong tube."

If Joe thought her sudden attack was from him mentioning babies, he said nothing and neither did Mel. She thought perhaps she had misunderstood him. They had been dating for only a few months; surely he couldn't be thinking that far in the future, could he?

Thankfully, Captain Jack kept them entertained by swatting and chasing his empty plastic bowl around the kitchen floor.

Joe collected their dishes while Mel took out Oz's cupcakes. She had to acknowledge that a part of her was nervous.

They looked good with their thick chocolate coating and pepper on top. She put one on a plate for each of them, and Joe handed her a fork.

"Here goes nothing," Mel said. She tucked into the cupcake, breaking through the chocolate exterior and into the seemingly moist cake. She raised the forkful to her mouth, knowing that their contest status was dependent upon the efforts of a supersized high school punk rocker with culinary aspirations, and her first impression of the taste was that it was exquisite.

She and Joe exchanged wide-eyed glances.

"This is fantastic!" he said. "This could be one of yours."

The taste of chocolate and chili rolled across her tongue in a burst of flavor that burned while it soothed, but neither flavor overpowered the other. It was addictive. She took another bite and another, and before she knew it, the cupcake was gone. She glanced at her empty plate and then at Joe.

"Don't look at me," he said. "You did that all on your own."

"But . . . oh, man, I have to get that recipe."

"Yes, you do," he agreed. His plate was empty, and he was looking at the box with longing.

"Oh, no you don't," Mel said. "The last one is for Angie. Speaking of which, I want to get back to her."

"Agreed," Joe said. "Will the little guy be okay?"

"I think so," Mel said. She watched Joe reach down and give Captain Jack a scratch under the chin. The white ball of fluff gave a contented purr, and Mel had a feeling her males were bonding. She refused to acknowledge how charming she found this entire situation or to dwell on how much it scared the baloney out of her.

It wasn't that she was commitment phobic, she told herself. Really. It was just that she'd been single for a long time, and although she loved dating Joe, she wasn't sure she was ready for the "24–7 together" thing or the "coparenting a pet" thing.

She reached down and rubbed Captain Jack's head, and he let out a big yawn. As they shut the door behind them, he was kneading a fluffy pillow on the futon, looking ready to pass out.

When they arrived in the waiting room, most of the De-Lauras were still there. They were watching a movie on the TV, and someone had brought in a load of subs from DeFalco's Italian Deli. They appeared to be camped out for the duration.

"How did it go, Mel?" Paulie asked. "Did you make the cut? Angie's been anxious."

"I think we may have pulled it out," she said. "Do you think I could go see her?"

"You might want to ask her husband," Dom said and gave Tate a firm nudge in the ribs.

Tate rubbed his side and said, "I'll call back and see if they're letting her take visitors."

He went to use the phone on the wall beside the door that led to the ICU. In a moment, he turned and waved Mel and Joe forward.

"It's a go," he said. As the door was unlatched, Tate grabbed Mel's arm. "Tell her if she needs anything, anything at all, to let me know."

"I will," Mel said.

The air in the ICU was suffused with the harsh astringent smell of disinfectant and body odors that Mel didn't care to dwell on. She forced herself to think of Oz's cupcake instead and tried to deconstruct the ingredients in her mind.

The corridor ended in a circle with the nurses' station in the middle and the rooms jutting off it. Joe paused beside Angie's room. Her curtain was pulled shut, and they eased around it, afraid to disturb her if she was sleeping.

Angie turned her gaze from the window, and her face lit up as soon as she saw them. She struggled to sit up, but Joe hurried forward and pushed her back down.

"Don't get excited or we're leaving," he ordered.

Angie ignored him. "How did we do? Did you make it in time? Did we win?"

"We did all right—better than all right, in fact," Mel said. "And we owe it all to Oz."

Angie's eyes went wide. "Explain."

Mel told her the entire story. Angie hooted with triumph when the story finished.

"We have to hire him," she said. "If we win, he gets a cut of the prize."

"Absolutely," Mel agreed. "I was so late. I never could have put together an entry, and his cupcake was superb."

"You have to check the leader board," Angie said. "First thing tonight when you go home and then call me. And Joe, you have to stay with her. Don't let her out of your sight."

"Angie—" Mel began, but Angie interrupted her, "No, this poisoning was no accident. I'm telling you it was meant for you."

"Joe said that before, but I just can't believe anyone would want to win this competition so much that they would poison one of us."

"I think both of our meals were poisoned," Angie said. "I've been lying here thinking about it, and I bet they were trying to take you out, but they would have to have poisoned both of our breakfasts since there would be no way for them to know what you had ordered. Mel, if you hadn't gone to the bathroom, we might both be dead."

"I hope you're wrong," Mel said. A shudder coursed through her at the thought that Angie might have died. "I couldn't stand it if some nut harmed you while trying to get to me. That would mean this is my fault."

"No, it isn't," Angie and Joe declared at the same time. Mel looked at them.

"It's not your fault if some wacko thought that poisoning you would give them a better shot at winning a cooking contest," Joe said. "That's out of your control."

"Does Dr. Patel have any more information?" Mel asked.

"No," Angie said. "He's still trying to figure out exactly what the poison was, but he did say he thought it was something that would have an immediate reaction, which means it had to be in my breakfast at the café. It was my first meal of the day."

"Did we see any of our competitors there?" Mel asked. "All I saw were a few of the judges."

"Just because we didn't see them doesn't mean they weren't there," Angie said.

The phone beside her bed began to ring. She reached for it, but the tubes she was tied to made it too difficult. Joe grabbed it for her and handed it to her.

"Hello," she said. There was a pause and then her voice got soft. "Oh, hi."

Mel figured it had to be Roach, Angie's boyfriend, and she glanced at Joe, who was watching his sister with a face full of unhappy.

"Come on," Mel said.

He looked exasperatedly at her as if he couldn't believe she was dragging him away from the perfect opportunity to eavesdrop on his sister.

She took him by the arm and pulled him away. She stopped only to wave at Angie to let her know she'd be back.

"I can't believe you're letting her have her privacy," Joe said. "Last I heard she was pouting because he wasn't calling as much as he had been."

"Yeah, then he sent her a cuckoo clock from Germany to tell her how cuckoo he was about her, and all was forgiven."

"How did Tate take that?" he asked.

"I believe he wanted to vomit," Mel said.

"I don't blame him," Joe said. "Poor bastard."

"And yet, he must have been the one to call Roach, because I didn't and I'm sure Angie didn't," Mel said. "It's like he wants to lose her."

They stopped beside the exit door to the ICU. Mel went to hit the electronic button that would release the door, but Joe grabbed her hand, stopping her.

"He doesn't want to lose her," he said. "Quite the opposite, I'm betting. I think he called Roach because he thinks it's the right thing to do, and that if he and Angie are meant to be together, he wants it to be because he won her fair and square, not because he withheld information from his competition."

"Is that what you would do?" Mel asked him.

Joe kissed her quick and hard on the mouth and then lightly brushed her bangs off her forehead with the back of his fingers. "Nope, when it comes to you, Cupcake, I play dirty."

And there it was, the grin that had made her weak in the

knees since the first day he had strolled into her life when she was twelve. Mel felt a little light-headed, and she shook her head, trying to clear it as he took her hand and led her back into the waiting room. To Mel's surprise, Uncle Stan was waiting there, and he looked grim.

"How is she?" he asked.

"Feisty as ever," Mel said. She noticed everyone in the room was listening, and at her words the tension level seemed to drop like the temperature on a winter's day.

"Good, that's good," he said. He glanced at the room full of DeLauras. "How about we take a walk and I buy you a cup of coffee. You look like you could use a pick-me-up."

"Am I invited, too?" Joe asked.

"If you must, but then the coffee is on you," Uncle Stan said. "Rule of deepest pocket."

"How do you figure?" Joe asked. "We're both public servants."

"Yeah, but the suits make more than the badges, so you can pony it up, pretty boy," Uncle Stan teased.

Mel knew that Uncle Stan was just yanking Joe's tie, as it were. They'd been friends even before Mel started dating Joe, and their affection for one another was always demonstrated through put-downs. She figured it had to be a law-enforcement thing.

"Fine, but we're not getting any of that vending machine swill you like," he said. "We're going to the cafeteria."

They left the ICU and made their way to the first floor. People in scrubs as well as visitors filled the room, but Mel, Joe, and Uncle Stan managed to get their coffee and then went to sit in the courtyard just off the cafeteria.

It was shaded from the direct blast of the sun, but the

afternoon air was still warm and Mel was grateful to be outside, away from the chilly air-conditioning.

Uncle Stan led them to a table in the back, and when they sat down, he said, "So, you're not just putting on a brave face for the family? She really is doing better?"

"Compared to being huddled in an unconscious ball under a table, yeah, I'd say she's doing better," Mel said. "Why?"

"Does the doctor know what did this to her yet?"

"He only knows that it was a fast-acting poison reminiscent of digitalis something or other, like foxglove, but he can't pinpoint exactly what it was. I'm just glad he's finding it treatable."

"She's going to have to keep the electrocardiogram on and they're still treating her with potassium chloride, but so far her recovery looks promising," Joe added. "Why the interest, Stan?"

"I care about her," Stan said. "She's always been my favorite DeLaura."

"No doubt," Joe said. He took a sip from his steaming cup of coffee and added, "But I know you. What's going on in that cop head of yours?"

"I talked to the medical examiner about Vic Mazzotta," he said. "It looks like he died of cardiac arrest, but we can't tell if it was before or after he ended up in the freezer."

Mel and Joe exchanged a glance.

"And?" Mel prompted him, knowing there had to be more.

"I got his doctor's name from his wife, Grace," Stan said. "When I talked to the doctor, I asked if he had a history of heart disease. The doctor said no."

"Well, that doesn't mean it couldn't have been natural

causes," Joe said. "Some people don't know they're high risk until they have a heart attack."

"Except Mazzotta just had a stress test a few weeks ago, and according to the results, he had the ticker of a twenty-five-year-old."

"You think he was poisoned by the same person who got Angie," Mel said.

"I'm just saying it's possible," Stan said. "I'm having the ME run some toxicology tests, and we'll know more soon. We've also questioned the kitchen staff at the café, and no one saw anyone in the kitchen who shouldn't have been. We were hoping to retrieve your breakfasts from the café's garbage to test them both for poison, but the city truck had already picked up by the time we got there."

"You know what this means," Joe said to Uncle Stan.

"We need to watch her around the clock" Uncle Stan said.

"I've got the night shift," Joe said. "And I can work out a schedule with the brothers to cover the rest of the hours in the day."

"What about me?" Mel said. "I want to help."

They both looked at her with identical expressions of confusion.

"I want to help watch over Angie, too," she said.

"Oh, honey, we're not talking about Angie," Uncle Stan said. "We're talking about you."

"Me?" Mel blinked.

"I think Stan is right," Joe said. "If Vic was poisoned, then whoever did it to him went after you."

"But why?" Mel asked. "There is no purpose in poisoning me. Vic, sadly, had a lot of enemies, but I don't."

"Don't you find it odd that Vic was judging the competition, you were his favorite student, he dies, probably poisoned, and then your sous-chef ingests poison that was most likely meant for you, too?"

"But that's mental," Mel said. "I mean it's not like we're having a million-dollar bake-off. It's ten thousand dollars and a plaque, not really worth murdering three people over."

"Mel, why are you in this competition?" Stan asked.

"Because it will bring prestige to the bakery, it's excellent publicity, and the cash prize is a nice chunk of change."

"Mel, we talked about this. You've got competitors who see this as the leap to a television career on the Food Channel," Joe said. "This is like *American Idol* for chefs to them."

"But that's ridic—" Mel cut herself off as she remembered Polly Ramsey, the cookie baker, telling her that her mother had high hopes that Polly would get noticed and picked up by the network.

"What are you thinking?" Stan asked. His gaze was shrewd.

"That I hate to admit it, but you might be right about some of my competitors. This is more than just a baking competition for them."

"And not just your baking competitors," he said.

"What do you mean?" Mel asked.

"Bertie Grassello is replacing Vic on his show, right?" Uncle Stan asked.

"Yeah," Mel said. "And he's taking Dutch Johnson along with him."

"Well then . . ." Uncle Stan trailed off, waiting for her to put it together.

"You think some of the celebrity judges don't want to be outshined by the competing chefs?" she asked.

"Namely, you and Angie," Uncle Stan said.

"I hate to puff up Stan's already substantial ego," Joe said. "But he's got something there. You and Angie are young, fun, and easy on the eyes. The Food Channel would be lucky to have a show featuring you two."

Mel frowned and said in a doubtful tone, "Maybe."

"Maybe?" Stan barked. A couple at the next table looked over, and he cleared his throat and took a sip of his coffee. "Look, I'm going to post a uniform in the ICU to look after Angie just to be on the safe side, but I don't think she was the target. That being the case, I'm also going to have some undercovers patrolling the festival and keeping an eye out for anything suspicious."

The three of them were silent for a moment, and then Mel blew out a breath. "Is there no chance that this is all just some huge mistake?"

"There's always a chance," Joe said, and he laced her fingers with his and gave her hand a squeeze.

"But it's unlikely," Uncle Stan said. "Now I'm only going to tell your mother the edited version, because you know how she gets."

"Yeah, now you're talking certifiable," Mel said. Uncle Stan frowned at her, and Mel added, "In a good way."

"All right, then," Uncle Stan said. "Mel, you're not to go anywhere or do anything without letting someone know—don't give me that look."

"What look?" she asked.

"That look that says you'll do as you damned well please, but that you're smart enough not to say it out loud," he said.

"I didn't—" she began, but Joe interrupted, "Yeah, you did. I've seen that look. It's not your best."

Mel glared and he grinned, diffusing her ire like snuffing a candle between his fingers. Damn it, they'd been dating for six months. She really should be able to maintain some annoyance with him.

"Here's the other thing, Mel," Uncle Stan paused, "and this is critical. If the killer's chosen method is a fast-acting poison, then you have to watch every bite you eat. That means, you shop for your own food, cook your own food, and you must have it in sight of you at all times."

For the first time, Mel felt the seriousness of her situation press upon her.

"He's right," Joe said. "No meals out. No sampling anything that someone gives you. You're going to have to be very, very careful."

Mel rested her head in her hand. "If anything had happened to Angie . . ." Her throat closed up and she couldn't continue. Joe pulled her into his arms and tried to comfort her, but Mel was too consumed with equal parts terror for her friend and rage that someone had harmed her.

"I'll have your word, Mel," Uncle Stan said.

She leaned into Joe and turned her head to face Uncle Stan, "I promise I'll do what you say."

He puffed out his cheeks with relief and checked his phone. "Okay, then, I'll call you later. Keep an eye on my girl, DeLaura."

"Always," Joe said.

Mel leaned against him, trying to feel comforted and ignoring the small part of her that was feeling suffocated.

She didn't know if she felt that way because a killer was out there or if it was because her relationship had just taken a claustrophobic turn. Either way, she felt an almost irresistible urge to run.

# Twenty-one

It was impossible for Mel not to stare at her competition during the next day's event. They were now in the fourth round with the field having been reduced by more than half. Twenty competitors remained, and tensions were running high.

In the lounge before the competition was to begin, Mel found Polly Ramsey in tears. She was convinced that she had nothing left and was going to fail out that day.

Mel tried to comfort her, but it was a halfhearted effort at best. She hated being here when she felt like she should be with Angie, but Angie had been very clear that she expected Mel to put her game face on, go out, and win.

Since he had been responsible for keeping them in the competition, Mel had brought Oz along as her sous-chef in Angie's place while Tony manned the bakery for them. Oz had dressed for the occasion by wearing his checkered Vans and his best wallet chain.

Olivia met Mel's gaze across the room. She had tried

to talk the festival official, Felicity Parnassus, into having Fairy Tale Cupcakes disqualified since Angie wasn't present, but given the extreme circumstance of Angie's illness, Felicity had refused. Now Olivia looked like she wanted to come over and trash-talk Mel. When she stepped toward them, however, and got an eyeful of Oz, she seemed to think better of it. Mel decided having a thug in her kitchen might prove to be a good thing on a lot of levels.

The whistle sounded, and they trooped into their kitchens awaiting Johnny Pepper's announcement for the day. When she passed by, Johnny whispered, "Sorry about your assistant—food poisoning, ugh, the irony."

Uncle Stan had told her that was the story they had told the rest of the festival participants, who were happy to keep it quiet, given that food poisoning would make them all look bad and be detrimental to festival attendance.

"Thanks, Johnny," she said. She squeezed his arm and their eyes met. For just the briefest second Mel was intrigued.

"Oh, sure, it wasn't enough to be teacher's pet; now you've got to be the host's darling, too," a snide voice hissed from behind her.

Mel whipped around. Apparently, Johnny's kindness to Mel was enough to make Olivia forget her fear of Oz. Well, that was fine with Mel. If Olivia was game, Mel was more than ready to have a smackdown with her. She never got the chance.

A deep growl from somewhere over her head said, "Shut it and back away . . . now."

Oz! He was looming over Mel's shoulder as intimidating as Lurch from the Addams Family. And he wasn't alone. Out of nowhere four of the DeLaura brothers—Sal,

Ray, Al, and Paulie—appeared, flanking him and creating a protective half circle around Mel.

"Oh, look at you, you've hired yourself an entourage," Olivia and her sous-chef snickered. "Think pretty highly of yourself, don't you?"

Mel went to dive after her, but two of the brothers grabbed her arms and held her back.

"Angie told us specifically not to let you fight, because you'll get kicked out of the competition," Ray said.

"Sorry, Mel, I'd love to let you kick her butt, but we promised," Al said. He sounded regretful, as if he understood just how much she wanted to rip Olivia's hair out by the roots.

"Fine," she said and yanked her arms out of their grasp. She waved her hands at them in a shooing gesture. "Now shoo before we're disqualified for having you onstage with us."

"Done," said Paulie. He jerked his head to the others, and they all trooped away, taking up spots just in front of her kitchen. "But I've got my eye on you."

Mel had always known that the brothers were overprotective. Her own brother, Charlie, could be overbearing, but at least he lived three hours away in Flagstaff. Angie had all seven of her older brothers here in the Valley and always up in her business. Mel wasn't sure how she could stand it.

She glanced down at the four DeLauras and noticed that Sal was talking to the female judge from *Food and Wine* magazine. He looked fairly intense about the point he was making, and Mel saw the woman look at her and then back at Sal. She looked nervous, and Mel knew she'd better call the brother off before he did irreparable damage.

"Sal," she called. "I need to get an update on Angie. Can you do that for me?"

"Yeah, sure, Mel," he said. He looked reluctant to end

his convo with the judge, but he sighed and fished his cell phone out of his pocket.

The judge gave Mel a furtive glance and dashed toward the judges' table. Mel hoped she had scored some brownie points for calling off the brother.

The twenty remaining contestants all looked nervous. Only two more rounds until they reached the final four. For those who had been hovering on the bottom of the leader board, today was do or die.

"Tate says she's doing fine," Sal reported. "She said she expects to see you two on the top of the board today."

Mel glanced at the board. That would be no small feat. Despite the brilliance of Oz's cupcake, they had dropped into fourth yesterday.

The scores were cumulative for the first five rounds. But for the round amongst the final four, it was winner take all. Sort of like college basketball, she thought. The key to this competition, Mel figured, was to get into the final four and then win.

Mel suspected their current fourth place ranking was a punitive move by the judges because she had been late and her intern had all but done it on his own. That was okay; they were still in the running.

Mel took her position beside Oz, who was looking uncomfortable in his chef coat and hat. Although she'd found ones big enough to fit him, somehow they still looked small on his bulky frame. With hair sticking out from under the lower edge of the hat, it appeared as if it barely managed to stay atop his shaggy mane. His coat was unbuttoned at the top, and she noticed sweat stains were beginning to appear beneath his arms.

"Are you okay?" she asked Oz as Johnny Pepper arrived with the big white box.

"It was easier yesterday when I was just doing it because I wanted to help you out," he said. "I didn't have time for nerves or doubts."

"Well, if it helps, you don't have time for that today either."

Oz snapped his head in her direction, but Mel was watching Johnny and had no more time to hold Oz's hand. He was just going to have to man up and deal with whatever they got handed today.

"And the mystery ingredient is . . ." Johnny began but then paused to fish it out of the box. He hoisted a bunch of bananas in the air, and the chefs were all quiet for a moment. After chilies, stout beer, and parsnips, bananas seemed sort of tame.

"The challenge today will be to create something new and spectacular out of bananas."

Ah, now Mel understood. Instead of giving them an odd ingredient, they were giving them something not so odd that would force them to really push the creative envelope.

"Chefs, are you ready?" he called into the microphone.

"Get ready, Oz," Mel said. "We need to get to the supply cart first. I want a bunch of fresh bananas—no green ones—as well as some of the smaller plantains."

Oz stretched his arms. "No worries. I have superior reach."

They waited on the balls of their feet. Johnny gave the countdown, and each chef and sous-chef charged the cart. It was mayhem. Elbows were thrown, kicks were issued, the fight for bananas was ugly.

Mel dove between Polly and her father and snagged a perfect bunch of bananas. She glanced over and saw that Oz had two fistfuls of plantains that he was holding high in the air as Olivia jumped and tried to snatch them from him.

Oz let out a warrior's bellow and strode out of the melee with Olivia hanging off his shoulders. Like a dog shaking off a tick, Oz shrugged his shoulders, and Olivia went down in a heap.

Mel high-fived Oz, and they hustled back to their station. Joanie was hopping from foot to foot on her trainers, and Mel ran through the list of extras that she needed. The other chefs were still hustling back to their kitchens while Mel and Oz quickly began to prep their bananas.

"Oz, take care of the plantains," Mel said. "I need them peeled and sliced on the diagonal, then spread onto a greased baking sheet. Bake them at four-fifty for ten to fifteen minutes."

"On it," Oz said.

Joanie came racing back with a basket from the supply cupboard. "Here you go."

"Excellent," Mel said. "Stand by in case I need you again."

Like a dutiful soldier, Joanie assumed a standing position beside the staging area.

Mel set to work. She set out her spring roll wraps to thaw and then grabbed her largest frying pan and poured in an inch of oil. While that was heating, she used her double boiler to start a thick chocolate sauce.

"Plantains baking," Oz said. "What next?"

"How is your burrito wrapping?" Mel asked.

"Please, that's kid stuff," he said.

"Good, then halve these bananas and wrap them burrito style in the spring roll wrappers," Mel said. "We're deep frying."

"Oh, oh, ah, ah, ah," he said while thumping his chest with his fists.

"Gorilla noises, really?"

"Sorry," he said, but his grin gave him away, and Mel found herself laughing with him.

She glanced up and saw Olivia standing on tippy toes watching them. It took every ounce of restraint she had not to lob a naked banana at the woman's forehead.

The halfway bell rang, and the contestants had to put on a burst of speed to finish up their desserts. Mel left Oz in charge of the deep frying while she thickened up the chocolate sauce and tended the baking plantains.

Finally, they were ready for plating. On each plate, they made a triangular stack of three fried bananas, drizzled them with chocolate sauce, sifted powdered sugar over the top, and then dusted them with just a hint of cocoa powder. Around the triangular stack of fried bananas, Mel scattered the baked plantain chips and drizzled chocolate over them as well.

"Those look amazing," Ray said from in front of their kitchen. Before Mel or Oz had a chance to stop him, he picked up one of the deep-fried bananas and bit into it.

"What the he—" Oz started, but Mel screeched over him, "Ray, that was for the judges, you imbecile!"

"What?" he asked through a mouthful. "Oops, well, it's really good."

Mel felt herself begin to hyperventilate. Thirty seconds left and one of the judges would be getting a mangled dessert.

Oz jumped in with an empty plate and an extra fried banana. With five seconds to go, he was able to re-create the plate that Ray had destroyed. It wasn't as pretty as the others, but it was damn close.

The final buzzer sounded, and Mel and Oz stepped away from their plates. There were a few whimpers and moans from the other chefs, and Mel was glad to see a sweat-soaked, red-faced Olivia, panting on the other side of the stage. Mel squinted to see her entry. It looked like some sort of cakelette. Mel hoped her banana burrito kicked its mini-cake butt.

The servers came and gathered their plates, and Mel saw Ray's head pop up again. He was reaching for the remainders off the plate he had mangled. Oz saw him, too, and without saying a word, Oz launched himself off the stage, tackling Ray to the ground.

"You almost blew that for us, you big dummy," Oz said. He was sitting on top of Ray, glaring down at him, looking decidedly menacing with his shaggy hair over his eyes and his multiple piercings.

"Well, I'm hungry," Ray said. "You can't expect a guy to stand there watching all that good food get made and not eat something, can you?"

"If it's the contest entry, yeah, I can," Oz argued.

The other three brothers ambled over.

"This was my bad," Sal said. "I should have taken into account Ray's sweet tooth when I assigned our designated areas. It won't happen again."

Paulie lifted Oz off Ray.

"You're right it won't happen again," Mel said. "Because as of right now, the DeLaura brothers are banned from coming into the festival."

"What?" Paulie balked. "You can't do that."

"Can and will," Mel said. "What do you think Angie would say if she saw this fiasco today?"

The brothers were silent.

"Exactly," Mel said. "You know how much she wants to win this. I can't have you all hovering while I cook or helping yourselves to the entry before the contest is finished."

"It won't happen again," Ray said. "I promise."

"Too late," Mel said. "You're fired—all of you."

"Sorry, Mel, but it's not up to you," Al said.

"Excuse me," she said.

"Yeah, Joe is the one who sent us here," Sal said. "Unless he pulls the plug, we're staying."

"Oh, he'll pull the plug," Mel said. "Just wait."

She took out her cell phone and dialed while the brothers shuffled their feet, looking decidedly nervous.

As they should, Mel thought.

She did not need the four of them making this competition any more difficult that it already was.

"Joe DeLaura's office," a female voice answered on the third ring.

It didn't sound like his secretary, but Mel forged on, too intent in her purpose to be dissuaded by a little thing like an unknown sexy voice answering her boyfriend's work phone.

"Hi, this is Mel," she said. "May I speak to Joe, please?"

"Hmm, no, I don't think so," the voice said.

"Excuse me?" Mel asked. "Is Joe not there?"

"Oh, no," the voice said. "He's here, but he's busy doing real work and can't be fielding calls from his little baker girlfriend."

Then it clicked. Mel had heard this voice before. It was the female colleague Joe had been working a case with about the same time Mel and Joe reconnected. If Mel remembered right, she was a knockout.

"Susan Ross, right?" Mel asked.

The woman didn't answer her.

"I'm sorry, do we have a problem?" Mel asked

"Not at all," she said. "I'm just making sure Joe gets his priorities straight."

"And how do you think Joe will feel when he finds out

you didn't let him know I called?" Mel asked. Her voice
was crisp with annoyance.

"You can't prove anything," the voice said, and with a
click the line went dead.

Mel closed her phone. "Well, it looks like a stay of exe-
cution for you four."

The brothers all perked up while Mel frowned at the
phone in her hand. She wasn't sure how to deal with this
new situation. She needed to find out from Joe what the
deal was with Susan. What if she had been calling about an
emergency with Angie? Would the woman not have put her
through? And if not, why not? Did Joe have unfinished
business with her? Mel so didn't need this right now.

"Come on, Oz," she said. "Let's get back to the bakery.
We need to sell some cupcakes."

Mel tried to ignore the DeLaura brother, Sal, who
tagged along behind them. She knew they had worked out
a schedule, and there was nothing she could do about it
until she convinced Joe to call them off.

Tony was manning the front counter when they stepped
inside. As soon as she took in her precious pink and chrome
bakery and heard Elvis's voice crooning form the jukebox,
Mel felt all of her tension slip away.

It seemed as if she'd been away for weeks instead of just
a day and a half. The sights and smells of all things familiar comforted her in a way nothing else could, and for the
first time since Angie had been poisoned, she felt her
shoulders sink down from around her ears.

"How's business been, Tony?" she asked.

"Steady," he said. "How did the competition go?"

Mel and Oz exchanged a look. "We don't know for sure,
but I think we pulled it out."

"I'm going to call Angie," she said. "Oz, will you and

Tony restock the front display case and make a list of what we're low on?"

Oz bobbed his shaggy head.

Mel went into her office and shut the door. She dialed Angie's room number at the hospital and waited. Angie picked up on the third ring.

"Speak to me," Angie said.

"It went well today," Mel said. "Oz has skills."

"I know. Ray already called me. He said your dessert was irresistible."

"Apparently."

"He also said you were unhappy with them and tried to have Joe call them off. What happened?"

"He didn't tell you he mangled a dessert?"

"No, he told me," Angie said. "I get that. I'd have kicked his butt myself, but he said you looked weird after you called Joe's office. He said he got the impression someone wouldn't put your call through."

"My god, that man has big ears," Mel said.

"You have no idea," Angie agreed. "So what happened?"

"It was no big deal," Mel said. "I'll talk to Joe about it later. How are you feeling?"

"Good enough that Dr. Patel is letting me out today. They're doing the paperwork as we speak," she said. "And I'll be assisting you at the contest tomorrow."

"Ange, do you really think you should?"

"It's one hour, and it's really important to me to compete, okay, more accurately, to win."

"All right, if the doctor says it's okay," Mel said. "Do you need me to drive you home?"

"Nah, Tate's got it," she said. Her voice sounded tight, and Mel knew it was none of her business but she asked anyway, "Has he moved into the hospital officially, then?"

"Pretty close," Angie said. Her voice sounded embarrassed, and she hastily added, "You know he'd do the same for you."

"No, he wouldn't," Mel disagreed.

"Well, that's because you have Joe, but if Joe was out of town, he would," Angie said.

"Yeah, keep telling yourself that," Mel said. "Call me if you need anything."

"Absolutely," Angie said. "See you tomorrow."

"Love you."

"Love you, too."

Mel hung up, feeling more grateful than she could express that Angie was okay and being released from the hospital. She never wanted to be that terrified ever again.

In the quiet of her office, she took a moment to go over the details of the past few days. Someone had murdered Vic. Although there were obviously several people with plenty of motive, she still had no idea who had the most to gain by his death.

She would have pinned it on Jordan just because she didn't like her, but Angie had been right—without Vic, Jordan probably would fade into obscurity. So that left Bertie, who had just gotten Vic's job, but then why did he need to kill Vic? He already had the job. Then there was Dutch. He hated Vic and blamed him for his failed career. But if he was working out a new situation with Bertie, then why risk it all by committing murder?

Mel felt her pupils contract. She was so tired of thinking about all of this. Every time she felt like she had a lead or an inkling of an idea, it slipped through her fingers like a puff of smoke, refusing to take any solid shape.

The only thing she did know was that Angie had been poisoned, and as much as Mel had balked about it, it did seem that it had been directed at keeping them out of the competition. Still, it seemed just crazy for a competitor to go that far to win. The only thing she knew for sure was that she had almost lost her best friend, and that made her angry, angry enough to take on a killer.

# Twenty-two

Mel spent the rest of the day in the kitchen, baking. It was the most therapeutic thing she could think of to do. She took a break about midafternoon and ran up to check on Captain Jack.

She opened the door to her apartment, half expecting to be attacked like he'd done to Joe, but no. No white little fur ball launched himself at her when she stepped inside.

In fact, he was nowhere to be found. She searched the bathroom, the kitchenette, and under all of the furniture. There was no sign of his little snow white body. Her heart began to pound in her chest. Had he gotten out? He was so little. What if he went back to the Dumpster? What if the garbage trucks came, and he got hauled away like so much trash? No, this was not trash pickup day. She checked the cupboards, thinking that maybe he had gotten trapped inside one.

She was on her hands and knees checking the cabinet under the sink when she felt someone watching her. It was a peculiar feeling. Slowly she turned around. There sat Captain Jack, studiously licking one paw, while he glanced at her with his pale green eyes.

"Where did you come from?" she asked.

He stretched his body in a long arc and ambled over to her. He purred as he rubbed his little face against her arm, and she had a feeling he was angling for more food. Joe had been good enough to pick up proper cat food and kitty litter and drop it off earlier that day, for which she was grateful.

Mel scooped up Captain Jack and held him until they were nose to nose.

"I'm feeling very fragile lately, so don't scare me like that again," she said.

He batted her nose with a paw.

"Fine, cuteness will get you a little snicky-snack," she said. She gave him a small portion of canned cat food and some dry as well and watched while he attacked his dish. When he was finished, they played an intense game of chase the yarn ball until Captain Jack started to look droopy and he began to knead her lap.

She put him on his preferred pillow and headed back downstairs. She had a special order for tomorrow that she needed to get done, and she wanted to help Oz lock up.

She really needed to do something about Oz. He had undeniable talent. He was still in high school, but he would be graduating soon. With his skills, she'd love to see him go on to the Scottsdale Culinary Institute. If only Vic were still alive. She could have asked him to use his influence to help get Oz in.

A wave of anger hit Mel low and deep. It was this sort of moment that brought the loss of Vic back to her like a punch in the chest. Yes, he had been the sort of person that sucked all of the oxygen out of the room, but he had also had an eye for talent and he nurtured it in those he deemed worthy. Mel had been one of the lucky ones. She couldn't help thinking what he would have done with Oz and how sad it was that Oz wouldn't get that opportunity.

The bakery was hopping when Mel returned. Oz and Tony were dashing between the counter orders and the tables. Elvis was keeping a moving beat, and the sound of laughter sprinkled the air with a mix of guffaws and giggles.

"Oz!" Mel called to him while she yanked on her apron. "Why didn't you call me for backup?"

"I figured you could use the break," he said. "Besides, it didn't get crazy busy until about ten minutes ago."

"I'll take the counter if you two can handle the tables," she said.

Oz and Tony nodded, and they split up to man their separate stations. Mel didn't have a chance to talk with them again for another hour and a half. By the time she kicked Tony out and they flipped the sign to Closed, it was eight o'clock, and the display case was all but empty. The walk-in cooler was looking pretty bare as well.

"It's official, Oz," she said as they both sank onto booth benches and put their feet up on empty chairs. "I am going to have to start paying you, and you're already due for a raise."

He gave a low laugh. "I think that's against the internship rules."

"So is skipping school to work here," Mel said.

Silence greeted her words.

"Oz?" she prompted.

"I hate school," he said. "It's a stupid waste of time. I've learned more since I've been here than I have in a whole semester there."

Mel was silent. Oz was huge for his age. Six foot three with a burly build, more piercings than she cared to count, and the few times she'd seen his eyes, he was wearing thick black eye liner.

She had come to suspect that although he looked pretty tough on the outside, he was a big marshmallow inside. Bullies loved targets like Oz. The bigger the victim, the tougher the bully felt.

Mel didn't doubt that the same type of bullies who had made her chubby years hell on earth found Oz an easy target as well. Still, he couldn't be missing school.

With the booth backs between them, she felt as if they were in a retro fifties confessional. Maybe that was why Oz had been square with her. She glanced down; she could see his size thirteens sticking out of his bench. The tips of his Converse high-tops kept tapping against one another. He was nervous; he was afraid he was in trouble. Mel decided to put him at ease.

"I was the fat kid in school," she said. "From grades K through eight, I was the porker, the one who always had a candy bar stashed in my cubby, my backpack, my locker. I even put one in my training bra once. It melted. Not a good plan, but it was an especially bad term."

She glanced down. The Converse had stopped tapping.

"I was lucky," she said. "My dad was a funny guy, and he always knew just what to say to make things better. I never realized what a gift that was until he was gone. But I also had a couple of friends, Tate and Angie, who got me through the worst of it. Oh, I still got picked on in high school, but it wasn't as bad."

"I never knew my dad," Oz said. "My friend Lupe looks out for me, but she's younger and we're not in a lot of the same classes."

"Do you feel afraid?" Mel asked.

Oz was silent for a while, and then he said, "No, just sad."

Mel lifted up her arm and rested it on the back of the booth. After a moment, almost hesitantly, Oz's hand appeared beside hers. She patted his hand and then asked, "Do you want me to come to your school and kick some bully ass?"

A shocked laugh erupted from Oz, and like the rest of him, even his laugh sounded too big and it boomed around the room, making Mel laugh with him.

He sat up and peered over the back of the bench. "That would be something."

"If I bring Angie, it'll be ugly," she said.

A grin appeared below his shaggy bangs.

"Oz, I'm going to write your counselor a note about what all has been happening here, and I'm going to take full responsibility for your absences, but you have to promise me you'll start going to your classes and maintaining your grades."

"Do I still get to work here?" he asked. His voice was just above a whisper.

"Absolutely, but not before your last class, which I believe lets out at noon, correct?"

"Yeah," he said.

"Okay, I don't want to see you before twelve thirty, then," Mel said. "And I wasn't kidding. We're going to work out a way for this to be a paid internship. You have certainly earned it."

His grin flashed back into place, and Mel felt relieved that she hadn't screwed up. Of course, she still needed to convince his counselor that this was a good idea, but she'd worry about that later.

Captain Jack was still asleep on his pillow when Mel went into her apartment. At least he hadn't slipped into that alternate dimension cats seemed capable of disappearing into on a whim. She did not need to be scared like that again.

Mel checked her messages. The first was from Joe telling her that he was on duty to watch Angie at her house tonight. Mel thought about stopping by, but knowing Angie, she was probably full up on people at the moment. Besides, it would be good for them to have some time together.

The second message was from Mel's mother, Joyce.

"Melanie, dear Joe told me that he is watching his sister tonight, such a good man, and we both agreed that you should spend the night with me." Here the message paused. "Are you there, Melanie? Please pick up. Oh, you're probably still closing up. All right, I'll call back in a half hour. Love you. Bye."

Even though Mel had always had voice mail, her mother always seemed to think she could hear the messages being recorded. Mel had tried to explain voice mail to her mother, but it hadn't taken.

She glanced at the clock. Her mother would be calling back in ten minutes. Mel didn't want to spend the night at her mother's. She knew she had to be careful, but really, who could poison her in her own apartment?

Now the trick was going to be avoiding talking to her mother at all costs. Joyce wielded guilt like a swordsman used a rapier. Mel would be tucked into her old bed at her mother's faster than she could say "no thank you" if she spoke to her directly.

She supposed she could go down and hide in her kitchen and get some baking done, but the idea did not appeal. She could unplug her phone and just ignore it, but then her mother would probably drive over to check on her.

She paced around the small room, trying to pinpoint what exactly was making her so reluctant to go stay with her mother. She couldn't describe it, except to acknowledge a feeling of restlessness that was consuming her from within, licking at her like the flames of a slow-burning fire.

There was so much on her mind between Vic's murder, the challenge to the chefs competition, and Angie's poisoning that Mel felt as if her brain was full. She knew she wouldn't feel better until she knew what had happened to Vic and who had poisoned Angie.

She thought about the conversation between Dutch and Jordan. If Grace hadn't interrupted, she may have learned more about what they had done.

Now what was she supposed to do? She couldn't exactly go to Dutch, admit she'd been eavesdropping, and demand an explanation. And she definitely couldn't approach Jordan, who was quite clear in her dislike of Mel. Who else would know if the two of them were in cahoots? And who would care other than the police, who really couldn't do anything without more than hearsay to go on?

Grace. If anyone cared about what happened to Vic, it was Grace. Mel glanced out the window. It was dark. She decided to take her car over to the Valley Ho and see if Grace had learned anything about how Vic had died. If Uncle Stan was right and Vic had been poisoned, too, then it stood to reason that the police would tell Grace first.

Mel left a light on, patted Captain Jack on the head, and locked up her apartment. With a renewed sense of purpose, she headed toward the lot where her car was parked.

# Twenty-three

Perhaps it was just the crazy week she'd been having, but Mel clicked the unlock button on her key fob and jogged to her car. She always parked under one of the two streetlights in the parking lot, and she climbed into her car and locked the door, feeling an urgency she couldn't explain.

She turned the key and stomped on the gas, moving the stick shift through the first three gears as she built up speed. Luck was on her side. Five traffic lights to get through and not one was red.

She pulled up in front of the valet. It wasn't the one she'd had watch her bike. She handed him her keys and hurried through the main door on her way to Grace's room. She supposed she could use a courtesy phone, but for some reason she didn't want to take the time.

She took the elevator up and hurried down the hallway. She knocked three times and waited. She felt awkward in the hotel hallway as if she were up to no good, but that was ridiculous. She was just checking on a friend. Yes, Joe would be furious that she hadn't taken someone with her, but this was Grace, for pity's sake. Mel had known her as long as she'd known Vic.

The door opened and a woman in a fluffy white dressing gown answered. Her hair was wrapped in a towel, but Mel could see right away that it wasn't Grace.

"I'm sorry," Mel said. "I'm looking for Grace Mazzotta."

"You and everyone else," the woman huffed. "You're the third person today to come knocking. I'm really going to have to complain."

"Do you know where she is?" Mel asked.

"No, like I've told everyone else, I don't know her," the woman snapped. "Now if you'll excuse me, I have a bath waiting."

She shut the door with a firm snap, and Mel knew there would be no point in trying to ask her any more questions.

Great, now what? She supposed she could call Uncle Stan, but he probably didn't know anything yet. She could try and talk to Dutch, but he was the king of deny, deny, deny. She'd seen him when he tried to date three girls at the same time when they were in cooking school. He had been such a cad back then, and judging by the conversation she'd overheard between him and Jordan, he hadn't changed much.

No, she needed to talk to Grace. She went back to the elevator, where there was a small table with a courtesy phone. She dialed the front desk and waited for the very gracious clerk to answer.

"Hi, this is Melanie Cooper," she said. "I'm a friend of Grace Mazzotta's. I was hoping to stop by her room for a quick visit, but I've misplaced the room number. Could you assist me?"

"Certainly, Ms. Cooper," the clerk said. "Let me check with Mrs. Mazzotta."

There was a few moments pause before the clerk came back on the line.

"Ms. Cooper? Mrs. Mazzotta said to let you know that she has moved to one of our ground-floor rooms. The number is eleven. Is there anything else I can help you with?"

"Oh, no, you've been very kind, thanks." Mel hung up the phone. Ground floor was good.

She went back to the reception area and out the patio doors to circle the pool area. She couldn't blame Grace for switching. She could only imagine that the reporters were dogging her every step since Vic's body was found.

She rapped on the door, It was answered swiftly as if Grace had been waiting on the other side for her. Mel blinked as she found herself face to face with Bertie Grassello.

"I'm sorry," she said. "I thought this was Grace's room."

"It is." Grace appeared from behind Bertie. "Thanks for the condolences, Bertie, it was good of you to drop by."

Bertie stared at them nonplussed, and then he pulled himself upright and gave a quick jerk of his head. "All right. I won't belabor my point, then. You'll think about what we discussed?"

"Of course," Grace said.

"Then good night," Bertie said and departed.

"What was that all about?" Mel asked as she followed Grace into the luxurious room.

"Bertie is having an identity crisis, I'm afraid." Grace shook her head. "He's been Vic's rival for so long, he doesn't quite know who he is if he's not the man battling Vic for the spotlight. He seems to think I'd like to manage his career for him."

"Would you?" Mel asked.

"A woman has to eat," Grace said. Then she shrugged.

"Interesting," Mel said.

"And what brings you by so late?" Grace asked. "Not an identity crisis of your own, I trust?"

"No, nothing so simple," Mel said. "Grace, you mentioned before that you thought Vic might have committed suicide. Do you really believe that?"

"I don't know what to believe," Grace said. She led Mel out onto her balcony. It was bigger than the last, and Grace lit up a cigarette. She stared out across the grounds as she blew out a plume of smoke.

"Vic was not an easy man, but the thought that someone might have murdered him . . ." Her voice trailed off and she shook her head. "I almost wish it was suicide so that at least it would have been on Vic's terms."

Mel could understand that. Vic had such a strong personality. She didn't like the idea that someone else had snuffed out his life against his will. It was very unlike Vic to be at anyone's mercy. It was one of the things she had always liked about him.

"How's your friend?" Grace asked.

"She's better," Mel said. "Thanks."

"I'm glad to hear it." Grace took another drag of her cigarette. As she blew out the smoke, she asked, "So, what can I do for you?"

"Tell me who you think killed Vic," Mel said. She hadn't been planning to say it quite so plainly, but now that the words were out, she felt relief.

Grace sat back on the cushy seat of her patio chair. She was quiet for a moment. Mel watched her face. She watched the lines get deeper around her eyes, the corner of her mouth turn down. Her shoulders drooped as if she were cloaked in a blanket of sadness.

Mel waited, knowing that she was being about as insensitive as a person could get, asking the grieving widow to speculate about her husband's death, but still she didn't take back the question.

Whoever had killed Vic had harmed Angie as well, making it all the more personal. Mel couldn't let it go. Not now, not until the person was caught.

"I don't know," Grace finally said. "I wish I did but I just don't know."

"But you must have some idea," Mel persisted.

"I don't!" Grace snapped. She stubbed out her cigarette in an ashtray that was already overflowing. "Don't you think I wish I did? Don't you think the police have grilled me for information that I wish I knew to give them? Don't you think I've lain awake every night since the murder, trying to recall some moment, some snatch of conversation, something that would tell me who killed my husband?"

"What about Jordan?" Mel asked. "She seems like the sort, doesn't she?"

"Yeah, the wife accusing the new girlfriend, I wonder how that would go over."

"Well, Dutch, then. He hated Vic and blamed him for the demise of his career."

Grace shook her head.

"Bertie!" Mel cried. "He hated Vic. Maybe he got carried away, maybe that's why he's having an identity crisis, maybe it's really just guilt that's dogging him."

Grace looked at her with sad eyes. "We may never know, Mel. But whoever did it, they're dangerous. Vic wouldn't want you to put yourself in harm's way to solve his murder. You need to let the police handle it."

"I am," she said, but even to her it sounded like a half-hearted protest.

"Come on," Grace said. "I'll pour you a nightcap."

Mel followed her into the suite. A bar was set up in one corner, and Grace took out two glasses and set to fixing them each a cocktail.

Abruptly, Mel's phone began to vibrate in her pocket. She checked the window. It was her mom. She'd better answer it before her mother called in the National Guard.

"Hello?" she answered.

"Young lady, you are not too big to be put over my knee," Joyce said. She did not sound happy. "I called dear Joe when you didn't answer your home phone, and he and I agreed that I should pop over and check on you, and what do I find when I get here? Not you. When I called him back to tell him, the poor man about had a heart attack. We've both been calling your cell. Thank you so much for finally answering."

"I have it on vibrate," Mel said. "This is the first time I felt it. I can't believe you called Joe."

"Of course I did. Now you get your butt on home, Melanie Cooper, right now."

"Mom, I am thirty-four years old. I do not need you or Joe looking after me."

"Well, apparently, you do," Joyce snapped. "Where are you?"

"Visiting a friend," Mel said. She gestured to Grace, who was studying her with her head cocked to the side, that she had to leave.

Grace nodded in understanding, offering Mel her drink if she wanted it.

Mel shook her head, crossed the room, and gave her a quick squeeze and whispered, "Better take a rain check."

"Who are you talking to you?" Joyce demanded. "You'd better not be offering me a rain check."

Mel strode to the door. "No, Mom, I'm not. I'm on my way. I'll be home in five minutes."

"Great, then you can explain to me why there is a kitten glaring at me from your great-aunt Sophie's water silk pillow."

"Fine," Mel said on a sigh.

Mel hustled out of the Hotel Valley Ho. The valet took one look at her face and raced to get her car. Mel tipped him heavily as she zipped out of the parking lot and headed back to the bakery.

Mel parked in her usual spot under a light. She locked her car by pressing the key fob and hurried up the back steps to her apartment. Joyce used to drop by all the time before Joe became a fixture in Mel's life, but since they'd started dating, she didn't pop in but called first, giving Mel a chance to straighten up before her arrival.

Mel hadn't tidied up since the contest insanity had hit a few weeks ago. She couldn't even imagine what her mother was going to say about her clutter gone wild.

She unlocked her door and pushed it open. Unexpectedly a giggle was the first sound that greeted her.

"Well, aren't you a clever little fellow?" her mother was cooing to Captain Jack while she rubbed him under the chin.

Mel rolled her eyes. Apparently, Captain Jack had charmed yet another person in her life.

"Mel, he is just precious," her mother said. "Look." She moved her duster, or more accurately Mel's duster, and Captain Jack hunkered down in a hunting position, wiggled his posterior, and dove for the feathers. Joyce kept it just out of his reach, and he put in a full-on chase. His tiny little body mimicked that of a great cat on the hunt, and

Mel felt her own lips twitch at the serious concentration on his kitten features.

Finally, Joyce let him catch the duster, and as he clutched it with his front paws, he kicked the feathers out of it with his hind legs. Joyce let it drop to the ground, and Captain Jack, assured that he had killed the offending duster, rolled to his feet, licked his chest, and walked with a swagger over to Mel, where he leaned against her and purred.

"You should take him over to Adobe Animal Hospital and have Dr. Newland check him out," Joyce said. "He's going to need to be fixed, or he'll start spraying."

"I don't suppose you want him?" Mel asked.

"Oh, no, he's picked you," Joyce said. "Besides, I still haven't recovered from the loss of your brother's iguana."

"Figaro did love you," Mel said.

Joyce sighed. Figaro had been Mel's brother's iguana technically, but it was Joyce that he loved. As loyal as a dog, Figaro had followed Joyce everywhere. And no one had cried harder when he died at the ripe old age of fifteen than Joyce.

The sound of a key turning in the lock turned their attention to the door as it swung open and there stood Joe, looking decidedly disheveled and more than a little miffed.

"Oh, dear Joe," Joyce said. "I am so sorry. I was so busy playing with the kitty that I forgot to call you and tell you I'd found her."

"What are you doing here?" Mel demanded.

Something in her tone must have annoyed him, because he frowned and said, "I came to check on you."

"You're supposed to be with Angie," she said.

Joyce glanced between them and worried her lower lip

with her teeth, obviously sensing there was tension in the air.

"I'll just be going," she said.

Mel and Joe both turned to look at her. Joyce gave them a little finger wave and scuttled out the door, shutting it behind her.

"Hurricane Joyce," Mel said. "Wreak havoc and vanish."

"That's a little harsh, don't you think?" Joe asked.

Mel went into the kitchen to pour herself a glass of wine. She held the bottle up to Joe, but he shook his head. So she poured herself a double.

"Who is with Angie?" she asked.

"Tate. He was more than happy to go and spend the night."

"I'll bet," Mel said.

"Are you jealous?" Joe asked. He crossed his arms over his chest and studied her.

"No," she said. She'd said it quickly, and she wondered if it had come out defensively, then she tried to convince herself that she didn't care. "I tried to call you today, but whoever answered the phone wouldn't put me through. Listen, you have to call off your brothers."

"What? Why?" he asked. "Wait a minute, who wouldn't put your call through?"

"I don't know," Mel said. She took a sip from her glass, hoping to appear casual. "She wouldn't give me her name."

"My secretary, Kayla, was out sick today," he said. "Probably, it was someone passing through the office."

"Someone named Susan Ross," Mel said. "I'm just guessing." She knew her tone made it clear that it was more than a guess.

"She was in the office," Joe said. "It could have been her, although that seems out of character."

"Didn't you two used to date?" Mel asked.

"Nah," Joe said. "I mean we sort of went out, but we never . . . and she wouldn't put you through? Oh, this is awkward."

"That's one word for it," Mel said.

"Sorry about that. I'll have a chat with her and send out an e-mail to all to make sure that never happens again. So what is the problem with the brothers?"

"They're doing more harm than good. Ray almost got Oz and I disqualified today," she said. Somehow, knowing that Joe would deal with his office situation, giving her priority status at his work mollified her irritation with him.

"But he didn't," he said.

"Only because Oz was thinking on his feet," she said.

"Angie plans to be back there tomorrow. Do you really want her to be unprotected after she was almost killed?"

"No, of course not."

"Then the brothers stay," he said. He said it in his prosecuting attorney voice, which made Mel's temper flare—so much for feeling mollified.

"Fine, but no more screwups," she said.

"Look, I know you're grieving for Vic and you're upset about Angie, but there is something else going on, and I think we need to talk about it," Joe said.

Mel looked at him over the edge of her wineglass. She felt her insides swoop at the sight of him, the way they always did. He was everything she had ever wanted, and yet she couldn't deny the feeling of suffocation she was beginning to feel in this relationship. It had to be temporary, a reaction to Vic's death, Angie's poisoning, and the stress of the competition, right?

She took a long sip from her wine. "I'm just tired."

Joe looked at her doubtfully. He even looked like he was

going to argue with her, but she put down her wine and reached out to hug him. He kissed the top of her head and held her close.

Mel hoped that this temporary insanity, this feeling of needing to run away, would disappear as soon as the competition was over. The itchy feeling inside her, however, made her fear that it wouldn't.

# Twenty-four

As she made her way to the conference room, Mel noted that the festival grounds seemed even more crowded than usual today, or maybe she just felt tenser than she had before. They were down to the semifinals. Out of today's twelve competitors, tomorrow's final four would be picked.

She had seen Angie and Tate earlier, making their way to the conference room. Angie looked pale but determined. Tate was shadowing her, not letting anyone get too close to her—not even her brothers or her parents. Mel couldn't blame him. Having almost lost her, she never wanted to be that terrified ever again.

Tony was manning the shop with Ray, who was under strict orders not to eat all the profits. After school, Oz would take Ray's place. Mel had called Oz's counselor that morning, and she had agreed to see if they could make the internship a paid situation for Oz, so long as it didn't interfere with his studies.

Mel took a seat next to Angie in the conference room

and studied her fellow competitors. Polly and Olivia were still in attendance and so was the chef from the Phoenix bakery, Molly's Moonpies. She couldn't help noticing that they all looked a bit worse for the wear as well.

"Are you sure you're up to this?" she asked Angie.

"Oh, yeah," Angie said. She was glaring at Olivia. Angie had pretty much decided that Olivia had tried to poison Mel but had gotten Angie instead. Mel didn't think so, but there was no talking Angie out of it. Mel hoped Olivia didn't come too close while Angie was dicing anything; she didn't think Angie would be able to refrain from giving Olivia a haircut.

The five-minute warning bell sounded, and they all stood up and stretched. Mel was relieved. She found sitting in the green room only made her more anxious. As if they were all eager to be done with today's competition, they headed out to the staging area in one big group.

Mel and Angie positioned themselves in their small kitchen. Mel saw her mother and Angie's mother, standing with Tate. They all waved and Tate gave them the thumbs-up sign.

Mel noticed that Angie's face turned a slight shade of pink as she locked gazes with Tate. Mel glanced between them.

"So, Tate took Joe's watch last night?" Mel asked.

"Yeah," Angie said with a shrug. "Since you decided to scare the pants off of everyone by disappearing."

"Oh, no, do not turn this back on me," Mel said. "We're discussing you and Tate."

"There's nothing to discuss," Angie said. "Oh, look, here comes Johnny Pepper."

"Saved by the master of ceremonies," Mel muttered.

Angie said nothing but turned her attention to Johnny and his box.

The crowd grew quiet as Johnny stepped onto the stage. He was wearing a bright yellow chef's coat today, making his trademark spiky blond hair seem pale in comparison.

"Good afternoon, everyone," he said into the microphone.

Mel watched as people from all over the festival drifted over toward the staging area. Johnny introduced the judges, and Mel noticed that with the exception of the lady from *Food and Wine*, they looked a bit wrung out as well.

"We are down to our final twelve," Johnny said. "Only four will remain after today's competition."

There was a murmur from the crowd, and Mel could swear she heard a few of them placing bets on the outcome.

"Let's see what they make of today's mystery ingredient, shall we?" Johnny shouted, and the crowd responded with a roar.

"Chefs, today your mystery ingredient is . . ." Johnny lowered the mic and reached into the white box. He seemed to be having a bit of trouble with it, which Mel found worrisome. "Your mystery ingredient is . . ."

Mel felt her chest get tight. They'd had parsnips, beer, bananas, and chili peppers. What could they pull out next?

"Goat cheese!" Johnny Pepper announced. The crowd cheered and murmured in an excited buzz. The chefs all frowned in concentration. Mel could feel her own forehead pucker as she scanned her cooking memory banks for the best and most unique way to present goat cheese.

The large supply cart was wheeled out and Johnny called, "Chefs, on my count, one, two . . ."

"Mel, what do I grab?" Angie hissed.

"The biggest hunk of cheese you can get your hands on," Mel said.

"Three, go!" Johnny Pepper shouted, and the chefs and sous-chefs mobbed the cart. With fewer and fewer chefs in the competition, it was easier to get what they needed. Mel saw Angie stomp on Olivia's instep, causing her to yelp and hop and allowing Angie to make off with a chunk of cheese the size of her head.

Mel grabbed two lesser blocks of specialty goat cheese and started mentally compiling a list for Joanie to go and get from the supply shack.

Once back in the kitchenette, she rattled off the list to Joanie, who gave a nod and bolted away as fast as her trainers could carry her.

"Cheesecake?" Angie asked.

"Too obvious," Mel said. "If we want to make the final four, we're going to have to dig deep."

Angie nodded. "What's your plan?"

"I'm feeling a bit tart," Mel said. "You?"

"I'd say I'm running more toward bitter, but I can scale it back to tart if you want," Angie joked. "What do you need?"

"Remember the cheesecake cupcakes we made last year? Yeah, well, same idea but more of a tart. I need you to make eight ginger-infused graham cracker crusts in eight tart tins," Mel said.

"On it," Angie said, and she dove into the cabinets to pull out the appropriate bakeware.

Mel considered her blocks of goat cheese. This was going to be good; even Vic would have approved. In her mind, she could even see the plating. A delicate goat cheese tart on a thin ginger-infused graham cracker crust with a caramelized top holding diced figs and drizzled with lavender honey.

She got her mixer and began prepping the tart. Joanie arrived with what they needed. Sadly, there was no lavender honey to be had, but she had gotten orange blossom honey, which Mel figured would do just fine. While she stood at the ready, Mel and Angie set to work.

Mel checked the tarts, and when they were slightly jiggly in the center and firm around the edges, she knew they were done. She and Angie hurriedly plated them as the five-minute alarm had already sounded.

With a glance at the eleven other competitors, Mel saw several variations of cheesecake, pastries stuffed with cheese, and even an ice cream, but no one else had gone with the tart. She took this as a promising sign.

When the final buzzer sounded and the servers came to collect their entries, Angie sagged limply against the counter. Two of her brothers and Tate vaulted onto the stage.

"You shouldn't have competed today," Tate chastised her as he slipped an arm about her waist in an attempt to help her off the stage. "You're not strong enough."

Mel blinked. Did Tate have a death wish? Angie was going to kick him into next week.

To Mel's shock and amazement, Angie leaned into Tate and said, "You're right. I overdid it. Can you give me a lift home?"

"'As you wish,'" Tate said, and he scooped her up into his arms.

They exchanged a long look, and Mel waited for Angie to identify the line from *The Princess Bride*, but she said nothing.

Mel and the brothers went bug-eyed. Was Angie really

that ill? She didn't get the chance to find out as Tate strode through the festival with Angie still in his arms.

"Well, it's about time, don't you think?" a voice asked.

Mel turned to see Joe standing there.

"You mean . . ."

"Angie's fine. She's just enjoying being the center of Tate's attention."

"But she . . . and he . . ." Mel stammered. She knew how Angie felt about Tate and how Tate felt about Angie, but they'd never listened when she'd told them how the other felt about them. Had Angie's near-death experience finally made them see reason? And if so, was Mel going to be forever on the outside looking in at their coupledom?

"You still have me," Joe said, correctly interpreting her thoughts. He draped his arm around her shoulders, and Mel was left to wonder why this didn't make her feel any better.

# Twenty-five

Mel was elbow deep in a luscious almond buttercream frosting when Uncle Stan came into the kitchen through the back door.

"So I was just chatting with your mother over at the festival," he said.

"How is she?" Mel asked. "I can't believe Ginny talked her into volunteering so she could meet men."

"What?" Uncle Stan asked.

"Oh, you know Ginny," Mel said. "She always has some crazy scheme that she gets Mom into."

"I didn't think your mother was looking to date anyone after that last . . ."

"Fiasco," Mel supplied helpfully. "I don't know that she really wants to be dating so much as she just wants something to do, but that's just a guess. You'd have to ask her."

"I may just do that." Uncle Stan looked thoughtful.

"So, can I tempt you with a freshly baked and frosted Blonde Bombshell?" Mel asked.

He looked about to say yes and then patted his stomach and shook his head. "I'm going to pass. I've got to start working on getting my girlish figure back."

Mel raised her eyebrows. "Any reason in particular?"

"Just want to be healthy," he said.

"Uncle Stan, you can tell me, you know," she said.

"Oh, all right," he glowered. "I failed my annual physical. If I don't drop some pounds and get in better shape, they're going to put me on a desk."

"Oh, harsh," Mel said. "I promise I won't bake another thing for you unless it's whole wheat and sugar free."

"If I give you my gun, will you shoot me?" he asked. He looked as if he had sunk into the lowest depths of despair.

"No," she said. "I'd miss you too much."

"Fine, be that way," he said. "I do have some good news, however. The leader board was up when I left the festival."

"And?" Mel tried not to look like she wasn't frothing at the mouth to get the results.

"Fairy Tale Cupcakes is sitting pretty at number . . ."

"Uncle Stan!" she cried as he dragged it out.

"Number two!" he said.

"Who is number one?" she asked.

"Confections Bakery," he said, looking none too pleased. He was not a fan of Olivia Puckett either.

Mel blew out a breath of relief. So they had made the final four. This was good, but still, she frowned. Tomorrow was a winner-take-all, do-or-die situation. She was going to have to bring her A game as it was her last chance to trounce Olivia.

"I have to call Angie," she said.

"Her brother Dom already did," he said. "She was happy

to make the final four but not pleased that Confections ranked higher today."

Mel grabbed two bottles of water out of the walk-in cooler and handed one to Uncle Stan.

"On a different subject," she said. "Has the ME said anything about Vic's death?"

"The tox screens won't be in for a while yet," he said. He looked longingly at the tray of Blonde Bombshell cupcakes and then took a long sip of water as if trying to wash away his hunger pangs. "As of now, the cause of death remains a heart attack."

"But why was he in the freezer?" Mel asked.

"The current theory is that he fell in when the heart attack hit," he said.

"I don't like that theory," Mel said.

"Neither do I, but until I can get proof of another method of death, I'm pretty much stuck."

"So many people hated him," Mel said. "On the morning Angie was poisoned, I heard a conversation between Dutch Johnson and Jordan Russell. She was upset and saying something about how she didn't want anyone to find out what they had done."

"I think I may know what that's about," Uncle Stan said. He sat on a stool at the steel table and inhaled the scent of the cupcakes before taking another slug off his water bottle. "Apparently, your friend Dutch faked some credentials for Ms. Russell so that she could be appointed a judge in the festival."

"What sort of credentials?" Mel asked.

"I believe he told Johnny Pepper that she'd been his intern on his television show, which of course she hadn't, since according to both of them, they hadn't even met until this food festival."

"That's a lie," Mel said.

Uncle Stan studied her face. "I thought so, too, but what makes you say that?"

"The very fact that he would vouch for her to Johnny Pepper to get her a spot as a judge. Why would he do that if he had only met her here?"

"He tells us it was love at first sight."

"Oh, please, the only thing Dutch loves is his own reflection," Mel scoffed.

Uncle Stan smiled. "Yeah, I had him pegged like that." The phone on his belt buzzed, and he checked the display. "Gotta go."

"Well, thanks for the update," Mel said. "You'll be there tomorrow?"

"Wouldn't miss it," he said, "and Mel, until we get the tox screens back and are sure that Angie's poisoning and Vic's death are unrelated, I want you to remain on your guard."

"I will be," Mel said. "I promise."

Her own phone rang as she waved him out the door. She pulled her phone out of her apron. It read *Angie*.

"So, you heard?" Mel asked. "We're going to have to implement some serious Olivia take-down tomorrow."

"Yeah," Angie said. She did not sound as fired up as Mel had expected.

"What's going on, Angie?"

"I have a checkup with Dr. Patel in an hour," she said. "Will you come with me?"

"Sure," Mel said. "I would have thought Tate was going to take you."

"I . . . he . . . needed to get back to work," she said.

"I'll be right there," Mel said.

She closed her phone and carried the loaded tray into

the cooler. Popping her head into the main bakery, she saw they were well into the midafternoon lull. Dom, who had stationed himself as her watchdog after Joe had returned to work, was asleep in a booth, while Oz was busy wiping down the bakery tables.

"I have to take Angie to the doctor," she said. "Are you all right with Sleeping Beauty?"

Oz grinned. "Don't worry. I'll kick him awake when the first customer comes in."

Mel hung up her apron and grabbed her purse. She cut through the back to her car in the lot. Angie lived in a small ranch house in the old neighborhood that surrounded Old Town Scottsdale. Mel pulled into her carport and knocked on the side door.

"It's open," Angie called. Mel strode in to find Angie just grabbing her purse. "Thanks for doing this. I promised Tate and Ray that I would let you take me; otherwise, I don't think either of them would have left."

"Oh, Ray was here?" Mel asked.

Angie looked chagrinned. "Yes, when Tate and I arrived home after the festival, overprotective brother number three was here waiting for me. It's just as well. Tate needed to get back to work."

Mel followed Angie back out of the house, and Angie locked it behind them. As they were getting into the car, Mel couldn't stand it anymore and asked, "What is going on with you and Tate?"

"Nothing."

"I saw him pick you up," Mel said. "That was not 'nothing.'"

"I'm dating someone," Angie said as if Mel could have forgotten.

"Tate cares about you," Mel said.

"As a friend," Angie said.

"He quoted *The Princess Bride*," Mel argued. "And not just any quote. It was *the* quote, the one that means—"

"Are you taking me to the doctor, or are we going to sit in my carport and argue, because if we are, I really should call and let them know I'm running late," Angie interrupted her, and Mel knew the conversation was over.

Mel blew out a breath. "Fine."

"I'm seeing the doc at his private practice office," Angie said. She fished a piece of paper out of her purse. "It's over on Hayden and Shea Road."

Mel left the old neighborhood behind and headed east toward Highway 101. Traffic shouldn't be too bad as yet, and they headed north on the raised highway, looking over the cotton fields on the Salt River Indian Reservation, with the jagged peaks of the McDowell Mountain Range looming at the horizon. It always amazed Mel that she only had to drive five miles to be out in the middle of farm country. The Valley of the Sun was amazing like that.

She took the Shea Road exit off the 101 and wound her way toward the street number Angie read to her. Dr. Patel's office was in a cluster of medical buildings that sat on the perimeter of Scottsdale Healthcare's Shea Hospital.

"You can go grab a coffee if you want," Angie said.

"No, I'm going with you," Mel said.

"There's no need."

"Yes, there is," Mel said. "I know if the wait is more than five minutes, you'll duck out the back."

"No, I won't."

"Angie, you can't even stand in line for ten minutes for a flu shot. You're possibly the worst patient ever, and I'm not letting you weasel out of your checkup."

"All right, but they'd better have good magazines in that waiting room."

Mel stood by her while she signed in. The desk person took Angie's insurance information, and they selected chairs by the window.

There was only one *People* magazine to be had, and Mel let Angie have it so she wouldn't get testy. She chose an old copy of *Food and Wine* for herself and settled in to wait.

Mel thumbed through the magazine, surprised when she saw a photo of one of their challenge to the chefs' judges pop out at her. How could she have forgotten? Candace Levinson was an editor at *Food and Wine* magazine.

She flipped through the pages, looking to see if she could learn anything about Ms. Levinson that might prove helpful for tomorrow's competition. The feature piece had been written by a celebrity chef and edited by Ms. Levinson. It was an excellent piece on the use of flower petals as edible ingredients. Mel was so engrossed in the article that she didn't hear Angie's name get called.

When Angie stood up, Mel automatically rose to go with her, but Angie shook her head and said, "Really, I think I can handle it."

"So sad, too bad," Mel said. "I'm coming with. I want his approval for you to compete tomorrow. You looked terrible after today's competition."

Angie rolled her eyes but argued no further, which to Mel was proof enough that Angie was not herself.

They sat in the exam room for a few moments after a nurse came and took Angie's vitals. There was a quick knock on the door and Dr. Patel entered.

"Ms. DeLaura." He smiled at her. "Well, you certainly look better than the last time I saw you."

"I feel better," Angie said. "All better. You're a miracle worker, Doc."

He frowned. "You have no idea how true that is."

Mel felt herself go still. "What do you mean?"

"I mean, I've discovered what the poison was that you ingested, Ms. DeLaura, and I have to say, you are very lucky to be alive."

# Twenty-six

"What was it?" Angie asked. Her voice sounded unusually high, and Mel suspected she had to be a little afraid to find out what poison had been coursing through her body just two days ago.

"It's a very rare poison—at least in this country," Dr. Patel said. "My father is a doctor in India, and I was reviewing my cases with him—we do that every week—and when I told him about your symptoms, he said it sounded like you had been poisoned by the seeds of a Suicide Tree."

"A what?" Angie and Mel asked together.

"There is a tree in India, commonly called the Suicide Tree or Pong-pong," Dr Patel said. His voice was grave. "Many people eat the seeds in order to commit suicide, thus the name."

"Well, don't look at me," Angie said. "I'm more of a 'swan dive off of a high building' type."

Dr. Patel frowned.

"Sorry, bad joke," she said.

Mel pinched Angie just above the elbow.

"Ouch." Angie rubbed her arm.

"Behave," Mel said. "Can you tell us more about the poison?"

"Its scientific name is *Cerebra odollam*, and it contains a heart toxin called cerberin, which is similar to digoxin, the poison found in foxglove."

"So that's why you were able to treat it because it was similar?"

"Exactly," he said. "The Suicide Tree grows only in India and Southeast Asia. I can't imagine how you could have come into contact with it, but if its seeds were crushed and served with spicy food, you may not have been able to taste it. It can shut down the body within an hour. Of course, it depends upon the size of the person and how much they ate. Ms. DeLaura is small so the poison would affect her more rapidly than a larger person."

Mel and Angie exchanged a glance.

"It must have been put in my food at the café," she said. "And it was probably in yours, too."

"There's no way to know," Mel said. "By the time I got to the table, you were already reacting to the poison, and I never touched my food. The police tried to retrieve it, but the trash had already been picked up."

"That's unfortunate," Dr. Patel said. "From an investigative standpoint."

"Indeed," Mel agreed. "Would you be willing to talk to my uncle about what you suspect? He's a detective with the Scottsdale Police Department."

"Of course," he said. "But I am just speculating."

"I know, but I think you're on to something," Mel said. She looked at Angie. "All right if I leave you for a bit?"

"Sure, I'm in good hands," Angie said with a smile at Dr. Patel.

Mel fished her cell phone out of her pocket as she left the patient room and walked outside. She stood on the side of the building while she waited for Uncle Stan to pick up.

"Hello, Mel, is everything all right?" he answered. Obviously he'd seen her name pop up in his caller ID.

"Uncle Stan, did you say that the ME was doing tox screens on Vic's body?" she asked.

"Yeah, we don't have the results back, however."

"I think I may have a lead on what killed him."

"I'm listening."

"Angie's doctor has a theory about the poison she ingested," Mel said. "It's not something found in the United States. If they run the standard screens on Vic, they're not going to pick it up."

"What kind of poison is it?"

"It's a toxin in the seeds from a tree in India called the Suicide Tree."

"Whoa," he said. "You have a number for this doctor? I want to talk to him."

Mel read it off to him.

"You know, if you ever get tired of the bakery," Uncle Stan said, "I could probably get you on the force."

Mel laughed. "I think I'll stick with cupcakes."

"Mel, if this is true and we can link Angie's poisoning with Vic's, then we have a real case for murder and attempted murder."

"I know," Mel said.

"Watch your back," he said. "I'll call you later."

"Thanks, Uncle Stan," she said.

Mel shut her phone. She studied the carefully xeriscaped land that surrounded the building. Decorative red gravel dotted with hesperaloe and spineless prickly pear cactus gave the squat red building a desert flare that was low on water intake and maintenance.

She watched as a hummingbird flitted over the aloe, looking for blooms. Her mind felt just like that tiny bird with its invisible wings. Her brain was flitting over all the information she had taken in over the past few days.

She was still standing there when Angie came out to meet her.

"What did Uncle Stan say?" Angie asked.

"He was interested," Mel said.

"So, what are you doing out here?"

"Thinking," Mel said.

"Oh, no." Angie shook her head.

"What, I'm not allowed to think?"

"You've got that look."

"What look?" Mel asked as they walked toward her car.

"The one that says you're going to stick your nose where it does not belong."

"That's a look?"

"Yes, and for your information, it's not attractive," Angie said.

"I'm just going to look up an old friend and have a nice little chat," Mel said. "No big deal."

"What friend?" Angie asked.

"An old cooking school buddy," Mel said. She was going for vague, hoping Angie would let it go. No such luck.

"Dutch. You're going to talk to Dutch," Angie said.

"Maybe," Mel said.

"You can't go alone," Angie said.

"I have to," Mel argued as they got into her car. She

turned on the ignition and hit the gas, sending them out of the parking lot and out onto the street. "He'll talk to me one on one. I'm sure of it."

"He could be the killer!"

"I don't think so," Mel said. Although, she had to admit, she could be wrong.

"Take me with you or I'm telling Joe," Angie said.

"No!" Mel argued. "You almost got killed. You're not going anywhere near this thing again."

"Fine." Angie fished her cell phone out of her purse. She began to dial.

"Angie, don't you dare!" Mel said.

"Then take me with you," Angie said. She had her finger hovering over Joe's name. One tap and the call would go through.

"All right, but I go in alone," Mel said. "We stay connected through our phones, and you don't eat or drink anything. Got it?"

"Roger, that," Angie said and closed her phone without placing the call. "I'm so glad you've come around to my way of thinking."

Mel rolled her eyes as she headed for the Hotel Valley Ho. She had a sinking feeling she was going to regret this in a big way.

Mel left her car with the valet, and they trotted into the lobby. Mel stopped at the desk and asked if they could place a courtesy call to Dutch Johnson's room. The desk worker graciously placed the call, and Mel waited.

"Do you think there is an issue of impropriety with us talking to a judge the night before the final competition?" Angie asked.

"Don't know, don't care," Mel said. "I'm not here to bribe him, so I don't see why it would be."

"I'm sorry, ma'am, he's not answering his phone," the desk clerk said.

"That's all right," Mel said. "Thanks for trying. We'll just go have a drink. Maybe he'll turn up."

"Excellent, ma'am," he said with a smile.

"We're not really going to stake out the place, are we?" Angie asked. "I mean we have a pretty big day tomorrow."

"There's more to life than winning a baking competition," Mel said as she strode toward the bar but then did an abrupt turn and went to the elevators instead.

"I have to disagree. There really isn't more to life than beating the apron off of Olivia Puckett for me. I still think she's the one who poisoned our breakfasts at the café."

"We have no proof that she was at the café when we had breakfast," Mel said.

"Oh, please, she's like the Wicked Witch of the West," Angie said. "She probably sent one of her flying monkeys over to do it."

"Call me crazy, but I think I would have noticed a flying monkey hovering over our food," Mel said.

The elevator doors opened and they climbed inside. Mel knew that Jordan's room had been next to Grace's, and she was betting that if Dutch was anywhere to be found, it was in the hot young protégée's room.

"You know what I mean," Angie said. "She probably had one of her lackeys do it."

"Do you really think it was Olivia?" Mel asked. "I know she's crazy, but murder?"

"You saw that wacko light in her eye when she tried to keep us from entering the competition," Angie said. "I'm telling you she'd do anything to beat us."

"Okay, well how does she know about the Suicide Tree?" Mel asked. "Whoever used this poison had to have had access to the seeds from that tree, which only grows in India and Southeast Asia. You heard Dr. Patel. This isn't a common poison."

"Maybe she went on holiday there," Angie said.

"And gathered deadly seeds just for giggles?" Mel asked. "No, I think someone planned this. I think it was someone who went to India recently."

The elevator doors slid open, and Mel stepped out and strode down the hall to the room she knew was Jordan's. She put her ear to the door, listening for voices, but there was none.

She gestured Angie to follow her, and they stood around the corner from the room. "Go ahead and call me."

Angie did, and Mel answered her phone, opening a line of communication so Angie could tell if she was getting in over her head.

"Are we connected?" Angie asked.

"Yep, and the signal is strong," Mel said. "Now, I'm going to knock and see if Dutch is there, but either way I'm going to talk to someone until I get some answers."

"Just be safe," Angie said, keeping her phone to her ear while Mel put hers in the front pouch of her purse.

"Will do."

Mel left Angie and went back to Jordan's door. This time she knocked.

She heard the rustle of someone moving behind the door. She waited, smiling into the peephole but not show-ing any teeth—yet.

The door swung open and Jordan stood there in high-cut white shorts and a red halter top with matching strappy red high-heeled sandals.

"What do you want?" she asked. Obviously, she didn't feel the need to play nice.

"I'm looking for Dutch," Mel said.

"Why would he be here?" Jordan demanded, looking perfectly outraged.

"Because you're sleeping with him and probably have been for a long time," Mel said. It was a punt, but she had nothing to lose.

"I don't know where you get your information—" Jordan began, but Mel cut her off.

"My Uncle Stan. You know, Detective Stan Cooper, we're like this." Mel crossed her fingers and held them up.

"Let her in," a voice called from behind Jordan.

# Twenty-seven

Jordan gave her a sour look and opened the door wide enough for Mel to stride through.

"Hi, Dutch," Mel said. She glanced around the room. A cart with champagne and strawberries had been wheeled into the sitting area. "Cozy."

Dutch ran a hand over his bald head and studied her through his dark eyes.

"What is it you think you know, Mel?"

Mel took a seat and helped herself to a strawberry, then she remembered that she wasn't supposed to eat anything for which she didn't know the point of origin. She placed it on a napkin as if saving it for later. Trying to look casual, she glanced up and studied them both. Dutch looked as smooth as ever, but Jordan appeared as twitchy as a treed squirrel.

"I think you know more about Vic's death than you're telling," Mel said.

"You think I murdered the old blowhard, don't you?"

Dutch asked. He sat in the chair beside hers, a look of scorn marring his handsome features.

Mel shrugged. She really hoped Angie could hear her.

"Let me quote something I heard in passing, 'What if someone finds out . . .' or here is another little gem, 'No one is going to find out what we did . . .'"

Jordan went pale and slumped into the chair beside Dutch's, while he glowered at Mel.

"That was a private conversation."

"Then why did I hear it?" she asked. "Maybe you shouldn't talk about murdering people when you're lounging poolside."

"We weren't talking about murder!" Jordan protested.

"Then what were you talking about?" Mel pressed.

"We borrowed something from Vic," Dutch said. "And we were concerned that if people found out, they would think we murdered him for it."

"Borrowed what?" Mel asked.

Jordan and Dutch exchanged a look.

"You may as well tell me," Mel said. "Or I'll tell Uncle Stan what I know."

"What's our guarantee that you won't?" Dutch asked.

"There isn't one," Mel said.

Dutch was silent. Mel waited. She wondered if Angie would think their call had been disconnected. She started to get antsy but tried not to show it.

"All right, you remember how we always suspected that Vic didn't give us his full recipes when we were in school?" Dutch asked.

Mel shrugged. "Of course, he always teased his students about having a secret ingredient for every recipe, but I never paid much attention. I thought he was kidding, especially since he said he wouldn't tell me until, well, he said until he died. But it was just a joke."

"That's what I thought," Dutch said. "But then, I found out it was true."

Jordan nodded vigorously, and Mel stared at them, thinking they were both daft. Her face must have shown her skepticism because Jordan leaned forward.

"It's true," she insisted.

"So, you're telling me that Vic really did withhold ingredients from his recipes to make sure that no one could replicate his dishes exactly?"

"Yes," Dutch said. "You realize what this means?"

Mel frowned. "No."

"It means he was a fraud," Dutch said. "He really wasn't a master chef, and he wasn't a great professor. He was just a con man with a few tricks up his sleeve."

"That's a lie!" Mel snapped.

"Is it?" Dutch asked. "Then why did he commit suicide after Jordan revealed that she had discovered one of his secret ingredients?"

"He didn't commit suicide," Mel argued. "He was murdered."

"I'm sorry, Mel, but that's not what happened," Dutch said.

Mel felt her throat get tight. "Have you told the police all of this?"

"No," Dutch said. His confidence was oozing forth like cookie dough out of a store-bought tube. Mel hated that prepackaged stuff.

"Tell me what happened the day he died," Mel demanded. "Don't leave anything out."

Dutch gestured to Jordan to speak with a wave of his hand.

"Well, I invited him to breakfast here in my room. I wanted to break it off with him gently."

Jordan looked at Mel, and Mel got the feeling she was looking for approval. Well, she wasn't going to get it. Mel gestured for her to continue.

"I was going to make omelets, but you know how fussy he was about his eggs," Jordan said.

Mel nodded. Vic had been known for his exquisite skill with eggs. The pleats in a chef's hat are supposed to represent the chef's knowledge of how many ways to use eggs. In Vic's case, Mel had thought they always needed to add a few pleats.

"So, I decided to make scones, you know how his scones were so rich and flaky and had that delicious but indefinable savory taste to them?"

"Oh, yes." Mel had envied Vic's scones forever.

"I wanted to show him that I did have some food skills, so I added his secret ingredient to them."

"Okay, put the brakes on right there," Mel said. "What secret ingredient?"

"It's the one he used in a lot of his baked goods," Jordan said.

"Yeah, I got that. What's the name of it?" Mel asked.

Jordan glanced at Dutch and then back at Mel. "I don't know."

"What do you mean, you don't know?" Mel asked. "Surely it had a name."

"Um, actually no," she said. "It was just in a plain spice bottle, and it had a handwritten label that said, *For baking*."

"Did you tell the police about your breakfast?" Mel asked.

"I told her not to," Dutch said. "I thought if they knew

he'd been here, she'd be in trouble. So she just told them that she'd broken things off with him."

"But left out that it was over a cozy little breakfast," Mel said. Jordan opened her mouth to protest, but Mel waved her off. "So then what happened?"

"He tried his scone, but when I told him I'd added his secret ingredient for pastries and asked him if he was surprised, he got the strangest look on his face."

"Strange how?" Mel asked.

"Well, he looked startled and then he got really pale. I thought he was going to have one of his temper tantrums, you know the kind where he yells a lot, so I quickly told him that I couldn't see him anymore."

"Nice," Mel said. "Announce that you have the apparent key to one of his recipes and then dump him. You're all heart."

"Hey, I asked him if he was all right," Jordan protested. Mel rolled her eyes. "But he just looked sickly. I thought maybe he was devastated that I had dumped him, but he got up from his chair and left without answering me. It was the last time I ever saw him."

Jordan dissolved into tears with a noisy hiccupping accompaniment. Mel wanted to tell her to put a sock in it, but then she wondered if Jordan had really had some feelings for Vic.

She turned to Dutch. "And you really thought not telling the police any of this was a good idea?"

"Look, I'm starting a new gig with Bertie, and I don't want any bad publicity mucking up my shot, you feel me?"

"Like a hemorrhoid," Mel snapped. "Honestly, is success so important to you that you don't care that Vic obviously left that breakfast in some distress and then he *died*?"

She jumped up from her seat and glared down at them.

"What did you expect us to do about it?" Dutch rose, matching her combative stance.

"Why did you really do it?" Mel asked Jordan. "Why did you cook him a meal using an ingredient that he supposedly kept to himself?"

"Well, to show him . . . that I . . . that we . . ." Jordan stammered and looked helplessly at Dutch.

"You made her do it, didn't you?" Mel asked, turning back to Dutch. "You did this. You stole his lover and had her serve him one of his own recipes just to destroy him. Admit it."

"I . . . it . . ." Dutch took a steadying breath. "Bertie made me do it. Bertie gave me the spice bottle and told me it was what Vic used in his baked goods. There wasn't much in it, so I told Jordan to use it all."

"Why?" Mel asked. "Why would Bertie have you do this?"

"Because he hated Vic; you know that. If I wanted a spot on his show, he told me I had to sleep with Jordan and reveal to Vic that we knew he withheld ingredients from his recipes and that we had figured out what they were. That was the deal I made with Bertie to be his costar— basically I agreed to humiliate Vic."

"What?" Jordan shrieked.

"Baby, I'm so . . ." Dutch reached for her, but she stumbled away from him.

"Oh, no, don't you 'baby' me! I thought you did all this for me. I thought you did this to prove to Vic that we didn't need him. I thought it was because you wanted *me*, not because you were involved in some twisted revenge scheme of Bertie's to forward your own career."

A knock like gunfire sounded on the door, but Dutch and Jordan were oblivious. Mel circled them and hurried to open the door. She had a feeling she was going to need backup.

There was Angie, holding two large soda spritzer bottles, looking ready to unload the contents should the situation warrant it.

"Where did you get these?" Mel asked as Angie handed her one.

"Passing bar cart," she said and strode into the room. "Very fortunate that it passed by right when it sounded as if someone needed a cool-down."

"You used me!" Jordan was shrieking now. "And I let you. I was just a way to get to Vic for you and Bertie, wasn't I? Wasn't I?"

Dutch raised his hands in the universal sign of surrender, which was an unfortunate mistake as it further enflamed the rage that was Jordan.

"Listen, sweetie," he began, but Jordan let out a grunt and started looking around for a weapon.

"Get your target sighted," Angie ordered. "I've got the brunette."

Mel aimed the business end of her spritzer bottle at Dutch. Jordan began to hurl strawberries at him, which landed on Dutch's shirt with a series of solid plops. When she was out of those, she grabbed ice cubes from the ice bucket. One nailed him in the eye, and he went down clutching his face. Jordan wasn't done, however. She took the chocolate dipping sauce and upended the entire bowl on Dutch's bent head.

"As much as I'm enjoying this . . ." Angie said, and Mel nodded. Enough was enough. Angie gave the order. "Fire!"

She and Angie squeezed their triggers. Angie got Jordan full on the chest, making her gasp and sputter. Mel fell a bit short and had to take two steps toward Dutch to hit him with the full impact.

"Hey!" he shouted as he reared back.

"I'm getting the stains out," Mel retorted when her bottle fizzled to a stop.

"Ah!" Jordan was doused from head to foot and seemed incapable of speech.

"I suggest you two separate until you calm down," Angie said.

"What are *you* doing here?" Dutch asked.

"Listening in," Angie said. She put her bottle on the table and fished her cell phone out of her pocket and ended their call.

"You . . ." Dutch turned hostile accusatory eyes on Mel.

"Backup," Mel said. "Don't leave home without it."

"I had thought this was just among friends," he said.

He took a pile of napkins off the champagne cart and dabbed at his shirtfront.

"We have never been friends," Mel said, "because you are not capable of friendship. You're so busy trying to be 'the man,' you've lost sight of everything that's important."

"I have not," Dutch protested.

"Eh, please," Mel said with a dismissive wave. "What is Bertie's room number?"

"Why should I tell you?" Dutch said. "So you can tell him what you found out and screw up my last chance at being a celebrity chef? Hell no."

"Fine." Mel fished her phone out of her purse and started to scroll through her contacts. "Let's see . . . Uncle Stan, where is Uncle Stan, oh, there he is."

She was about to push the dial button when Dutch said, "All right, all right. He's in the suites on the first floor, number fourteen."

"Thank you," Mel said. She turned and looked at Angie. "Shall we?"

"After you," she said. Then she turned around and looked at Dutch. "Maybe you should leave with us?"

He glanced at Jordan, who was soaked and whimpering, and back at them. "Maybe you're right."

Mel and Angie trailed Dutch out the door, closing it with a snap behind them.

Dutch headed to his own room down the corridor, and Angie followed him.

"Hey," she called. "Wait for me. I don't want you calling Bertie and warning him that we're coming."

He turned to look at Angie with one eyebrow raised.

"If you wanted to be alone with me, all you had to do was ask."

"Oh, hurl," Angie said. She turned to Mel. "I see what you mean about becoming immune to his charm."

"Yeah, it wears thin after a while."

Dutch looked offended but they ignored him.

"Let's set up our phones," Angie said.

They both pulled out their phones, and Mel rang Angie's number. Angie opened her phone and then disappeared into Dutch's room. Mel wasn't worried. She knew that even in Angie's weakened state, she could take him. Dutch really was a big baby.

Mel went back to the elevator. It was a short ride down, and she was once again in the lobby. She turned right and headed out toward the suites that lined the pool.

She got to number fourteen pretty quickly and paused to check her phone.

"Angie, I'm here, can you hear me?" she asked.

"Loud and clear," Angie answered.

"Is everything okay there?" Mel asked.

"Yeah, he went to take a shower after I made sure I had

his phone, and I checked that there was no phone in the bathroom," she said.

"Good thinking," Mel answered.

Mel walked across the flagstones to Bertie's door and gave it three hard taps. No answer. To her surprise, the automatic door hadn't closed all the way. She glanced down and saw a bit of towel wedged in the door frame, keeping it from shutting. She pushed the door open.

"Hello? Bertie?" She could hear the sound of running water, so she raised her voice and called out again, "Bertie, it's Mel. I need to talk to you."

There was no answer. Mel wondered what to do. Should she push forward and demand to speak to him or swiftly retreat and come back later?

If he was in the kitchenette, he would see her if she just moved farther into the room. She decided to risk it.

"Sorry to barge in, Bertie," she said as she stepped over the towel that had been dropped in front of the door. "I just need to . . ."

She stopped and glanced at the kitchenette. No one was there. The sound of running water was coming from the bathroom. Oh, man, now she was embarrassed. She didn't want to see Bertie in the altogether. She'd need therapy for months.

She started to back away when she noticed that water was bubbling out from under the closed bathroom door. It was flooding the tile floor like a fast-moving wave headed for the carpet in the living area. Didn't Bertie realize he was causing a small disaster?

Oh, ish. She was going to have to knock on the bathroom door. Mel stood to the side, trying to avoid soaking her sneakers, and banged on the door with a closed fist and yelled, "Bertie, you've got a mess out here. Bertie!"

There was no answer. Oh, man, she did not want to go in there, but he obviously could not hear her over the water. She had no choice.

Clapping one hand over her eyes, Mel pushed the door open and yelled, "Bertie, shut off the water!"

She waited for him to yell back or for the sound of the water to stop. Nothing. With a sinking feeling in her gut, Mel lowered her hand and opened her eyes.

Floating amidst the suds in his large circular tub was Bertie. Mel raced forward. Losing her footing in a bout of panicked uncoordination, she slid into the side of the tub, bruising her hip on its hard edge.

She reached into the water and grabbed Bertie by the shoulders. He was slick and slippery, and she had a hard time keeping a grip on him.

"Bertie, damn it, help me out," she yelled at him. He slid back under the water, but not before she saw that his eyes were open and his mouth was slightly agape in a grimace of pain. Bertie Grassello was dead.

# Twenty-eight

"Are you sure there wasn't anyone else here when you entered?" Uncle Stan asked.

"Quite sure," Mel said. She was sitting outside Bertie's suite with a large, fluffy pool towel draped over her shoulders. Angie was on one side of her while Joe and Tate were on the other.

"Was it a heart attack?" Mel asked.

"It appears to be," Uncle Stan said. His gaze met Mel's, and she knew he was thinking the same thing she was. It was too much of a coincidence, and now that they knew what poison to look for, Bertie needed to be tested immediately.

Uncle Stan had sent another detective to interview Dutch and Jordan, but until the ME said otherwise, it appeared that Bertie had had a heart attack while enjoying a nice long soak with his loofah and his Mr. Bubble.

They all watched silently as Bertie was taken out of his suite on a stretcher.

"Are you all right?" Joe asked.

"Two bodies in six days. I've been better," Mel said.

As the stretcher was wheeled away, Felicity Parnassus came racing over to their little group. "Is it true? Is Bertie Grassello dead?"

"I'm sorry, ma'am, you would be . . ." Uncle Stan frowned as if he couldn't quite place her.

Small wonder, Mel thought. Felicity had changed her hair color again, and now it was the raven black of midnight.

"I am the chairwoman for the food festival," she announced this as if it held the same importance as ambassador to China.

Uncle Stan squinted at her. "Oh, you changed your hair. Any particular reason?"

Felicity looked nonplussed. "It's what I do."

"Oh, so you're a hairdresser," he said.

Mel saw the twinkle in his eye and had to duck her head to keep from laughing. Judging by Joe's bowed head, he was having the same reaction. Uncle Stan loved to play the dimwitted cop with society's ridiculous matrons.

"I most certainly am not!" she declared hotly. "Now, I need you to tell me how dead is Bertie Grassello?"

"Excuse me?" It was Uncle Stan's turn to look nonplussed.

"How dead is he?" she demanded.

"I'm sorry." Uncle Stan shook his head. "He had a heart attack in the bathtub."

"Is there no chance that he'll recover by tomorrow's festival?" Felicity huffed.

"Because 'there's a big difference between mostly dead and slightly alive. Mostly dead is slightly alive. With all dead, well, with all dead there's usually only one thing you can do,'" Angie said, keeping her voice low enough so that only Mel, Tate, and Joe could hear her.

"'What's that?'" Joe joined in with the next line.

"'Go through his clothes and look for loose change,'" Tate and Mel finished the quote.

"*The Princess Bride*," Angie said, identifying their shared quote. Her gaze met Tate's, and they watched each other for a moment. Mel wondered if they were remembering the other quote from *The Princess Bride* that they had shared yesterday, the one that meant "I love you."

She glanced back at Uncle Stan, who was staring at Felicity as if she were completely demented. He turned and walked away from her without saying a word.

"How rude!" Felicity glared at his retreating back.

"What is all this?" Grace Mazzotta walked across the terrace toward them. "Isn't that . . . Has something happened to Bertie?"

"Grace!" Felicity raised her hands in the air as if her own personal salvation had come. "You can do it."

"Do what?" Grace looked wary.

"You can take Bertie's spot in the judging tomorrow," Felicity said. "It's the last day. We can't end it without declaring a winner."

"I don't understand. What's going on? Has something happened to Bertie?"

"Well, yes, there was a tragedy," Felicity said. "It seems he had a heart attack in the bathtub."

Grace clapped a hand over her mouth and rocked back on her heels. Mel bolted up from her seat to grab Grace's elbow and steady her.

"Are you all right?" she asked.

"Now, Grace," Felicity continued, "I'll just slip you in

as Bertie's replacement. Don't be late—the judging will start at noon tomorrow."

Felicity hurried away on her skinny high heels, and they all stood staring after her.

"Real bleeding heart, that one," Mel muttered. She helped Grace into her empty seat. "Are you okay?"

"I'm just shocked," Grace said. "I suppose given all of the events of the past week, it's not unlikely that the stress would cause a heart attack, but still . . ."

"I know," Mel patted her hand. She pulled the towel tighter around her shoulders. "I can't believe it—first Vic and now Bertie."

"I'm beginning to think this competition is cursed," Angie said.

"Don't let Felicity hear you say that," Tate said. They all shuddered at the thought.

Uncle Stan strode over to their group. "Mrs. Mazzotta, may I ask you a few questions?"

"Certainly," Grace said. "I don't know what help I can be, but I'm happy to try."

"It's just a formality. Since you knew the deceased, perhaps you can help us with some background on him." The crowd that had been loitering while the body was carried out began to surge forward and Uncle Stan frowned. "We'd better do this inside."

Grace rose to follow him, and Joe stood as well.

"Stan, can I take Mel home before she catches a cold?" Joe asked.

Uncle Stan glanced at Mel, and his cop eyes softened with affection. "You okay?"

"Yeah, I'm good," she lied.

"Call me if you need anything," he ordered.

"Will do," she said.

"Tate, can you take Angie home?" Joe asked.

"On it," he said.

Angie popped out of her chair and gave Mel a fierce hug. "Call me if you need me."

"I promise."

Joe put his arm around her waist and led Mel away from the suites, away from the scene of yet another death, and she was relieved to let him.

'´ ` ` ´ `

**Mel awoke to the sound of a soft snoring purr.** Captain Jack was curled up in the crevice where her and Joe's pillows met. She reached out a finger and stroked his downy fur. He responded by purring louder, stretching out his paws and giving her a big yawn with his pink tongue out and curling up.

He really was the cutest darn thing, and he had slipped himself so seamlessly into her life. She couldn't imagine her apartment without him. And just like that, she knew that this little guy had found his forever home with her.

Mel looked at his white fur nestled against Joe's dark hair. Her gaze moved over Joe's face relaxed in sleep, giving his handsome features an unusual vulnerability that made her feel a flash of protectiveness for him. She felt so lucky to have them both, so lucky that it scared her, no, it terrified her.

Joe's eyes fluttered open as if he was aware of her watching him. His warm brown eyes took a second to focus on her, but when they did, he smiled.

"Good morning," he said. He stretched out his arms, much like Captain Jack, and pulled her close. "How did you sleep?"

Mel took comfort in his warmth, letting his body heat melt the icy clutch of fear that had her in its hard grip.

"Better than expected," she said.

"You must have been exhausted," he said. "I have to tell you, I will be so glad when this challenge to the chefs is over. I feel like I have been worried about you from the moment it started."

"Yeah, if I could throw in the oven mitt today, I would, but we've worked so hard. Angie would be crushed, besides . . ."

"Yes?"

"I want to beat Olivia," she said. "And I want to know what really happened to Bertie."

"What do you mean?"

"It just seems awfully fishy to me that he takes Vic's television host spot and then ends up dead from a heart attack."

"You think Vic haunted him and gave him a heart attack?"

"If anyone could do that, it would be Vic, but no, I think there is something more going on here," she said. "I think, well, what if Bertie killed Vic and the stress of it all did him in?"

"It's possible," Joe said.

"Anything is possible," Mel said. "It's what's actual that is driving me batty."

"Do me a favor," he said, gently plucking Captain Jack's claws out of his pajama top while rolling him over to pet him. "Don't do anything that would piss Vic off so that he feels compelled to haunt you."

Mel smiled. She thought it spoke pretty well of Joe that he didn't even waste his breath telling her to mind her own business.

They shared a quiet breakfast in her apartment. Thankfully, Captain Jack kept her busy with his shenanigans; otherwise, she might have gone the teensiest bit mental. It was Sunday, so her bakery wouldn't open until one o'clock, and both Oz and Angie's brother Al had agreed to man the fort for them.

Mel had already lost track of how many people she had to thank for getting them through this past week.

Finally at eleven, she and Joe made their way over to the festival. Angie had texted that she was on her way, but she made no mention of Tate, and Mel had to wonder what had happened with them when Tate had brought her home last night.

"Melanie and dear Joe," Mel's mother greeted them at the entrance. She gave them each a hug and ushered them through the gate. "Can you believe it? The last day!"

"So did Ginny's plan work?" Mel asked.

Her mother turned a faint shade of pink and looked away.

"What plan?" Joe asked.

"Oh, nothing really . . ." Joyce waved her hand but Mel ignored her.

"Ginny thought Mom might meet a man if she volunteered to work at the festival."

Joe raised his brows. "So I expect you're beating them off with a spatula, then."

"Oh, dear Joe, aren't you a love?" Joyce said, blushing an even deeper shade of pink.

He grinned and Mel rolled her eyes. Her mother and Joe adored one another, which was fabulous most of the time. It was only when they ganged up on her that she found it problematic.

"I hate to cut the love fest short, but I have to go," she said. She kissed Joe's cheek and then her mother's. "I'll see you two later."

"Oh, Melanie, wait," Joyce called after her. She hurried to Mel's side, drawing something out of her pocket. "This came for you at the house. It looks very official."

Mel glanced at the envelope before shoving it in her pocket. She didn't have time for junk mail right now. "Thanks, Mom."

She hurried to the conference room, where they were to cool their heels until showtime. She wanted to visit with Johnny Pepper and see if he knew anything.

With only four of them competing, the room was empty when Mel got there. She crossed it and knocked on Johnny's door.

"What?" a snippy female voice called.

"It's Mel, Johnny, open up," she called.

The door was yanked open and out popped Johnny's trademark blond tips.

"Mel, this isn't a good time," he said.

"Sorry," she said. "I'm just wondering what you've heard about Bertie's death and what you think about it."

Johnny stepped forward and leaned on his doorjamb. Mel glanced over his shoulder and saw a woman, holding a hair dryer, looking like she meant business.

"Heart attack in the bathtub seems pretty straightforward to me," he said.

"Yeah, I suppose," Mel said. "But don't you think it's odd that two of our judges are dead?"

"Yeah, I'm sort of feeling like this food fest is cursed," he said without humor. "I'm surprised Felicity was able to strong-arm Grace into taking Bertie's place. I'd have passed."

"Agreed," Mel said.

"Johnny, your product is going to dry out," the hair lady called.

"Gotta go. Don't tell anyone," he said and glanced over his shoulder at the dominatrix-looking stylist, "but I'm afraid of her. See y'all on the stage."

The door shut in her face, and Mel was left in the prep room alone. She had been leaning toward Bertie as Vic's killer. It made the most sense. He was the one with the most to gain from Vic's death. With Vic dead, there could be no more rivalry, meaning the studio couldn't replace Bertie with Vic if they decided they didn't like how it was going.

Of course, Dutch had a lot to gain, too, by joining forces with Bertie. But Bertie's death was going to set him back. Without Bertie to give him another shot in front of the camera, how was Dutch going to get back into the spotlight?

The door opened and Olivia Puckett entered. She had her usual sneer in place, and her eyes lit up at the sight of Mel.

"Well, well, well," she said as she sashayed across the room. "Is poor little Melanie all alone?"

Mel felt her teeth clench as Olivia talked to her like she was a lost little toddler likely to burst into tears.

"Can it, Olivia," she said and added with a smile, "Then it will taste just like your frosting."

Olivia glared daggers at her but kept up the baby talk. "What's the matter, don't you have anyone to protect you from the big, bad world anymore?"

"I don't need protecting," Mel said, frowning. "What exactly is your problem with me?"

"You mean, other than the fact that you're a spoiled little rich girl who pretends to work when really you just have your rich friend Tate Harper dump money into your business to make it look successful?"

"Let me get this straight: You're mad because I have an investor in my business?" Mel asked. "For your information, I happen to work my butt off in that bakery. Those cupcake recipes are all mine, and I do most of the baking. Yes, Tate gave me start-up capital, but he also gets a cut of the profit, which given our success, is substantial."

"Blah, blah, blah." Olivia made a talking motion with her hand. "Try selling that somewhere else. I am not buying it."

"You are such a . . ."

The door opened, halting Mel's rant as Felicity Parnassus entered.

"Ladies," Felicity greeted them with a bob of her head.

They barely had time to greet her in return as she trotted past them to Johnny's door. She gave it a swift knock and then entered without even waiting to be invited.

Olivia was too much of a suck-up to continue their spat while an official was present, so they gave each other mutual looks of loathing before Olivia turned on her heel and headed for the coffee in the back of the room.

Mel glanced at her phone. She had another half hour of waiting at least. She was not going to sit in this room with Olivia. She felt weary all the way to her bones, and even though she would have given it her best, she was not up for another confrontation.

The festival was open, and the crowds were gathering. Mel noticed that the cooks from the restaurants that had booths looked as tired as she felt, and she wondered if the charm had worn off for them as well. Six days of cooking outside for gobs of visitors would do that.

"Mel!" a voice cried, and she turned, expecting to see Angie or her mother. Instead, it was Polly Ramsey, the cookie baker, who had also made the final four, running toward her.

"Hi, Polly," she said. The young woman was breathless as she stepped into the shade with her.

"Can you believe the news about Mr. Grassello?" Polly asked, her breath still rasping.

"No," Mel said, feeling suddenly sad for Bertie even though she had never been very fond of the old blowhard.

"It's been such a crazy week," Polly said. "Two judges dead and that mean Olivia Puckett giving me such a hard time. I can't believe I made the finals."

"Polly, come here!" an imperious voice commanded.

Mel looked past Polly to see her mother standing a few feet away from them, carrying an old-fashioned round cosmetic bag.

"I thought you weren't going to let her in," Mel said.

"I had to," Polly sighed. "My dad asked me to, and he's been working so hard during the competition, I couldn't refuse. Now she's going to have me wearing red lipstick and stinking of Shalimar."

"Well, there's no time like the present to tell her no," Mel said. "If you don't, she'll be like this forever."

"Forever?" Polly asked.

Mel nodded.

"Oh, gees, and I've just been offered an opportunity to test for a new television cooking show," Polly said, fretting her lower lip.

"What?" Mel asked.

"I'm not supposed to say anything," Polly said, cringing. "Promise you won't tell."

"Absolutely," Mel said.

"Well, Grace, you know the woman married to Mr. Mazzotta, she asked me if I had any interest in television," Polly said. "I was shocked, but she seemed to think that with my youth and skill, I would have real audience appeal, so she wants me to come with her to Los Angeles for a screen test next week."

"That's exciting!" Mel said. "You must be thrilled."

Polly frowned. "I don't know. I'm not sure that life is for me."

"Well, you won't know unless you try it," Mel said. Polly was cute. Mel could see an audience loving her big smile and genuine warmth. With Vic gone, it made sense that Grace was looking for someone else to represent.

"It's lucky for her that she discovered you, given Vic's passing and all," Mel said. She knew her voice sounded sad. "It'll be good for Grace to have a new talent on whom she can channel her management skills."

Polly frowned. "I suppose. Although she asked me the day before he died when I was just touring the staging area to get my bearings. She seemed very excited to make the offer."

"I'm sure she did," Mel said. She felt her mouth curve into a smile while her stomach twisted into a knot. There was something about this that she didn't like.

"Polly Alexandra Ramsey, come here right now!" her mother demanded.

"I'd better go," Polly said apologetically.

"Say no to the red lipstick!" Mel called after her.

Polly shot her a grateful grin over her shoulder and walked away with her mother nattering behind her.

Mel turned and looked out over the festival. She could see people clutching their taste-testing coupons. She didn't know what to make of Polly's news.

Grace had approached Polly about testing for a show. She could certainly see why—Polly was perky enough to be the next Rachael Ray—but still it didn't sit well with Mel that Grace had approached her before Vic passed away, almost as if she had known that Vic's career was over . . . for good.

Mel thrust her hands into her pocket and found the letter that her mother had given to her. It was probably just junk mail, but she opened it anyway, as it gave her muddled brain something to do.

It was a letter from an estate attorney. It was short and to the point. The attorney represented Vic Mazzotta's estate, and as per the deceased's request, upon his death the enclosed letter was to be sent to Mel.

An envelope, looking to be a bit yellowed with age, was included. She carefully pried open the seal and pulled out a small sheet of matching stationary.

Vic's characteristic squiggly script appeared on the page, and Mel felt a lump form in her throat, as she read.

*Dear Mel,*

*If you are reading this, it means I have gone to the great kitchen in the sky. I promise your dad and I will stink up the joint with smelly cigars while we enjoy the finest wines.*

Mel laughed and had to pause to wipe the tears off her face before she could continue reading.

*As everyone knows, you have always been my favorite student. And so I share with you my secret ingredient.*

*It is simply this: Always cook with love. It makes everything taste divine.*

> *Your friend and teacher, always,*
> *Vic*

Sobs cut through Mel's chest like her sharpest knives. Her tears dropped onto the paper, and she wiped them away, wanting to save this last bit of Vic so that she could keep him with her always.

Damn him, she would miss the old bastard so much, and as usual, he had managed to have the last word.

She stared at the letter in her hands. Vic had always joked that he would tell her his secret when he was dead. She had assumed it was a joke, but she knew he was serious. Vic did cook with love. His food was better than anyone else's because he loved the food he cooked with and the people for whom he cooked.

She stared off into the crowd. Then what the hell had Jordan and Dutch been talking about? All the rumors that Vic left out seemingly insignificant but ultimately critical ingredients were just that—rumors. Vic didn't leave out any ingredients in his recipes; he was just a better cook than the rest of them because he'd honed his skills and cooked from a place deeper inside himself than the rest of them.

So, what had Bertie given them to use on Vic's scones? Mel felt fear's chilly fingers creep up her spine in a scary tickle.

"Mel, where have you been?" Angie raced down the sidewalk, ducking around visitors in her hurry to reach her. "Didn't you notice the time? We have to get to the staging area, like now!"

"Oh!" Mel stuffed the letter back into her pocket and wiped her face.

"What's wrong?" Angie asked.

"Nothing," Mel said as she snuffled. "Just an allergy attack."

"Well, shake it off," Angie said. "We have to go."

Mel bolted up from her spot in the shade. She followed Angie as they made their way against the crowd toward the stage.

Now that it was the finals, the area seemed even more congested than ever. Mel and Angie took their spot in their kitchen. The chefs from Molly's Moonpies were in theirs while Polly and Olivia hurried into their spots, too.

Mel looked out over the crowd. Her chest still hurt when she thought of Vic's letter, but she saw Joe in the crowd and the sight of him bolstered her. His brothers, including the married ones with their families, and Mr. and Mrs. De-Laura were also there. She and Angie waved, and the whole group waved back, and one of them let loose an air horn that made everyone in the vicinity jump.

Mrs. DeLaura spun around and gave them her scary-mama look. Mel didn't think she imagined it when Tony got noticeably shorter.

Next to the DeLauras, Tate was standing with Mel's mother, who gave them a thumbs-up and jumped up and down in excitement.

In no time, Johnny Pepper was taking the stage. His hair didn't have a blond spike out of place, and he was carrying his usual large white box.

Mel leaned close to Angie and said, "I'm beginning to hate the white box."

"Maybe he'll let us burn it when this is over," Angie said.

They exchanged a smile, and Mel was grateful to have Angie by her side for this final round.

"Many of you are aware that we lost a dear friend last night. Our judge Bertie Grassello, a legend in the food world and a close personal friend to many of us, passed away from a heart attack early last evening," Johnny said. "Bertie, you will be missed. Let us observe a moment of silence for our friend."

A hush swept over the crowd as Johnny lowered his head in a sign of respect. Mel noted that not a sound could be heard other than the trickle of the distant fountains and the twittering of the birds that inhabited the park.

"We are fortunate enough to have Grace Mazzotta taking Bertie's place," Johnny said, raising his head and addressing the crowd. "As we all know, Bertie would have wanted this competition to reach its natural conclusion with a winner."

"Call me unsentimental," Angie muttered to Mel, "but I really don't think Bertie would give a rip."

Mel felt her lips twitch. She had to agree.

"The challenge to the chefs, pastry division, is now down to its last four contestants," Johnny announced. He introduced each of them in turn. Mel and Angie, in second place, were introduced second to last. When Confections was announced, the applause noticeably dimmed. Mel wondered if it was just her ego or if the crowd really had cheered louder for them. Then again they had the DeLauras on their side.

"And the ingredient is . . ." Johnny reached into the box and pulled out a long wiggling black thing. "Eels!"

"Ya!" Olivia shouted. In a blink, she jumped forward, grabbed the eel out of Johnny's hand, and using one of the larger knives from her kitchenette, she whacked off its head.

In her peripheral vision, Mel saw Angie jump, but she couldn't be sure if it was the eel or Olivia's knife wielding that caused it.

"I am so out of here," Angie said, and she made to leave.

"Um . . . it was rubber," Johnny said. He picked up the remnants of the eel, looking worriedly at Olivia.

Angie glowered at him while Olivia slid the sharp edge of her knife against her thumb as if checking its post-eel beheading sharpness. Then she smiled.

Mel moved their set of knives away from Angie's throwing arm—just in case.

"Okay, enough fun and games," Johnny continued, "the final ingredient is . . . beets!"

"Oh, ish," Angie said. "I hate beets. I think I'd rather have the eel."

"No, trust me," Mel said. "Beets are good. Beets are perfect."

"What are you thinking?" Angie asked.

Mel covered her mouth with her hand and whispered, "Red velvet cupcakes."

Angie's eyes got wide. "You can do that with beets?"

Mel nodded. "Get ready. When they reveal the cart, try to get the best-looking beets you can find."

The whistle blew, and Mel and Angie raced to the cart.

Olivia looked wild eyed and tried to muscle Mel out of the way. Polly looked very focused while her father yipped and stayed out of the fray. The other two bakers were the first to beat it back to their kitchenette.

Mel mentally composed a list and gave it to Joanie, who shot off for the supply cupboard. Mel set to work on the beets while Angie gathered the dry ingredients.

The judges walked amongst their kitchens while they worked. Mel noticed that Grace lingered at Polly's station, and she wondered if Grace was watching her with a mind toward her future career as a celebrity chef.

Mel glanced at the other judges. Dutch and Jordan were not circulating; they both looked tired and stayed huddled in the judges' booth as if they could not wait for this to be over.

Candace Levinson, the judge from *Food and Wine*, passed by Mel and Angie and gave them an encouraging smile while she paused to watch them work.

Mel added the wet ingredients to the dry and let the mixer take over. Angie started prepping the cupcake pan, while Mel began to make the cream cheese frosting.

Grace passed by and Mel looked at closely at her. "How are you holding up, Grace?"

The older woman gave her a wan smile. "I've been better, but Felicity is not exactly someone you can say no to. Besides, I think Vic would have wanted me to see this through to the end for him."

Mel nodded. "Yeah, he was like that. He finished what he started."

Grace moved on to Olivia's station. Olivia was red-faced and sweaty, and she stopped chastising her sous-chef in order to give Grace an ingratiating smile.

Mel wondered what Vic would have made of her. For the millionth time, she wished he were there, and she felt a surge of rage at the killer who had taken him away.

"Mel, *psst*, Mel!"

She glanced up to see Uncle Stan by the side of the staging area.

She hurried over to him. "Kind of busy here, Uncle Stan, what's up?"

"Well, first, good luck," he said. Mel nodded and motioned with her hands for him to hurry. "And I wanted to warn you to be careful. We got a preliminary tox screen on Grassello. It's not conclusive yet, but it looks like the same poison used on Angie was used on him."

"Really." Mel sat back on her heels with a thump.

"Be careful," Uncle Stan said. "There's a nut job mixed up in this food competition, and I won't be happy until you're out of it."

"Mel, clock ticking!" Angie shouted. "Come on!"

Mel raced back over to her kitchenette. Her hands were shaking. The secret ingredient that wasn't.

Dutch was finally circulating, working his way around the kitchenettes. When he got to Mel's, she grabbed him by the shirtfront.

"Hey, easy on the silk," he said.

Mel leaned her head close to his and hissed, "Who gave Bertie Vic's secret spice for pastries?"

"What?" he asked.

"The one that you had Jordan use on Vic's scones—who gave it to you?"

"I told you," he said. "Bertie wanted us to use it to bring Vic down, to humble him."

"I know that, but where did Bertie get it?" she asked.

Dutch frowned. "I don't know. He never said, so I assumed he stole it from Vic."

"Did he tell you what it was made from?" she asked.

"No, I badgered him, believe me, but he refused to tell me. All he would say was that it was a very rare spice from Southeast Asia."

Mel released his shirt and nodded. She hadn't known she'd been clinging to the hope that stress had done Bertie in until Uncle Stan took it away. She had almost convinced herself that guilt had caused Bertie to have a heart attack, but she'd been wrong. So wrong. They'd all been wrong.

She glanced up and looked around the stage. They'd all played a part. Unbeknownst to one another, they'd all played a significant role in the death of Vic Mazzotta, and it hadn't been suicide—it was murder, and Mel knew exactly who had orchestrated the entire thing. The question now was how to prove it.

She and Angie placed red nasturtium blossoms on top of the cream cheese frosting. She did not know where Joanie had found them, but she suspected one of the flower beds in the park had been denuded just a touch. If the *Food and Wine* lady liked edible flowers, these would be sure to get her attention.

Mel had to admit the red color from the beets was stunning. She only hoped they tasted as good as they looked. If they did, she fully intended to make these at the bakery and lose the ones that used too much bottled dye.

The final buzzer sounded, and the chefs all slumped back away from their creations. Glancing over the stage, Mel noticed their competition offered up a beet mousse, beet ice cream, and beet cookies. This was going to be an interesting showdown.

The servers gathered up their entries and began to make their way to the booth where the judges sat waiting.

The crowd shuffled restlessly on their feet, and Mel couldn't blame them; it had been a long hour already.

"Ladies and gentlemen, we are asking our chefs to remain while the judging commences. I will be introducing each chef and have them talk us through their creation while the judges rank them."

"From Polly's Kitchen, let's start with Polly Ramsey and her beet-infused white chocolate–chip cookie."

Mel tuned out Polly with her perky giggle. She saw Polly's mother standing in front of the stage, trying to hiss pointers at her daughter.

"Smile, bigger, show me those teeth, Polly!"

Polly smiled and frowned at her mother at the same time, lost her concentration, and ended her explanation in mid-sentence. Awkward.

"That woman should be kept in a padded cell," Angie said, tipping her head at Polly's mother.

The Moonpie bakers were next, and the crowd cheered loudly after their interview.

Next was Olivia. She was still sweating profusely and looked uncomfortable at the front of the stage. She towered over Johnny Pepper, and when she spoke into the mic, she yelled as if uncertain that it was really making her heard over the festival grounds.

Johnny cut the interview short and waved Mel over.

She glanced at the table where the servers were just putting out her red velvet cupcakes.

"Lastly, we have Melanie Cooper from Fairy Tale Cupcakes. What inspired your red velvet cupcake, Mel?"

Mel took a deep breath and studied the judges. This was it. Now she was going to get her tell. "Vic Mazzotta," she said.

"Oh, so you made these in honor of Vic. He was your mentor, am I right?"

"Yes, he was. He was also my friend," Mel said. "You know, Vic was such an amazing chef that when I was his student, we thought he didn't tell us every ingredient he used in his recipes, because we could never get our food to taste as good as his. So as a tribute, and with the help of some of his associates, I decided to use his secret baking ingredient in my cupcakes."

One of the judges dropped their fork with a clatter. Mel felt her heart fall like a soufflé in her chest. It had been a bluff, but the killer had revealed herself by reacting with shock.

Their eyes met, and Mel forgot she was still talking into the microphone. "Why did you do it? Why did you kill him?"

# Twenty-nine

Grace Mazzotta jumped up from her seat at the table and bolted to the side of the stage. Joe DeLaura was standing there. She turned and raced for the other side, but Uncle Stan was there. She was trapped.

"I didn't do anything," she protested. "You can't prove anything. It was them!"

She pointed at Dutch and Jordan. They looked at Grace and then at each other. Their expressions were blank, and Mel knew them both well enough by now to know that they had no idea what was happening.

"No, it wasn't," Mel said. "It was you. You had Vic poisoned, you tried to poison me, and you poisoned Bertie. What happened? Did Bertie figure it out?"

"What is the meaning of this?" Felicity Parnassus stormed the stage. She glared at Mel and Grace. "You are supposed to be tasting her cupcakes—taste them."

Mel gave Grace a slow smile. "Yeah, taste them."

"You're bluffing," Grace said. She backed away from the table until she was pressed up against the wall.

"What's the matter? Are you afraid I used the spice that you gave to Bertie to murder Vic?" Mel taunted her.

Both Dutch and Jordan sat up higher in their seats at that.

"What are you talking about, Mel?" Dutch asked.

"I know what Vic left out of his written recipes," Mel said. She fished his letter out of her pocket and waved it in the air before tucking it safely back into her jeans. "He told me in this letter, and it isn't what you thought."

"But Bertie . . ." Jordan began, but Dutch shushed her.

"Bertie gave you something that he said was one of Vic's secret ingredients, correct?" Mel asked. Dutch and Jordan exchanged a look and then reluctantly nodded. "And he wanted you to serve it to Vic to let him know that all of you knew what his secret was. How am I doing so far?"

With hundreds of festival attendees watching and his hopes of stardom rapidly diminishing once again, Dutch had the grace to hang his head.

"Yeah, here's the problem with that," Mel said. "What Bertie gave you was poison."

Jordan sucked in a breath and Dutch swore.

"So, what happened, Grace?" Mel asked. "Were you and Bertie in cahoots? That seems most likely."

Grace glanced away, and Mel knew she had guessed right. "You took a hell of chance. I'm guessing it was Bertie's idea to have Jordan serve Vic the poison. How did you know Jordan and Dutch wouldn't try it first? Or didn't you care if they died?"

She heard Dutch and Jordan gasp together.

"This is crazy talk," Grace said. "You're just grief struck since your mentor is dead, and the stress of this contest is getting to you. Vic died of a heart attack. It hit while he was walking the grounds, and he took a wrong turn into a freezer and died. It's just a tragedy. I'm sorry. I know you want to blame someone, but there is no one to blame."

Grace gave her a heartbroken look, and Mel realized the real acting talent in the Mazzotta family had been Grace.

"You're lying," she said.

"Mel, I would never have hurt Vic. He was my whole life," Grace said. Her voice even trembled as if she was wrought with emotion.

"Really?" Mel scoffed. "He was cheating on you. That had to hurt. And you, you were scouting new talent before he was even dead, because you knew you were going to have to replace him, didn't you? Because you planned Vic's death. You planned it so well that everyone did your dirty work for you."

"You're delusional," Grace said.

"Not as much as you'd think," Mel said. "You see, Angie here was lucky enough to have a doctor from India, and he was quite familiar with *Cerebra odollam*, or as they call it in India, the Suicide Tree."

Grace's face went pale.

"Yeah, I meant to ask you before," Mel said. "How was your trip to Southeast Asia? Informative?"

"I dedicated my life to him," Grace snarled. "And how was I repaid? Pushed to the side and forgotten for that—a pair of tatas and taffy for brains! You're right. I wished him dead, and I got my wish."

The seething rage that poured off Grace in waves contorted her features into a person Mel did not recognize. It was frighteningly easy to see this stranger as a murderer.

"But why me? Why did you try to poison me?" Mel asked. Her voice was small and she hated that, but she had to know.

"Because of the letter," Grace said. Her voice was full of contempt. "I knew he had written you a letter about his secret ingredient—love. Ha, what a joke! That man only loved himself. I knew if you got the letter from his attorney, you would try to piece it all together. Why did you care so much about that miserable bastard? He wasn't worth it."

"He was worth it to me," Mel said. "What about Bertie? Why did you kill him?"

Grace glowered at her and pressed her lips together. She was not going to say another word.

"Let me take a wild guess," Mel said. "He figured it out, didn't he? I mean, he had to have been suspicious. You give him one of Vic's secret ingredients, Jordan serves it to Vic, and he dies. You must have been counting pretty heavily on Bertie's hatred of Vic, which was admittedly epic, to keep him silent. It didn't, though, did it?"

"I don't know what you're talking about," Grace said.

"That night I came to your door and Bertie was there and he said, 'You'll think about what we discussed,' tell me, had he already started blackmailing you?"

Grace fumed but said nothing.

"You know the one thing I can't figure was why Vic was in the freezer," Mel said. She turned to Jordan. The brunette was watching her as if mesmerized. "Jordan, what exactly did you say when you served Vic that fatal scone?"

Jordan looked wretched. Tears were streaming down her cheeks, and most of her makeup was dripping from her chin.

"I don't know," she said. "I guess I said something to the

effect that I didn't need him anymore now that Bertie had told everyone that he really did withhold secret ingredients from his recipes and that the key to his perfect pastries was a simple spice from Southeast Asia. Then I asked him how it tasted."

The entire festival was silent, straining to hear Jordan's words.

She swallowed and said, "He looked confused and then he clutched his chest. He asked me what I had cooked with, so I showed him the spice jar. There wasn't much left, so I used all of it in the scones."

Mel could see that the truth was really just beginning to dawn on Jordan.

"Oh my God, *I* poisoned him," she said. She started trembling and her teeth chattered. "That's why he did it!"

"Did what?" Mel asked.

"He threw the plates," she said. "I thought he was angry because I was breaking it off with him and because I knew his secret, but he did that so that I wouldn't . . . so that I wouldn't eat the poison. He took the bottle and staggered out of my room, and that's the last time I saw him alive."

Jordan collapsed into a sobbing heap against Dutch, who looked as if he'd just been shot. Mel was sure the two of them had no idea that they'd been pawns in a game of murder.

"So that was it. Vic knew he was dying. He knew he'd been poisoned. You know, finding him in the freezer did make it seem like he had fallen in there by accident or was trying to kill himself, but that wasn't it at all."

Grace glowered at her, her nostrils flaring, and Mel could tell she wanted her to shut up. Well, tough.

"Vic knew he was dying, he knew it was too late, so he fell into the freezer to preserve the poison in his body, didn't he? Man, he always was one step ahead."

"You don't know anything!" Grace yelled. "It's all lies, lies, I tell you. You were always Vic's favorite. You'd do anything to protect him even though he was a lying, cheating son of—"

Uncle Stan stepped forward and grabbed Grace's elbow. "Mrs. Mazzotta, you need to come with me." It wasn't a request.

Mayhem broke out on the stage as everyone began to talk at once.

Felicity Parnassus was yelling that Uncle Stan couldn't take Grace. They had to finish the contest. People were staring in openmouthed shock as Grace was hauled across the grounds to a waiting squad car, and Olivia was demanding that the judging be finished or she was going to sue.

Angie slid an arm around Mel's shoulders. "Are you okay?"

Mel nodded. "Better now that Vic's killer has been caught."

Finally, drowning out the shouting and shocked whispers, Johnny Pepper took over the mic and began to use his charm to soothe the crowd.

"Well, we've lost another judge," he said. "It looks like the only thing I can do is jump in and finish the judging myself."

He leaned over toward Mel and whispered, "You didn't actually poison those, did you?"

"No, it was a bluff," she said.

"Good one," he said. "Remind me not to play poker with you."

He strode over to where Felicity Parnassus stood, still looking outraged. They quickly conferred with the other judges. Jordan, still in shock, was obviously useless, so Felicity took her place while Dutch and the other judge rallied. Murmurs and quick glances were exchanged, and the four judges returned to the judges' table and began to sample the desserts.

The scoring cards for each dessert were handed to Felicity, who quickly tabulated the results. It was as if each of them could not get out of there fast enough.

Felicity then handed the results to Johnny Pepper, who took up his mic and said, "Well, after much consideration, we have concluded that there is only one bakery worthy of the distinction to win this year's challenge to the chefs."

Mel felt Angie grab her hand and squeeze. Having just seen Grace hauled off by her uncle Stan, Mel really couldn't care less about the contest, but she respected that the others had devoted a week of their lives to this event. She squeezed Angie's hand in return, although her heart was not in it.

"The winner is . . . Fairy Tale Cupcakes!"

The grounds exploded into a frenzy of cheers. Mel saw the DeLauras, her mother, and Tate jumping up and down. Oz and Al had appeared just in time for the announcement, and Mel watched as they shot each other high-fives. Angie hugged Mel close and shook her, she was so excited.

Mel was happy for all of them, but she couldn't smile and she couldn't cheer, not when her mentor wasn't here to share it with her when he should have been.

She saw Joe across the stage. He was watching her with his head turned to the side as if he understood how bittersweet this moment was for her. She wanted nothing more than to run to him and bury herself in his arms. She never got the chance.

"No, no, no!" Olivia Puckett cried, drowning out the giddy cheers. "I demand a do-over! This is my competition. Mine!"

As Felicity Parnassus was trotting across the stage to give the large crystal bowl to Mel and Angie, Olivia leaped forward and snatched the trophy out of her hands.

She tucked it under her arm and looked as if she were going to bolt off the stage with it. As one, the brothers fanned out; even Joe jumped down from the stage to join them, and they looked like an NFL defensive line. With a lionlike roar, Olivia jumped off the stage and made to plow through the crowd.

"Let's do this!" Angie nudged Mel, and they leapt off the stage after her.

Tony tried to take Olivia out at the knees, but she body-slammed him back into Sal and Paulie, taking them out like bowling pins. Dom made a diving tackle, but she tucked her shoulder and he rolled over her, taking Ray and Al with him. Joe and Tate linked arms to form a human chain, but Olivia grabbed Tate's free hand and pulled them as she ran, then she did a one-eighty and cracked them like a whip, sending them sprawling.

Mel and Angie exchanged a look. Like it or not, Olivia was impressive in her crazed state. She had managed to take out seven DeLaura brothers plus Tate.

"Let's get her!" Angie snarled. They made to plunge into the crowd, but all of a sudden Olivia disappeared from view.

Mel raced into the thick of the crowd with Angie hot on her heels. In the midst of the festival visitors, they found Olivia facedown on the ground, with Oz sitting on top of her and Mel's mother and Mrs. DeLaura each with a foot planted on her backside.

Joyce was holding the crystal bowl, which she held out to Mel and Angie.

"No one takes our babies' trophy," Joyce said.

The moms exchanged a high-five, and Oz raised a fist and shouted, "Huzzah!"

"Yeah, what he said!" Ginny, Joyce's friend, raised her fist and took a long swig from her water bottle.

"Angie!" a voice yelled into the crowd. They turned to see a tall, lanky man with his long black hair flowing over his shoulders striding toward them. It was Roach.

Angie's eyes bugged, but she didn't have a chance to say anything as he swept her up into his arms and planted a kiss on her that weakened the knees of every woman watching.

"Oh, my . . ." Ginny muttered.

"Roach." Angie clasped his face in her hands. "What are you doing here?"

"I came to see you," he said. "I had to see you. I had to know you were okay."

"But I thought all of the planes in Germany were grounded because of the bad weather," she said.

"They were." He gazed at her tenderly and said, "But you didn't really think that would stop me, did you?"

"Well, I . . ." Angie stammered.

"When it comes to you, there is nothing I won't do," he said. He tucked her hair behind her ears and said, "So I took a train, and a bus, and a ferry, and another train and finally three flights just to be sure that you're okay."

"What about your tour?" she asked.

"It'll keep," he said. He glanced around at the DeLaura brothers, who were brushing themselves off; the crowd that had gone speechless at the scene before them; and finally at the crystal cup in Mel's arms. "So, you won?"

"I . . . yes, we did," Angie said.

"That's awesome!" he said. "I'm so proud of you, babe. I knew you could do it. Let's go celebrate!"

"All right," Angie said. She looked at Mel, who nodded at her that it was fine.

"Go, I'll see you later," Mel said.

Roach wrapped his arms around Angie, and they made their way toward the exit. Mel couldn't help glancing at Tate. He looked as if he'd been sucker punched, and her heart ached for him.

He watched as Roach led Angie away and then looked down as if he couldn't bear it. Mel glanced at Angie and Roach. Just before they disappeared from the festival, Angie turned and glanced over her shoulder at Tate, and her eyes held a longing that made Mel's breath catch.

A pair of arms encircled Mel's waist from behind and a voice said, "Yes, she's still in love with him, but no, there's nothing you can do. They have to figure this out for themselves."

Mel fell back against Joe and sighed. She wouldn't give up his strength and support for anything. Had she really started to feel claustrophobic about them?

She realized now that it was just fear. To have something so precious, it was easy to see why she'd want to push it away. She didn't want to be heartbroken again like when she'd lost her dad. Vic's death had brought that fear home to her. But wouldn't the greater tragedy be not to have Joe in her life and never have Vic's secret ingredient—love?

She turned in his arms and hugged him close, with one arm still holding the crystal bowl.

"I want to go see my cat," she said. "Let's go home."

"Now you're talking." He grinned at her.

They paused for a brief moment to watch as Olivia was carted off the festival grounds by security. Mel stopped to congratulate Oz on his excellent tackle and let the DeLaura brothers admire the trophy.

Joyce and Maria gazed at Mel and Joe with pleased expressions, and then Maria leaned close to Joyce and said, "They're going to have beautiful babies, don't you think?"

Joyce beamed. "Oh, yes, very beautiful."

Mel felt her face get hot and assumed it was now the color of her beet-infused red velvets. "Mom! Mrs. D!"

"Call me Mama, dear," Mrs. DeLaura instructed her.

"We have to go—now!" Mel said to Joe.

Much to her chagrin, he was grinning at her. He kissed her temple and led her from the festival. As they crossed the street, putting some distance between them and their families, Mel felt her breathing become more normal.

She felt Vic's letter crinkle in her pocket, and she pulled it out and placed it carefully in her glass bowl. It seemed only right that Vic's secret ingredient should find its resting place inside a winner's trophy.

# Recipes

## Parsnip Cupcake with Ginger Cream Cheese Frosting

A parsnip spice cupcake with ginger cream cheese frosting topped with a toasted walnut.

*2 cups peeled, shredded, and lightly steamed parsnips*
*1½ cups all-purpose flour*
*1 cup sugar*
*1 tablespoon ground ginger*
*2 teaspoons baking powder*
*1 teaspoon ground cinnamon*
*¾ teaspoon salt*
*¾ teaspoon ground nutmeg*
*¾ teaspoon ground allspice*
*¾ teaspoon ground cloves*

*3 large eggs*
*½ cup vegetable oil*
*½ cup whole milk*
*1 teaspoon vanilla extract*
*½ cup walnut halves, toasted*

Preheat oven to 350°F. Steam the shredded parsnips lightly in a vegetable steamer for 5–7 minutes; set aside to cool. Put cupcake liners in a muffin tin. Combine the flour, sugar, ground ginger, baking powder, cinnamon, salt, nutmeg, allspice, and cloves in a large bowl; whisk to combine. Whisk the eggs, oil, milk, and vanilla in a medium bowl to combine. Pour the wet mixture over the dry, stirring until just combined. Stir in the parsnips. Fill each muffin cup ⅔ full with the batter and bake for 23–25 minutes, until a knife inserted in the center comes out clean. Let the cupcakes cool completely. Makes 12–16.

## Ginger Cream Cheese Frosting

*8 ounces cream cheese, softened*
*1 stick unsalted butter, softened*
*½ teaspoon vanilla extract*
*2 teaspoons crystallized ginger*
*3 cups powdered sugar*

Beat the cream cheese, butter, and vanilla in a large bowl until smooth. Add in the crystallized ginger. Gradually add the powdered sugar and beat until the frosting is smooth. Put the frosting in a pastry bag and pipe onto cupcakes in thick swirls, using an open tip. Top with a toasted walnut.

**Toasted Walnuts**

Spread walnuts in a single layer on a cookie sheet; bake at 350°F for 8–10 minutes.

\'\'\'\'

# Chocolate Stout Brownie Torte

A chocolate stout brownie served in a chocolate shell and topped with thin layers of chocolate mousse and brownie and a dollop of whipped cream.

## Chocolate Stout Brownie

*12 ounces chocolate stout*
*1 cup cocoa powder, unsweetened*
*2 cups sugar*
*½ cup butter, melted*
*2 teaspoons vanilla extract*
*4 eggs*
*2 cups all-purpose flour*
*¾ teaspoon salt*
*1 cup semisweet chocolate chips*

Preheat oven to 350°F. Line a 13 X 9 X 2-inch baking pan with aluminum foil. In a large bowl, whisk together the stout and cocoa powder until blended and smooth. Whisk

in the sugar, butter, vanilla extract, and eggs, one at a time.
Blend well. Add the flour and salt, mixing until the batter
is smooth. Stir in the chocolate chips. Spread the mixture
in the prepared pan. Bake 35–42 minutes, until a knife inserted in the center comes out clean or with just a few
crumbs. Set aside to cool. Makes 32.

## Chocolate Mousse

*8 ounces bittersweet chocolate, chopped*
*10 ounces heavy whipping cream*

Place the chocolate in the top of a double boiler, or in a
microwave-safe bowl; cook until melted. Stir the chocolate
until it is smooth. Allow to cool slightly. Whip the cream
in a large bowl with an electric mixer until soft peaks
barely form. Fold the chocolate into the cream and chill 30
minutes in the refrigerator, until set.

To make Mel's torte, use a premade chocolate shell and
cut a 2 X 2-inch brownie in half so that you now have 2
layers. Put one layer in the chocolate shell then spread
chocolate mousse over it. Place the second layer on top and
garnish with a dollop of whipped cream.

# Chocolate Chili Cupcakes

A spicy chocolate chili cupcake dipped in a
chocolate candy coating and garnished with a
chili pepper.

1¼ cups flour
½ cup cocoa powder
1 teaspoon baking powder
1 teaspoon cinnamon
½ teaspoon cardamom
½ teaspoon nutmeg
1 teaspoon chili powder (Mexican)
¼ teaspoon salt
5 tablespoons butter, softened
½ cup sugar
2 eggs
½ teaspoon vanilla extract
12 small red chili peppers for garnish

Preheat oven to 350°F. Put cupcake liners in a muffin tin.
In a large bowl, whisk together the flour, cocoa, baking
powder, spices, and salt. In another bowl, mix the butter
and sugar until it is fluffy; slowly mix in the eggs and vanilla. Then add the wet mixture to the dry until thoroughly
blended. Fill each muffin cup ⅔ full and bake for 18–22
minutes, until a knife inserted in the center comes out
clean. Makes 12.

## Chocolate Candy Coating

*8 squares of chocolate candy coating, melted*

Once the cupcakes are cooled, melt the chocolate candy coating in either a double boiler or use a microwave-safe bowl. Stir the melted chocolate until it is smooth. Carefully remove the chocolate chili cupcakes from their cupcake paper. Using a fork, stab the top of the cupcake and dip it into the chocolate until it is completely covered. Let the excess chocolate drip back into the bowl and carefully place the cupcake on the wax paper to harden the candy shell. Top with a fresh chili pepper.

# Deep Fried Bananas with Baked Plantains

Bananas with brown sugar, wrapped in a spring
roll and deep fried, served with chocolate sauce
and baked plantain chips.

*2 large bananas*
*8 (7-inch-square) spring roll wrappers*
*1 cup brown sugar*
*1 quart hot oil for deep frying*

Preheat the oil in a deep fryer to 375°F. Peel the bananas and slice them in half lengthwise and then across to make

4. Place one piece of banana on a spring roll wrapper and sprinkle with brown sugar to taste. Roll up the spring roll wrapper; as you roll, fold up the edges to seal the ends as you don't want the banana to get saturated with oil. Wet the final edge of the spring roll paper to seal it. Repeat with remaining bananas. Fry a few banana rolls at a time in the hot oil until evenly browned. Place on paper towels to drain. Makes 8.

## Plantain Chips

*2 green plantains (green ones bake better than yellow)*
*Cooking spray*

Preheat oven to 400°F. Coat a nonstick cookie sheet with cooking spray. Cut the ends off the plantains and peel. Cut each plantain on the diagonal into ½ inch-wide slices. Arrange in a single layer and coat the tops with cooking spray. Bake 15–17 minutes, turning after 8 minutes.

## Chocolate Sauce

*⅔ cup unsweetened cocoa*
*1⅔ cups sugar*
*1¼ cups water*
*1 teaspoon vanilla extract*

In a medium saucepan over medium heat, combine the cocoa, sugar, and water. Bring to a boil and let boil 1 minute. Remove from heat and stir in the vanilla.

# Goat Cheese Mini Tarts

A delicate goat cheese tart on a thin ginger-
infused graham cracker crust with a caramelized
top holding diced ripe figs and drizzled with
lavender honey.

*2 packages honey graham crackers, to
    make about 2¼ cups of crumbs*
*5 tablespoons sugar*
*2 tablespoons ground ginger*
*10 tablespoons unsalted butter, melted*
*8 ounces spreadable goat cheese*
*2 cups ripe figs, diced*
*1 cup caramelized honey*

Preheat oven to 350°F. In a food processor, grind the graham crackers to form fine crumbs. Add the sugar, ginger,
and butter, and pulse to combine. Press the mixture into a
mini-cheesecake pan, pressing the crumbs into the bottom
until ½-inch thick. Bake for 10–12 minutes. Cool slightly
before carefully removing from the pan. Once the crusts
are cool, spread a ½-inch layer of goat cheese onto the
crusts and sprinkle with the diced figs. Pour caramelized
honey on top and serve.

### To caramelize honey

In a heavy-bottom saucepan, heat 1 cup of honey with 1
tablespoon of water (it keeps the honey from scorching)
and a few drops of lemon juice (it keeps the honey from

hardening). Stir the honey constantly with a wooden spatula. Once the honey is a deep brown hue, it is ready to use.

\`,',',`

# Red Velvet Cupcakes (Using Beets)

A red velvet cupcake made with beet puree and topped with cream cheese frosting and an edible flower (optional).

*1¼ cups all-purpose flour*
*1 cup sugar*
*2 tablespoons cocoa*
*1 teaspoon baking powder*
*¼ teaspoon salt*
*⅓ cup canola oil*
*¼ cup lemon juice*
*1 teaspoon vanilla extract*
*1 egg, room temperature*
*¾ cup beet puree*

Preheat oven to 350°F. Put cupcake liners in a muffin tin. In a large bowl, whisk together the flour, sugar, cocoa, baking powder, and salt. Set aside. In another bowl, add in the oil, lemon juice, vanilla, and egg to the beet puree. Pour the beet mixture into the bowl of dry ingredients, and mix just enough to combine. Fill each muffin cup ⅔ full and bake for 18–22 minutes, until a knife inserted into the center comes out clean. Let cool completely.

## Cream Cheese Frosting

*8 ounces cream cheese, softened*
*1 stick unsalted butter, softened*
*½ teaspoon vanilla extract*
*3 cups powdered sugar*

Beat the cream cheese, butter, and vanilla in a large bowl until smooth. Gradually add the powdered sugar and beat until the frosting is smooth. Put the frosting in a pastry bag and pipe onto cupcakes in thick swirls, using an open tip. Decorate with an edible flower, such as a nasturtium.

Turn the page for a preview of Jenn McKinlay's
next book in the Cupcake Mysteries . . .

### Red Velvet Revenge

Coming soon from Berkley Prime Crime!

"What are we going to do about the business?" Angie DeLaura asked. She was sitting across the table from Melanie Cooper, dishing up her Twenty-three Skiddoo sundae while Mel sipped on her Camelback soda.

They had escaped their cupcake bakery, leaving it under the supervision of their two employees, and were sitting in the Sugar Bowl, Scottsdale's landmark ice cream shop. Mel always had the Camelback soda, vanilla ice cream scooped into old-fashioned soda with a pitcher of extra soda water on the side; it was her longtime favorite.

She glanced around the pink and chrome interior and noted that the Sugar Bowl hadn't seemed to age a day since it opened in 1958. Not that she had been around then, but her mother, Joyce, had been, and she remembered coming here when she was a little girl, just like Mel remembered coming here with her father and her brother when they were kids. There was something about the thick glass ice cream dishes served on paper doilies on the classic white plates that was charmingly nostalgic.

Growing up, the Sugar Bowl had been a favorite hangout of Mel and Angie's, along with their other childhood chum Tate. The three of them had practically owned the table by the window where Mel and Angie now sat enjoying the respite from the scorchingly hot July day outside.

Summer in the Valley of the Sun was as mean as an old man with sciatica. The sidewalk heated up so much, Mel was sure the bottoms of her flip-flops were going to melt. Just walking around the corner from their shop, Fairy Tale Cupcakes, had made both Mel and Angie sweat like marathoners, which they were definitely not, given that the relentless heat had them moving about as fast as a pair of desert tortoises.

"What do you mean, what are we going to do about the business?" Mel asked. She was staring out the window, watching the midday heat rise from the street, making everything shimmer as if it actually were melting under the ferocity of the sun.

"It's 114 degrees out there," Angie said. "Our tourist business has completely dried up, and the last special order we had was for the Levinsky bar mitzvah two weeks ago."

Mel made a very loud slurp with her straw and reached for the pitcher to add more soda. She looked at Angie and said, "Your point?"

Angie blew out a breath, stirring the dark brown bangs that hung across her forehead. The rest of her long hair was piled up in a clip on the back of her head. She gave Mel a level look as she scooped up another gooey spoonful of her sundae.

"I think we should close for a week or two," Angie said. Mel opened her mouth to protest, but Angie barreled ahead. "Hear me out. It's costing us more money to be open than to close; we can both take a vacation until monsoon season hits, and then when we open, our regulars will be back and our tourists will slowly trickle on in again."

"You know, if you want to go to Los Angeles to see Roach, you can just go," Mel said. "We don't have to shut down the bakery so you can go be with your boyfriend."

Mel knew her tone was a little harsh, but sheesh! Close down the bakery? She couldn't help but think that it would be the kiss of death for their small business.

Angie's eyes narrowed, and she plunked down her spoon with a plop. She looked like she was winding up to argue, and Mel braced herself as Angie's fiery temper was hotter than the desert sun and known for leaving scorch marks on the recipient of her ire.

Angie never got the chance to let loose her volley of mad. With a bang and a puff of blue smoke, an ancient, oversized van lurched into a parking spot on their side of the street. Mel and Angie whipped their heads in the direction of the noise.

"Is that . . ." Angie began, but Mel was already rising to her feet.

"Yup, it is," she said. "I'd recognize that shaggy mane and that bald head anywhere."

Angie began to shovel the last of her sundae into her mouth. She slapped her free hand to her forehead, and Mel knew Angie had just given herself a walloping case of brain freeze.

They hurried to the cashier's window by the exit and paid their tab. Mel rushed back to leave their waiter's tip tucked under her soda pitcher.

"But Oz and Marty are supposed to be watching the bakery," Angie said as she followed Mel out the door.

Mel was pretty sure the blast of heat that struck her full in the face as she stepped outside singed her eyebrows. She tried to look on the upside, as in no waxing or plucking, but people without eyebrows just looked weird. She ran her fingers over her brow bone just to reassure herself that they were still there, and then felt positive that the acrid smell that was assaulting her nose wasn't burnt hair but rather the noxious blue smoke coming out of the tailpipe of the decrepit van in front of her.

"Oz," she called to her young intern. "What are you doing here?"

The young man, who had been the bakery's paid intern since last spring, turned his head from under the hood of the van to look at her.

"Hey, Mel," he said. He stepped back and opened his arms wide. "Check it out. Isn't she a beauty?"

"That depends. Is she a contestant in a demolition derby?" Angie asked. She was fanning the back of her neck with one of the thick paper napkins from the Sugar Bowl.

"Heck, no," Marty said, stepping forward. He was a dapper older gentleman who had come to work in the bakery several months before, when Mel and Angie had discovered if they were to have any sort of personal life, they needed backup.

Oz and Marty exchanged excited glances and then spoke together, "She's your new cupcake van."

Mel looked at Angie and assumed her dumbfounded expression mirrored her own and then looked back at the van. She took in the oversized white behemoth, which reminded her of an old bread truck. It was covered in faded Good Humor and Blue Bunny ice cream stickers, and she felt her powers of speech evaporate as she tried to form a response.

"I know it isn't much to look at now," Marty said. "But we could trick this baby out, and it would be sweet."

"Where did it come from?" Angie asked.

"Mi Tio Nacho, er, my Uncle Ignacio left it to me when he died last year," Oz said. "It's been in my cousin's garage down in Tucson, and they finally drove it up."

"That's great, Oz," Mel said. "I'm so happy that you're going to have some wheels."

"No, it's not just for me," Oz said. "You two gave me my first job at the bakery, and I want to give back. Marty and I are thinking we can motor around the hood and sell cupcakes."

"In that?" Mel asked. She had visions of her carefully cultivated image for the bakery going up, well, in a puff of blue smoke.

"Come on," Marty said. He took Mel and Angie's elbows and half guided, half dragged them toward the back of the van. "You just need to go for a ride, and you'll see the potential."

"All right, I'm going," Angie said, and she shook Marty off. Oz hefted up the rolling door in the back, and Mel and Angie climbed aboard. Vintage steel freezers lined both sides, and Mel took in the scratched sliding window on the left side of the truck that appeared to have been retrofitted.

There was no seating. Angie plopped down on the floor, and Mel sat beside her while Marty and Oz scrambled into the front. Mel wrinkled her nose. Something smelled bad, like an expired dairy product. She suspected the smell lingered in the beige shag carpet, but she didn't want to get close enough to verify her suspicion.

It took three turns of the key and a punch to the top of the dashboard to get it going, but the van finally coughed itself back to life, and Oz backed out of the parking spot, using the overly large side mirrors to guide his way.

The polyester shag carpet that covered the narrow strip

of floor between the banks of freezers stuck to Mel's sweaty legs and itched. She sat with her knees drawn up and noticed that Angie did the same.

They puttered around Old Town Scottsdale, and then Oz headed out to the open road.

"Let me show you what she can do," he said as slick as any used car salesman.

"Really not necessary," Angie said. "Around the block will do."

But it was too late. Oz took Indian School Road out toward the highway. They were idling at the on-ramp traffic light when a big pink van pulled up beside them. Mel got a bad feeling in the pit of her stomach.

Marty and Oz had their windows down, because in addition to the sour milk smell, blue exhaust, and itchy shag carpet, the van's air conditioner didn't seem capable of cooling the van to a temperature of less than one hundred.

Mel peered out the window over Marty's shoulder and groaned.

"What is it?" Angie asked. She rose and moved to kneel beside her.

"Olivia Puckett from Confections bakery just pulled up beside us."

THE WHITE HOUSE CHEF MYSTERIES FROM
ANTHONY AND BARRY AWARDS WINNER

# JULIE HYZY

Introducing White House
executive chef Ollie Paras, who is rising—
and sleuthing—to the top…

"Hyzy may well be the Margaret Truman
of the culinary mystery."
—Nancy Fairbanks

"A must-read series to add to the
ranks of culinary mysteries."
—*The Mystery Reader*

## STATE OF THE ONION

## HAIL TO THE CHEF

## EGGSECUTIVE ORDERS

## BUFFALO WEST WING

# The delicious mysteries of Berkley Prime Crime for gourmet detectives

**Julie Hyzy**
WHITE HOUSE CHEF MYSTERIES

**B. B. Haywood**
CANDY HOLLIDAY MURDER MYSTERIES

**Jenn McKinlay**
CUPCAKE BAKERY MYSTERIES

**Laura Childs**
TEA SHOP MYSTERIES

**Claudia Bishop**
HEMLOCK FALLS MYSTERIES

**Nancy Fairbanks**
CULINARY MYSTERIES

**Cleo Coyle**
COFFEEHOUSE MYSTERIES

*Solving crime can be a treat.*

penguin.com